Doc Silence:
The Cost of Magic

Matthew Phillion

Doc Silence: The Cost of Magic

Lost Continuity Press
P.O. Box 1044
Salem, MA 01970

Printed in the United States of America

ISBN-13: 979-8-9850132-0-7
(also available in eBook format)

Front cover design:
Sterling Arts & Design

For my family, always and forever;
For Casey, born in the strangest of times;
And for Harley, who was here for every story until now.

From the Author

I've always known I wanted to tell the story of Doc Silence, and I was always worried I'd run out of time.

Doc's journey has been hinted at all along through the Indestructibles series, mostly in silent musings about the places he's been and the people he's known. But those books were their story, not his. He was there to support them, to help Jane, Billy, Kate, Titus, and Emily grow. His time in the sun had passed, and it was their turn.

But now it's Doc's.

Each section in this book is intended to be its own journey and genre: coming of age, eldritch horror, supernatural, tragedy, a love story. I wanted it to feel like flipping through someone's memories, old photos tucked between the pages, images of places he's been, the people he loved and lost. It's been a personal journey writing it, because unlike the Indestructibles in their first few books, Doc is old enough to have made a lot of mistakes and remember and regret them. It's a story of magic and regret, of making hard choices, of trying to not resent who you were for the decisions you've made along the way.

It's about the cost of magic, which is the cost of living a life.

I hope Doc's story surprises you. I want this book to cast a little bit of a spell as well: I believe it will transform the older Doc Silence we've known all this time in such a way that we never look at him the same way again.

I need to thank my fellow travelers on this journey: Stephanie Buck, who listens to every idea, good and bad, that I throw out into the wind; Colin Carlton, who helps me look at story from another perspective; Sterling Arts & Design, for another beautiful cover; and Christine Geiger, always the last and sharpest set of eyes on a new manuscript.

Thank you for accompanying me on this strange, mystical journey. We'll meet on the other side.

Matthew Phillion
Salem, Massachusetts
October, 2021

Prologue: Name magic

Sometimes, in quiet moments, Doc Silence could hear ghosts.

The magician moved among the spectral and the arcane; that literal spirits might speak to him was almost mundane, given the life he'd lived. But these were not true ghosts. He wished that they were. Instead, they were just echoes, hollow cries from the past, the voices of those who no longer existed, calling out from places Doc had been a lifetime ago.

When those voices called out, Doc would close his eyes and listen.

Tonight was one such time, as a heavy rain poured down on the City, tapping a slow, sporadic song across the surface of the Tower. Doc sat in his darkened chamber, removed the red-lensed glasses he wore to hide the burning light that eternally brimmed from his now-closed eyes. Names crossed his tongue, names he wanted to call out, but he knew he could not summon them forth. There is a cost to everything he has ever done, and admitting that some things are lost forever is one of those costs.

A soft rap came at his door. Doc placed his glasses back on his face and turned the lights on with a flick of his wrist, a wisp of a spell flicking the switch on the wall.

"Come in," he said.

Jane stood at the door. It was perhaps a trick of the light, or the remnants of the shadowy reverie she'd drawn him from, but she seemed, in that moment, two people at once; the fire-haired superhero he'd helped her grow up to be, and the infant he'd pulled from the wreckage of a plane, a squishy little creature without a scratch on her among the burnt and twisted metal, the burnt and twisted bodies.

She looked at him with worry. Jane often worried about him, he knew. Their entire relationship had been in many ways defined by their mutual worry for each other. Doc was so very used to losing people now. The dead drifted alongside him like dolphins riding the wake of a fast-moving ship.

But Jane was the one he'd fight for the most. The one he most needed to outlive and outlast him.

"Sitting in the dark again?" she asked. "I saw the light flip on before I opened the door. Don't lie to me."

"I like sitting in the dark."

"Creepy old wizard," she said.

"I'm not that old," Doc said.

"But you don't deny the creepy part."

"Creepy is what wizards do," Doc said, smiling warmly. "What can I help you with?"

Jane sighed, walking a circular path around his chamber. She ran a hand over the cover of an old grimoire, gently picked up a crystal ball and placed it down with equal care, examined a jar of silver powder. Her hunt seemingly finished, she flopped down in a chair across from him, legs dangling in front of her.

"I had a thought," she said.

"Nothing wrong with that."

"I thought: why hasn't Doc ever told me his real name?" Jane leaned forward, elbows on her knees. "I've known you my entire life. You've always just been Doc."

"Any particular reason you're asking this now?"

"Because we almost keep dying," Jane said. "And if some day we go off to save the world again and don't come back, I'd hate to never learn your real name."

Doc smiled, but he could palpably feel the lack of joy in it, and this made him immediately sad. Jane was far too empathetic to not pick up on it, too. He saw her eyes narrow suspiciously.

"What's wrong?" she asked.

Doc shrugged, then rubbed the bridge of his nose with his

thumb and forefinger.

"It's a bit more complicated than I can explain, but… I gave my name away," he said. "Doc Silence is all I have. I had to give up my name when I learned magic."

Jane's mouth twisted in a flash of irritation. She did not trust magic. Never had. And for good reason.

"You mean you can't tell anyone else your name?"

"I mean I can't remember it," Doc said. "Once upon a time, I made a bargain, and the price of that bargain was my name. I gave myself away to become who I am now."

"Do you remember your family's names? Could you ask them what you were called?"

Doc's heart twisted in his chest. The air caught in his throat.

"I… that was part of the deal, Jane. When you give your name away, you give away what comes with it. Who I was… he's gone. He's been gone a very long time."

"And you can never go back," Jane said.

Doc Silence shook his head.

"Part of the deal."

"Why would you give your name away?" Jane asked. "Was magic so important to you?"

"No," Doc said. "But something needed doing, and I thought I was the only one who could do it, and I thought that my name was a fair trade to be able to do so."

"Do you regret it?" Jane said.

"No," Doc lied. He gave up his name to change the world; that seems a fair trade. But on nights like this, when memory called out to him like a siren song, he wondered if the world could have got on without him just fine. He wondered if it was necessary.

But Jane didn't need to know that. She worries, he thought. She worries more than anyone I've ever known.

"Are you okay just being Doc?" Jane said. "Did you pick that name?"

"If I weren't who I am, I would never have found you," Doc said. "And you saved the world. I would give up all my names to make sure that happened. And I didn't pick the name. The name picked me."

"I don't understand."

"Honestly, neither do I," Doc said. "The naming of things is powerful magic. I think this name came to be because it took the place of something else I might have become. And also, maybe something I should always remember to be."

"Were you going to be a doctor? Were you a doctor when this happened?"

Doc shook his head.

"No," Doc said. "I wasn't a doctor. I was just a little boy. And there was someone I needed to help. That's all I really remember."

More lies, Doc thought. He remembered who was in need of his help. He heard that voice in the darkness all the time. Ghosts from the void, calling him home.

Jane nodded and climbed out of the pillowed chair she'd selected with some difficulty. She studied Doc's face deeply, then sighed.

"Sorry I bothered you."

"You never bother me." Not a lie.

"Will you ever have to give up your name again?" Jane said.

Doc shook his head.

"We only have one true name to give away," Doc said. "Other names follow, but none is as precious as the first."

"And you can never have that back."

"And that's okay," Doc said.

"Well," Jane said. "Good night, Doc. I'll leave you to your sitting in the dark alone, all creepy-like."

"Thank you, Jane," Doc said.

Jane left, pausing at the door one last time before closing it behind her. Doc flipped the light switch one more time with his mind, then leaned back into his chair and listened.

The past called out to him. And every voice he heard almost, almost said his true name, like a memory of something that never happened.

Chapter 1: Two boys

There was one boy who wanted to be a magician when he grew up, and one who did not.

The former was the younger of two brothers, a dreamer, often lost in his own thoughts. He believed in things that did not exist, and saw magic where there was none. He was a hopeful child, and he admired his older brother very much, in that innocent, selfless way little brothers sometimes overlook the flaws in their older siblings.

The latter was a serious boy, practical, but not the useful kind. He worried about everything and looked for ways to solve those worries, and this made him grim, and though he dreamed grand dreams as well, he assumed that there was little chance those dreams would ever come true. He tempered his expectations in all things. He loved his little brother very much, but in that gently neglectful, absent-minded way older brothers sometimes do, before they learn the brevity of time.

These boys lived in the City, on the edge of the metropolis where the buildings never quite looked clean, where the people always seemed just a little more tired than everyone else. But this was all they knew of the world, and their neighborhood, Queen's Garden, was where they belonged.

Queen's Garden was named as such because a stretch of the neighborhood was dominated by what once was a beautiful greenspace, dotted with sculptures that were a gift of the wife of a powerful industrialist a hundred years before the boys were born. But the garden often flooded, and it fell into disrepair, as much of the neighborhood did, the statues soon growing green and black with mold. The garden was built on swampland, after all, and the swamp will always reclaim its own, with time.

There were, of course, stories about Queen's Garden, or more specifically, about the Stone Fens, which was what the overgrown garden and statuary had become known as. Rumors of a giant snake that ate pets; of ghostly figures who wandered the night, glowing pale and ethereal in the darkness; stories of children going missing, though those stories were often true. Queen's Garden had more than its fair share of stories about children who never came home, though in any large metropolis, especially among the downtrodden, runaways were sadly commonplace. There needn't be a haunted swamp for young people to choose to never come home.

The boy who wanted to be a magician heard these stories, and they did not fill him with fear. He wanted to conquer the Stone Fens, to explore it like a brave magician would. He wanted to delve into its secrets, to find ghosts and free them, to face down the giant snake and make the world safe. The younger brother dreamed of being heroic, and dashing, and brave.

The older brother had no interest in the Stone Fens. He'd heard it was infested with rats. Certainly mosquitos. Quite possibly ticks. None of this was appealing. It was a trash-strewn, muddy mess in the middle of a grubby city, and he worried what else might lurk there—not supernatural, not monstrous, but human, because the older boy knew that humans were more dangerous than monsters, sometimes.

On a Saturday afternoon, the older boy took his younger brother to the local magic shop. They'd been given a gift by a generous aunt, and little brother wanted to buy new tricks. They had little else to do, so older brother hopped on his bike and led the way, the boys responsibly stopping at intersections, avoiding pedestrians, following the rules in an almost sadly boring manner. Younger brother wanted to fly on his two-wheeler, but older brother was worried about getting in trouble, and he set the pace.

The magic shop was also a costume shop, and it was overflowing with mundane wonders. Even the older brother, in his grim practicality, found the place exciting. Superhero costumes hung on the wall, in spandex and heavy rubber, standing alongside movie monsters, cowboy hats, and surplus army gear.

Meanwhile, the little brother had his nose pressed against a glass cabinet protecting a number of gimmicks and tricks. He pointed to a colored cloth, and the proprietor, a graying man with an easy smile, genuinely entertained by his younger brother's enthusiasm, withdrew the cloth and handed it to the boy.

There was a simple mechanism inside, enabling the would-be sorcerer to slide a wooden ring quickly to invert the silken cloth. Outside, the cloth was red and blue, but once the ring passed through, it appeared to become yellow and green.

"Look!" the little brother said, enormous, dark eyes looking up at his older brother with joy. The elder boy favored his little brother with a smile, entertained by the simple trick.

The shop owner demonstrated to the younger brother a trick wand which could, with the flick of a wrist, release a spring-loaded payload of fake flowers from its tip. The younger boy laughed and repeated the trick for his brother, who feigned surprise.

As his little brother tried on top hats, the older boy became lost in a comic book rack, old, battered back issues jammed in without any particular care or order. He pulled a few issues out that caught his eye, costumed heroes and detectives in trench coats and fedoras, and counted out the money in his pocket. He discovered he had enough for one more comic, this one with mutated reptiles on the cover.

He turned back to see his little brother wearing glasses with red-tinted lenses. He stuck his tongue out at his older brother when he saw him looking, then removed the glasses from his face and looked at the tiny paper price tag on the arm.

"Oh," the little brother said, looking crestfallen.

"Let me see," the older boy said, checking the price. He counted his own money, returned a few comics to the rack, and kept the glasses. He called over to the shopkeeper. "I'm going to buy these for him, too, if that's okay."

"Sure," the owner said.

The little brother looked up at his older brother, face wrinkled, mouth a tight line of concern.

"It's okay," older brother said. "I've got plenty of comics at home. You need these for your act."

The shopkeeper worked his way behind the long counter until he was just behind the older boy and spun the comics rack. With a curator's eye, he pulled one, two, three comics from the rack, then added one more for good measure. He handed these to the older boy.

"On the house," he said.

"I can't," the older boy said.

"Call it a good deed paid forward," the gray-haired man said. He leaned in conspiratorially. "My brother used to raid my piggy bank. I like your style better."

The boys paid for their purchases, thanking the shopkeeper, and headed back out onto the main drag, walking their bikes. The younger brother put the glasses on and looked around.

"Everything's red," he said. "Here, you try."

The older brother placed the glasses over his eyes and squinted.

"Looks weird," he said. "Don't wear them too long. You'll give yourself a headache."

On their way home, they passed by the Stone Fens on their left. Below them, a sewer grate offered an escape for the swamp's overflow. It smelled faintly of rot, but over the stink there was just the hint of flowers.

"Hey," the younger brother said. He'd placed the red sunglasses back on. "I heard a story."

"Yeah?" his older brother said, trying awkwardly to thumb through one of the comics while wheeling his bike one-handed and failing. He looked up at the graying sky. The air felt thick and damp with pending rain.

"Yeah. It's about the Fens."

"None of the stories about the Fens are true," the older boy said. "Except maybe the one about the giant rats. I heard there are wharf rats in there the size of puppies."

"That's gross."

"The Fens is gross."

"Well, that's not the story I heard," the little brother said.

The older boy stopped walking so he could adjust the comics in the little bag the shopkeeper had given him, surrendering in his attempt to bike and read at the same time. The younger brother leaned up against the stone railing looking down over the Fens. In his red glasses, he looked like a parody of cool, one sneakered foot kicked up casually, mimicking a pose he'd seen in a movie poster.

"I heard there's an old woman who lives in the Fens, and if you meet her, she'll grant you a wish," the little brother said.

"Literally every old lady in every swamp in every fairy tale is a bad person," the older brother said, joining his sibling in a comedic, laid back lean on the wall.

"Can we go look for her?"

"You want to look for a little old lady in the swamp," the older boy said.

"Yep."

"Why?"

"Because I want to make a wish."

"What are you going to wish for if we catch her?"

The little brother lowered his glasses to make direct eye contact.

"For real magic, of course."

"It's going to rain."

9

"I'll be fast," the younger brother said.

"And someone might steal our bikes."

"We'll hide them."

"This is a terrible idea."

"You're no fun," the little brother said.

"You're crazy," the older brother said.

"So, can we go look?"

"Fine."

Chapter 2: Trespassers

The boys dragged their bikes down into the marshy ground off the sidewalk and hid them behind a large tree. The wheels were probably visible from the street, but someone would have to be looking for them, and nobody went down into the Stone Fens. Mud sucked at their shoes, threatening to engulf their feet. Unidentifiable birds and bugs chirped and sang, offering a symphony of alien sounds. The older brother found himself marveling at the sound; it's so strange, he thought, that you can't hear this from the street. It's so loud. But you can walk along the bridge and never hear more than distant peeping, maybe frogs in the late evening.

Here, though, you entered a different world.

His little brother darted ahead, fearless. The forest rose to meet him, and trees that felt too tall to be contained by the Fens surrounded him. The marsh seemed to have a fairy tale quality to it, awash in exotic greenery, small creatures darting through the underbrush to avoid his heavy footfalls.

He looked into the murky water of a vernal pool and watched a snake slither away as if startled by his approach.

There was nothing like this elsewhere in the City, he knew. The City was a great expanse of concreate and glass. Some of the nicer streets might have trees dotting the sidewalk, but nothing was this wild, nothing this ferocious. The Stone Fens hummed with a chaotic energy. It sent a thrill through his heart.

The younger brother raised his eyes just in time to see a woman's face staring back at him from a twisted knot of green vines. He yelped and stepped backward, putting his entire foot into an ankle-deep pool.

"A statue," the older boy said, grabbing his little brother under the arms and helping him extricate himself from the puddle. He was right, of course. One of the statues that gave the Stone Fens its name, built for the industrialist's wife. Time had been unkind to them, leaving them grimy and blackened, furred with lichen. This one, a young woman wrapped in a flowing robe, reached out to him with a long-fingered hand. Her other arm lay on the ground beside her, broken off by time and the elements.

"Do you think she was a real person?" the little brother asked.

"I don't know," the big brother said. "Maybe? We shouldn't stay long. Someone might steal our bikes."

"Nobody's going to steal 'em," the little brother said. He looked up just in time to see a massive bird fly overhead—a heron, silent, massive, so out of place he felt as though he'd spotted a dinosaur.

"See that?" he asked.

"Sure did," the older brother said.

The younger boy picked up a branch, long enough to be a walking stick, and proceeded to use it to check for solid ground in front of him. He walked up a small incline and then onto a fallen tree. The bark cracked and fell away beneath his sneaker-clad feet.

"I think this place is magic," the younger boy said.

"It smells like farts," the older brother said.

"Yeah, it kinda does," the younger brother said. "Doesn't mean it can't be magic."

The younger boy skittered down the log and dropped to the

ground beside his brother.

"Thanks for taking me down here," he said.

"You all set now though? Can we go home?"

"I just want to stay a little longer," the younger boy said.

His older brother gave a non-committal shrug of his shoulders. The younger boy took this as his assent and darted off into the woods.

"Oh, come on," the older boy said, dashing to catch up.

He watched the light at the edge of the trees, maintaining an eye on civilization. He knew the Fens was not that big. Even if they got lost, the worst thing that could happen, he knew, was to come out on the wrong side and have to walk all the way around to get their bikes. But still, this made him nervous. It felt bigger than it should here. He couldn't hear street sounds. No voices, no cars. Was it the trees? Did all the foliage muffle the noises of the City? His stomach twisted fearfully. This place, he thought. It didn't feel right.

"Hey, let's get out of here," he said to his little brother. "I don't want to get in trouble for coming home covered in mud."

"Okay," the younger boy said.

And then they heard the woman speaking.

The older boy looked to his little brother, who had turned his head to follow the sound. Both boys exchanged a curious glance.

"We should go," the older boy said.

"What if it's someone who needs help?"

"Out here?" the older boy said. "You're just wishing it's the old woman in that fairy tale."

"Maybe," the younger brother said. "But I mean, it's an old lady's voice. How bad can it be? Maybe she's in trouble. Or it's nothing."

"Or it's some creep pretending to be an old woman," the older brother said. "Come on. Let's get back."

He turned and started toward the road, following the light spilling between the trees. He turned to make sure his little brother was following.

The younger boy wasn't there.

"Hey!" the older brother said. He felt a spike of rage ram through his chest, furious that his brother had run off. But that lasted only a second. Just long enough to realize his brother did not yell back. He always answered, even if it was to give him a hard time or say something sarcastic. The silence that answered his call turned his blood cold.

The older boy ran back in the direction he'd last seen his brother looking. He skirted fallen trees, splashed in mud, tripped and fell in the muck. His breathing became ragged as he fought back fury and tears. He told himself he would drag his brother home if he caught him hiding, but it was a weak argument. His mind had already gone far in a darker direction.

He came upon a larger pool of water, black in this shadowy place—this shouldn't exist here, he thought, how is there a pond in the Fens? And then he saw his brother standing perfectly still, face to face with a small, hunched woman. Her skin was jaundiced, almost green; her hair whitish gray, like the color of mold. She was speaking to his brother, her voice too quiet to make out from here.

And then the older brother saw the vines.

It seemed like an optical illusion at first, a trick of the light, but no, it was true, it was right there in front of him: vines hanging like power cables from the trees, a tangled mass of greens and browns, all leading to the old woman's back and shoulders. They spread out behind her like a train on a wedding gown, then up into the trees.

A vine fell down from the treetops and wrapped itself around little brother's torso. Arms and legs limp, the younger boy was pulled into the trees. The older boy followed him into the air and saw that the trees were dotted with small human shapes, completely covered by leaves and moss. They looked like apples waiting to be picked.

The old woman turned to face the older boy. Her eyes seemed unnatural, like a stuffed animal's.

"Oh look," she said. "Two for dinner."

And the older boy ran for his life.

Chapter 3: There are such terrible things

The older brother, covered in mud, lacerated by tree branches, exploded out of the Stone Fens, almost crashing into a pedestrian strolling by. The passerby, a woman walking her dog, gave the boy a stern look and carried on.

I should go back, he thought, the guilt coursing through him like poison. I left him. I have to go back. But what can I do against... a monster? Was she a monster? What was that? Was it even a person?

He started to run again, this time not out of fear for himself, but in a panicked search for help. He couldn't go home. What would his parents do? Would they even believe him? His brother was his responsibility. This was his fault. He had to fix this.

He barely noticed as the streets rolled by. Twice he was almost struck by a car crossing the street, but that felt almost trivial now. Where could he go? The police? The police would call his parents. And that's if they believed him. He needed something else. He needed...

He looked up from his silent ranting to see the sign of the

magic shop just above him, the brownstone building quiet and still in the gray, late afternoon light. Maybe I can ask to use the phone, he thought. I can't do this on my own. I have to do something.

He sat down on the sidewalk outside the shop, drawing his knees to his chest and lowering his head. His lungs felt heavy. Breathing was almost impossible. He felt the first few drops of rain. My brother is out there, alone, in the rain. A monster has him and there's nothing I can do.

To his left, the shop door jangled. Weirdly, he hoped to see the shop owner—maybe he couldn't help, but he'd been kind, and kindness is rare. It is memorable.

But he did not see the shopkeeper. Instead, he looked up to see a lined face framed by a close-cropped silver beard. The man wore a dark coat, long, nearly to mid-calf. He had a high forehead, framed by more silver hair, kept very short. In his hands, he held a small bag emblazoned with the shop's logo.

"Oh," the man said. "You're a mess."

The boy nodded once, saying nothing.

The man approached, then sat down beside the boy, flipping his coat a bit so it wouldn't be crushed into the pavement.

"What seems to be the trouble," he asked.

"You wouldn't believe me," the boy said.

"I just walked out of a magic shop," the man said. "I'll believe a lot."

The boy looked at the older man, studying his eyes. There was no malice there. The opposite, in fact. He seemed genuinely concerned.

"I lost my brother in the Fens," the boy offered.

"Oh dear," the man said. At first the boy thought he caught a hint of condescension, but once again, he looked long and hard at the man's face, but it was grim, deadly serious.

"What were you looking for in the Fens," the man asked.

"My brother wanted to try to find the old woman who gives wishes," the boy said. "But I think... I don't know. This is stupid."

"Better to say it than keep it to yourself, kid," the man said.

The boy took a deep breath. Somehow, it felt better saying this to a complete strange than to his parents. At least if a stranger thought he was lying it wouldn't matter.

"She took him," the boy said. "The old woman wrapped him up in vines and stole him."

"I honestly thought she was gone," the man said.

The boy's breath caught in his throat. It felt cruel, that he'd make fun of him like this. Worse than not believing him. He's making fun of me. My brother is gone and this cruel old man is teasing me.

"She's real," the boy said defiantly.

"I know," the man said. He sighed. "I shouldn't do this."

The last words sounded more to himself than to the boy.

"What shouldn't you do?" the boy asked.

The old man's face twisted. Not in a monstrous way, the boy thought—the way a grownup's face changes when you know they're angry, or sad, but don't want you to see it.

"I can't do it myself," the man said. "Adults can't see her, you understand. That is her power. That is her camouflage. It's why she's been able to fester there for as long as she has."

"You believe me?"

"Oh, kid," the man said. "I believe you. There are such terrible things in this world. Were that it not so. Yes, I believe you."

"You have to help me get my brother back!" the boy said. "She stole him! He's my best friend and she stole him!"

"How long ago was this?" the man said, standing up and brushing off his pants. He held out a hand to help the boy up.

"Just now," the boy said, realizing he wasn't sure how long he'd been wandering, terrified. "I don't know how long. Maybe an hour?"

"That's good," the man said. "There's still time. But as I said, I can't do this myself. Tell me something—what would you do to save your brother?"

In another moment, the boy would have felt as though this were a ghastly threat. But there was something so efficient about the way the man said it, almost like a teacher.

"I'd do anything. He's my brother."

"Show me where you lost him," the man said.

The boy led him back to the Stone Fens, no more than a ten-minute walk. The boy expected strange looks from anyone who saw them, a muddy child and strange old man, but it was as though they were invisible. Not a soul made eye contact. Nobody looked at them askance. At one point the old man strode out into the street and held up a hand a car, moving fast toward them, slowed and stopped as though he commanded it.

They reached the edge of the Fens where the brothers had left their bikes. Rain began to fall in earnest now. The boy left a puddle of mud at his feet.

"Here is what you must do," the man said. "I know her true name. When you speak the true name of a thing, it must listen to you. But I can't see her to stop her. Only a child can find her."

"Give me the name," the boy said, as if it were the most normal thing in the world.

"I intend to," the old man said. "But to use a thing's name in this way, to command them with a true name, you must give up your own name. You have to surrender your true name."

The boy shook his head, not understanding why the man's voice had a quiet, worried tone.

"I can't use my own name anymore? I don't care! It's just a name!"

"Not the name you are called," the man said. "The name you are."

The boy stared at him blankly. He looked into the woods and thought of his brother, wrapped in vines like a fly in a spider web.

"You say that like something bad will happen," he said.

The old man sighed. He looked up into the sky, rain falling on his face, soaking his beard.

"Just once, I wish it were different," he said, again to no one at all. He turned his attention to the boy. "When you give up your true name, your life forgets you. You fade from the memories of

18

those who love you. You give up who you have always been to become something else."

"My life forgets me," the boy said. "So, my brother will…?"

"I'm afraid so."

"But he'll be safe."

"He will."

"And she won't be able to hurt anyone else ever again," the boy asked.

"That is the hope," the old man said. "Magic is an art, not a science. But the magic of names is more powerful than almost any other kind."

"Will I… Will I remember him? And my parents? Or do they fade away too?"

"I wish I could tell you that you would forget them," the old man said. "It would be easier that way."

The boy felt tears well up in his eyes, hidden by the falling rain. He bit his lip. He thought about the room he and his brother shared, covered in superhero posters. His parents, probably worried now, maybe even looking for them. He thought about going home without his brother. And he thought about his brother going home without him.

"Give me her name," the boy said.

The man said a word. It made no sense. The boy could not call it to mind, could not form it with letters in his head, but it rung like a bell in his years.

"And now your name," the man said.

"I don't know how," the boy responded.

"Yes, you do," the old man said. "Just say it."

And the boy said his name out loud, and felt a pang in his chest, as though a piece of himself was ripped from his flesh. The pain was unbearable, but just for a split second. And then it was gone. The rain seemed louder, then. Clearer. He turned toward the Fens and saw it not the way he'd always seen it from the road, but the true form, the medieval swamp he'd discovered within.

"Here," the man said, removing a chain from around his neck.

A tiny medallion hung from it. He placed it over the boy's head. "This will hide you from her, at least until she can see you with her own eyes and not through spying magics. You'll be able to get close."

"And then what do I do?"

"You say her true name. You say you know her true name and call upon her to let your brother go. To leave this place and never come back. With this name, she must listen to you."

The boy nodded and started toward the Fens. Before hopping down into the muddy soil below, he paused.

"Will I be able to say goodbye?" he asked.

"Say it quickly," the old man said. "You'll fade from his mind so fast. But say what you can. It will echo through time."

Chapter 4: Your true name

The boy charged into the murky Stone Fens with a fearlessness he did not know he had. Where once he had an anxious dread, he now had only one thought: find his brother, and creature who stole him.

The wetlands seemed more alive than before, the sound of birds, frogs, and bugs almost deafening. The evening grew late quickly, and soon he found himself in a gray-black mire of shadow and mud.

The flora, though, seemed to entirely ignore him. He passed easily through vines and scrubs, leaving no trace wherever he passed. The medallion around his neck felt warm to the touch—not burning, but a soothing heat, as if keeping the chill of the swampy air off his skin.

He almost strode right past her. More strangely, she seemed also to be unaware of his presence. Closer than he'd been before, he could see how deceptively big she was—hunched forward, gnarled like an old tree and almost as big, a winding, twisting body of green flesh and knobby growths. He paused in front of her, and she turned her strangely large head toward him, black, iris-less eyes blinking slowly as though needing to focus on him more actively to even see him.

"You came back," she said, her voice friendly, grandmotherly. "They never come back."

The boy said nothing at first, taking in this alien creature, limbs too long, eyes too large, teeth like slats of wood. How did we ever think she looked like old woman? He thought. Vines stretched out of her back like electric cables, and he thought: she's not an old woman. She's part of the Fens. The vines weren't wrapped around her, he saw. They were a part of her. She was connected to the circulatory system of the swamp, as if it fed her, and she fed it.

He stole a glance into the trees and saw his brother hanging there, motionless and silent. When he returned his attention to the creature, she had leaned in close, examining him. Her breath smelled like stagnant water.

"Too old for my tastes," she said appraisingly. "But not without a certain appeal. Yes. You can stay for dinner. I think you'll do nicely. There's still a gleam of childhood on you. Not much, but it will do."

The boy stared at her defiantly. The creature laughed.

"And a fighter, as well. That's why I don't like them too old, you see. Harder to show them just how inevitable this all is. The older ones think they have a chance. What's your name, boy?"

The boy clenched his fists and took a deep breath of the swampy air. He exhaled sharply.

"I have no name," he said.

"Everyone has a name," the creature with a grandmother's voice said.

"I have no name anymore," the boy said. "But I know yours."

This time, the creature laughed more heartily. It felt as if the entire swamp laughed with her. Somewhere in the distance, birds cawed in unison with her laugh.

"Which one do you know?" she said. "I have so many names."

"I know your true name," the boy said. "And you're going to let my brother go."

The creature waved a hand at him dismissively.

"I have no time for bravado, boy," she said. "Either sit down for dinner or try to flee. Fleeing sounds good. I haven't had to chase one of you in a long while."

The boy said the creature's true name.

It felt as if no sound passed his lips; he said the words, but his vocal chords struck nothing. He worried, for just a second, that the old man had fooled him.

But then the creature began to scream.

"How dare you!" she said, slamming hands that had grown to nearly the boy's own height in to the ground, gouging much and mud everywhere. "I'll tear your guts out and use them as a necklace!"

The boy said her name again, and again the creature wailed.

"No! No, you can't. You have no art! How can someone with no art do this to me?"

"Let my brother go," the boy said.

"No!" the creature said.

"And all of them," the boy said, gesturing around at the darkened shapes in the trees, the bodies of dozens of stolen children left to die here in the dark. "Let them all go. Now!"

"You are a cruel boy," the creature said.

"Now," the boy said. "You will let them go and never hurt the children of the City again. I know your true name. You have to do as I say."

The creature snorted furiously, huffing and blustering. She knocked down a tree, then another, in a fit of petulant rage. Finally, she waved a dismissive hand at the treetops. The boy risked a glance to his brother and saw him falling peacefully to the ground.

"I curse you," the creature said. "I curse you until the end of your days. A dark cloud will follow you until the end of your days, nameless boy. You will know only enough happiness to feel pain when it is gone. This is my promise."

The boy thought of his brother forgetting him. He thought of his parents and if they would see an empty bed and not know how it got there. He imagined a world with them in it, where he did not exist for them.

"I think I already made that deal," the boy said. "Now leave. You are not welcome here anymore."

He said her name once more, and shocked even himself with the viciousness the syllables left his lips. The name felt like a curse word. Like an epitaph.

The creature backed away, black, gleaming eyes never leaving his face.

"We will meet again, nameless child. My kind do not take slights such as this lightly."

Before the boy could respond, she faded into the green and disappeared.

Beside him, his little brother called his name. Or at least the older boy thought so—the word the younger boy said was meaningless to him. But there was a familiarity to it that made him turn his head.

The younger boy crashed into him with a hug.

"You came back for me," he said.

"I did," the old boy said. "I could never leave you behind."

"I…" the younger boy said, looking at his brother's face. He blinked a few times, as if trying to refocus his eyes. "I'm sorry, I feel really confused…"

All around them, children were lowered from the trees, deposited on the ground. Some, wearing modern clothing, looked around, suddenly awake, and ran without asking a question. Others lay still. Often, these wore clothing from bygone eras; some of these the older boy recognized from television, and a few even reminded him of photos he'd seen of his parents as kids. There were even a few dressed in strange garb like something out of a historical movie. These, particularly, lay forever still.

"Let's get you out of here," the older boy said, making sure his little brother did not look behind him where the bodies were abandoned. Together, they ran back toward the street, stopping to take their bikes out from behind the tree where they left them. As they walked up the embankment toward the sidewalk, the older boy caught the younger by the shoulder.

"Hey," he said. "Something is going to happen."

"I… why can't I see your face?" the younger boy said. He blinked a few times, then smiled. "There you are. What's wrong with me?"

"There's nothing wrong with you," the older brother said. "But listen, I just… I love you, okay?"

"I love you too. This is weird. You never say that."

"Nobody does until it's too late,' the older boy said. "I should have said it more. I'm really sorry. About all of this."

"But you came back for me."

"I will always come back for you," the older boy said. "Just know I'll never forget you, okay?"

"Where are you going? Don't leave me here!" his little brother said.

"I'm not leaving you here," the older boy said. "I'll always be here."

The younger brother looked to be on the verge of tears. But then his eyes went blank for a moment. He looked at his older brother like a stranger. He backed away slowly, letting the older boy's hand fall from his shoulder.

"Thank you for helping me," the younger boy said. "I thought I was going to die."

"Of course I helped you," the older boy said. "You're my…"

"Who are you, though?" the younger boy interrupted. "Do you go to school with my… Do you go to… Um. I should go home. It's late. My parents might be worried."

The older boy bit the inside of his lip, felt his eyes growing hot. He smiled at the younger boy and nodded.

"Yeah. You… you should get home. They'll be worried."

"Thank you again for what you did back there. Was that magic?"

"I think so, yeah."

"Huh," the younger boy said. He wheeled his bike back to the sidewalk, checked his bag from the magic shop, somehow still secured to the handle of his bike this whole time, and then looked back one more time.

"Bye?" the little boy said.

"Goodbye," the older boy said. He watched him ride away into the darkening evening as streetlights lit up one by one.

And as soon as the younger boy was out of sight, the older brother burst into tears.

Chapter 5: All magic has a cost

The old man found the boy there, sitting beside his bike, crying silently. The rain had soaked him through, but the boy didn't know where to go. He'd seen his little brother forget him. Going home seemed impossible.

The old man took off his long black coat and draped it over the boy's shoulders before sitting down beside him in the rain.

"Was that really the only way?" the boy asked.

"Unfortunately," the old man said. He looked terribly sad, the boy noticed. The man's eyes glistened in the rain as though he might cry himself, though it may have just been an illusion in the rain.

"But why?"

"Because all magic has a cost," the man said. "This is the first lesson every magician must learn. Nothing is free. When you change the world with magic in one place, an equal shift must happen elsewhere. It doesn't matter what kind of magic you use. There is always a cost."

"So, the cost of my brother was myself," the boy said.

"Your connection to him, yes," the man said. "I made a similar choice myself when I was your age. Maybe a little older. It wasn't a creature like this, of course. It was something else. But... I will tell you, this is the loneliest you will ever be. Going down this path you will face hardships, but nothing, nothing ever compares to this."

"Down this path?" the boy said.

The old man sighed.

"I didn't come to the City to take on an apprentice," he said. "Gods above and below, that was not what I thought I was doing here. But here we are, and we are forever responsible for the things we break. I helped you break your life. It's now my debt to make sure you're safe."

"Is that your cost?" the boy asked.

The old man smiled at this, nodding approvingly. He almost laughed.

"Look at you," he said. "Yes. I think you'll be a fine magician. I can see it already."

"I never wanted to be a magician," the boy said. "That was my brother's dream."

"Then he got off lucky," the old man said. "The best magicians are those who find magic because they have to, not because they want to. I think perhaps today you saved your brother twice."

"And I took on the cost," the boy said. "I was right? I'm your cost?"

"You are my responsibility," the man said. "If you'll have me. You can say no. There are others you can learn from, if you want. At least let me teach you a few spells so you can eat and stay warm. But if you want to learn more, you are my responsibility. I will teach you everything I have to teach."

The boy chewed on a fingernail and studied the old man's face. He had been taught to fear strangers, like most children are; but there was something in this lined face that radiated trust. And a tiredness to his eyes that said he was too weary to be cruel.

"What's your name?" the boy asked.

"I'm called Erasmus Hawksmith," the old man said.

28

"Is that your true name?'

"No, it's just a name I'm called," he said. "It does the job. It's a bit overdramatic, isn't it? But that's what magicians do. We're all overdramatic. It's how we find something to laugh at when the dark places like this one make us tired."

"What should I be called then?" the boy said.

Erasmus Hawksmith laughed, a quick, barking laugh. There was no meanness to it.

"You can call yourself whatever you'd like," the man said. "This is a cruel life, but at least you get to choose your name."

"I don't know what I want to be called."

"Well, you need a placeholder at least," the man said. "I can't call you kid forever. You can always change it later. In fact, most magicians change their names a lot. Mostly because we get bored."

The boy shifted and felt something crunch beneath his hip. He reached down and pulled out the dented and soaked comics he'd been given. He pulled one out.

"Can magicians be... good?" he said.

"What you did today, kid, was the definition of good," Erasmus said. "But it takes all kinds."

"Can they be heroes?"

"Some have been, over the centuries."

On the cover of the comic was a masked man, in a cape. Fighting a monstrous villain in a strange place, full of colors and strange shapes. The hero's name was emblazoned across the top of the page. For some reason, this hero was a doctor. Of what, the boy wasn't sure.

"Could take his name if you want," Erasmus said.

"I don't want to take his name," the boy said. "But maybe I can just be..."

"How about we call you Doc. There's a lot of heroes named Doctor, you know. Doc Holliday was a great gunslinger, for one. There's been adventurers and scientists, time travelers... even a few magicians in old stories."

"I can change it later if I want, right?"

"You absolutely can, kid," Erasmus said.

"Okay. I'll be Doc. For now. Until I think of something better."

The old man hoisted himself to his feet, grimaced at the squishing sound in his boots. He offered a hand once again to help the boy up, and the boy accepted. As he stood up, he noticed an object on the pavement, a glint of red. His brother's red-tinted glasses. He reached down and scooped them up, holding them just below his heart. He held them there tightly as though they might fade away, the edges of the arms digging sharply into his palm.

"Okay, Doc," Erasmus said. "First spell you'll learn."

Erasmus made a symbol in the air with his hand and said a single word. The rain around them ceased to fall, as if they were sheltered by an invisible bubble. Doc watched as the rain splattered against that invisible bubble like glass.

"Why didn't you do that before?" Doc said.

"Because you are my responsibility, and your pain is my pain. If you sit in the rain, so do I," he said. "Also… I forgot I could do this one."

Doc almost laughed. A smile caught in the corner of his mouth, but stopped, remembering why he was here. What he'd lost. Who he'd never see again.

"Come on," Erasmus Hawksmith said. "There's much to learn. There's a wide world to explore. And I think it will be better for having you in it."

Chapter 6: Save everyone

"You can't save everyone."

Erasmus Hawksmith said this to young Doc Silence so often in the early years it was nearly a mantra.

It was followed, almost every time, by: "Why?"

It was a hard lesson for Doc to learn, far harder than the magic Erasmus taught him. His specialty, and therefore the specialty he taught Doc, was naming magic.

"You learn the name of a thing, you can either command it, or you can ask it for a favor," the old wizard told him. "And how you use that name defines you as a magician."

"If you can learn the name of a thing and make it do your bidding, why are there hungry people in the world?" Doc asked. "I could learn the name of water and make sure no one is thirsty. The name of medicine so nobody ever runs out. What's stopping someone like us from doing that?"

Erasmus puffed out his cheeks and exhaled loudly. He did this often, because Doc asked many questions, and none of them were simple. Sometime Erasmus smiled when Doc questioned him, because his apprentice never asked about power for himself. It was always why magic did not leave a better imprint on the world. And the answer was always the same.

"You can't save everyone."

"But you have unlimited power," Doc said. "You can save everyone."

"No," Erasmus said, patiently but firmly. "Here is what you must understand, Doc Silence. Magic always has a cost. When you do a good thing here, the scales tip elsewhere. The good and evil of magic never happen in a vacuum. Science, which is damned near magic by another name, has taught us that energy is never destroyed, it is simply transformed. And magic is the same. You can rip a cancer from one man's gut, but that dark energy will find a home elsewhere. You might use magic to create enough bread to feed a nation, but somewhere else, you've bankrupted a resource others need to live."

"Then how does magic work at all?" Doc asked. "How can you do any good with it?"

"By understanding your limitations," Erasmus said. "Once, when I was a little older than you, I found myself in a war. I wasn't a soldier. I refuse to take orders from any mortal man. But I was there, and I saw a great weapon of war, a tank, leveling its massive canon at a village."

"And you did nothing, because you can't save everyone," Doc said.

"No," Erasmus said. "I turned the tank into a pillar of salt."

Doc thought about this for a moment.

"You didn't destroy the tank. You changed it."

"That's right," Erasmus said. "Let me tell you the simplest thing I've ever learned. If you have no idea what to do, turn it into a pillar of salt."

"Why?"

"I don't know," Erasmus said. "Because it'll dissolve in the rain?"

"So you did a good thing. You saved a village by turning the tank into salt."

"I did," Erasmus said. "But I learned a lesson that day as well."

"That salt is water soluble?"

"There were men in that tank," Erasmus said. "And then, because of me, they were nothing but salt.

"They were going to destroy a village," Doc said.

"Because they were told to, by worse men. Maybe they would learn from that terrible deed and go home to change their people. Maybe one terrible act would lead them to be better men. But I turned them to salt and the universe will never know what else they might have become."

"You told me energy is never destroyed," Doc repeated.

"But potential can be," Erasmus said.

"And maybe if you hadn't saved that village, a kid there never grows up to change the world," Doc said.

Erasmus shrugged.

"Potential is fragile," he said. "All we can really do is give it a chance to grow."

"Because we can't save everyone."

"No," Erasmus said. "We can't."

***

Quite a few years passed before Doc had this lesson put to the test.

He grew up under the teachings of Erasmus, who guided him with other kinds of magic beyond the naming of things, methods to evoke the elements, spells of conjuration, and each had a different kind of cost than naming magic. They began to wear on him. That was the other cost, Erasmus explained. Not just the one in, one out balance of mystical energy, but that by their exposure to magic, the magicians themselves were changed.

"After a while," Erasmus said, sipping a cup of coffee at a café in Manhattan. They'd teleported there for lunch, Erasmus using his desire for coffee from his favorite shop as an excuse for Doc to practice his ability to move them across great distances. "After a while we find we're barely human anymore. That's the burden we carry."

"What do you mean, barely human?" Doc asked. In his late teens, now, he'd taken up an affectation Erasmus referred to playfully as knock-off Goth, dressed mostly in black, baggy jeans and Doc Marten boots, his hair a messy fringe that flopped down into his face.

"It's hard to explain," Erasmus said. "Part of it is time—magic sustains us, in some way, and we tend to outlive our peers, and suddenly a hundred years go by and the only people who know you are other magicians."

"I'm going to live that long?" Doc asked.

"If you're unlucky," Erasmus said. "I've been around too long myself, I think."

Doc sipped at his own coffee, still getting used to the bitterness. It was helping with the weariness teleportation magic left him with, though, and was beginning to understand why Erasmus drank so much of it.

"How else do we change?"

"After a while, we start caring less," Erasmus said. "It's the time thing again, I think. You start thinking in terms of decades, and then centuries, and it becomes hard to focus on the little things. You look exhausted."

"I'm fine," Doc lied. "How do you stop yourself from not caring anymore?"

"I think it's time for your first mark," Erasmus said. "And it's hard not to get lost. I'll be honest, it's things like teaching you that help me not to disconnect."

"My first mark?" Doc said. His stomach twisted with nerves. Marks were what Erasmus called the untold number of tattoos he wore on his body. His arms were blue-green sleeves of artwork and arcane symbols. He was like a living spell book. Doc hadn't gone under the needle yet and he worried about the pain, though Erasmus had told him the marks helped make casting spells easier, like a bookmark in space, a shorthand for eldritch energy that would be stored in his skin. "And should I, like, start now? To not disconnect?"

"Well, you don't need an apprentice yet, that's for sure," Erasmus said. "But I think maybe you should do some work on your own. Do something good for the world that helps you feel human."

"We are human, though, right?" Doc asked.

"More or less," Erasmus said. "Feel up for one more teleportation spell?"

"Sure," Doc lied again.

"Great. My favorite artist is in Dublin. We'll go there and get you marked."

Doc felt the color drain from his face.

"Trust me," Erasmus said. "Once you have your first mark you'll be worrying about running out of skin to tattoo."

"Right. Sure. Of course." Doc took another sip of his coffee and choked it down as waves of nervous nausea seized up his insides.

"Y'know what," Erasmus said, throwing back the dregs of his drink and standing up, stretching his back with a crack. "I'll cast the teleportation spell. I don't want us ending up in Dublin, Ohio because you're afraid of needles."

"I'm not afraid of needles."

"One more thing we get really good at in our old ages, as magicians," Erasmus said with a smirk. "We're really hard to lie to."

Matthew Phillion

36

Chapter 7: The missing girl

Doc Silence reappeared in the City alone, fighting the urge to scratch at the new ink etched into the flesh on the soft underside of his wrist. The tattoo artist, a woman with dark hair, rosy cheeks, and a tired expression named Bláithín, had done a beautiful job on the mystical mark, which resembled an ouroboros etched with tiny runes. As much as Doc had not wanted the mark, he did find it made casting a teleportation spell easier, as though a weight had been lifted from his shoulders as he spoke the words of the spell.

Erasmus remained in Dublin, telling Doc he had to talk to an old contact, and sent the young magician home ahead of him. Go get into some trouble, Erasmus had said before nudging Doc through the portal.

The old wizard's words stuck in Doc's mind. You can't save everyone. It bothered him. Statistically, he supposed, this had to be true. There were just too many people in danger at all times for them to even know who to save, let alone reach them all. Still, Doc wished he'd voiced the follow up question properly. Why not? Even with the limitations magic set upon itself, there had to be a way to do more.

What other reason was there for learning to change the world if you couldn't make it better for everyone?

He held back, though, which he still often did when Erasmus got on a tear. Doc had been training with him for a few years now, but he was still vaguely afraid of the man. Not that he'd harm his apprentice; more that Doc worried he'd be looked at as a failed experiment and cast aside.

He was distracted from his wandering thoughts by a twinge in his wrist from where the tattoo still gleamed freshly. Doc looked up to shake off the daydreams and get his bearings, and found himself face to face with a sign stapled to a telephone pole. It was a poorly printed photo of a little girl, maybe five or six, with the word MISSING printed boldly above her face.

Missing. It seemed impossible to truly disappear in the modern world. Something about the sign set off his alarms in his mind. He wasn't quite sure why. Maybe it was the old-fashioned, almost pathetic condition of the sign itself, like a parody of a missing person's milk carton photo. Maybe it was the thought of someone so small out on her own.

Or if he was being honest, it reminded him of his life before magic.

Get into some trouble, Erasmus had said.

You can't save everyone.

But maybe I can find someone who is lost, Doc thought. He studied the photos for a moment, then called to mind the words and gestures of a finding spell. He'd never used it on a human being before, but rather tested it on lost keys, the remote control to his television, once to help find a missing cat for a neighbor. This seemed a more noble use of the spell.

He began the incantation for the finding spell, willing it to materialize in the form of a small, spectral sparrow. A tiny, glowing, winged shape appeared on the ground in front of the telephone pole and looked up Doc expectantly.

"Well, go on," Doc said, taking the poster with him and stuffing it in his pocket almost as an afterthought. "Go find her."

The semi-translucent bird took off, ambling through the air with a meandering purpose. The spell itself was a successful casting, though twice the spectral bird was dive-bombed by real birds protecting their nests, and led Doc into moving traffic no fewer than three times, which Doc gracelessly, but successfully, managed to avoid being flattened by. He followed the summoned creature across town, and then into a small park along the river that cut the city in half like a book's spine. The bird disappeared over a railing attached to a low cement wall used to keep pedestrians from falling off the fifteen-foot drop, where a narrow, concrete walkway ran alongside the river, just inches above the river's edge. Doc checked to make sure no one was looking, then leapt over the rail, casting another minor spell to slow his descent until his feet touched the paved walkway.

The young magician had been so proud of himself, so impressed with his own spell craft, that it was only now that he realized the grim implications of the bird's journey. A missing child, a river alongside a park. Icy fingers grabbed at Doc's heart as he envisioned what might have become of the little girl.

You can't save everyone, he heard Erasmus say in his mind.

Doc pressed on, shaking off the dark thoughts.

The bird continued to flit along the riverside, the walkway frequently wet or even slightly submerged. Doc kept an eye on the other bank of the river, which was not poured concrete like this side, but rather a sloping green space leading up to a street above. He would be visible to anyone who happened to look over, but Doc noticed that few people paid much mind to this underbelly of the City, a forgotten path, like the ones Erasmus talked about when describing how teleportation worked. Magicians walk trails others have forgotten, Erasmus said. And if we're not careful, we are forgotten as well.

Along the way, Doc passed several vertical grates, which he knew were used either for runoff from the ground above, or to help manage the flow of the river should it flood. Every time he passed one, he held his breath, worried that this would be the place the bird led him to, and that there would be a grim discovery waiting for him. But each time, the bird continued on, ignoring the grate.

It came to rest above one final opening. Doc stopped walking and waited for the bird to renew its flight, but it remained still, waiting for him to dismiss it from its duties. Doc reached the grate, and found to his dismay that, unlike the others, it was not barred shut, but rather open, the metal door itself removed from the hinges. It was a low pipe, a thin trickle of gray water drizzling out from the mouth, short enough he'd need to duck to walk inside, but not so small he'd need to crawl.

Small enough for a child, though, Doc thought. It's small enough for a child.

"Go do something on your own, he said," Doc muttered to himself. He looked up to the spectral bird and nodded. "You did well, little friend. You are free of your duties. I thank you."

Doc repeated the phrase again in an old, forgotten language that Erasmus had been teaching him, and the bird puffed out its chest, and then fluttered away, seemingly becoming one with the sunlight as it disappeared. Doc cast another spell, uttering a single word and making a strange, almost elegant pattern with his hand, and a tiny ball of light appeared in his palm. He held it out like a flashlight in front of him.

I know I can't save everyone, he thought. But please don't let this be one I fail.

***

The tunnel started out ordinary, a wide tube of man-made construction, grimy and old, smelling of sewage and river water. But perhaps two hundred feet in, Doc found a break in the tunnel on his left, a hole of raw stone where the normal construction broke.

He stared down into the runoff pipe, then looked into the gap, and chose the latter.

Doc found himself in a rough-hewn, five or six foot hole in the concrete. The stone here was natural, and unskillfully chipped away. Beyond that, the new pathway opened up, and what he saw turned his guts to acid.

It was a place that should not exist. A manmade tunnel, the ceiling held up by spires carved with images of illogical monsters and eyes, its walls made of cracked greenish brick. Water dripped from the shadowed ceiling, though whether because of the river or simple condensation, he could not tell.

Doc placed each step cautiously, careful to not scrape the sole of his shoe or kick a stray stone. He listened. The space sounded as though the walls themselves were breathing. He tightened his grip on the small globe of light in his palm to dim it, offering just enough light to see by, and he walked deeper inside.

He came to a split in the tunnel and cocked his head, listening for voices. When he heard nothing, he whispered an incantation.

"Show me the way," he asked, his question directed as if to the air itself. He felt the softest breeze from the right-hand tunnel and carried on.

The tunnel was not straight, winding in a serpentine motion in the darkness. Twice more he came upon forks in the path, and asked the air to guide him. Eventually the path opened up into a larger room. The sound of breathing was louder now, and he heard the faint sound of a man chanting. This pulled his attention immediately. Doc followed the sound of the voice, emanating from the largest of several carved archways leading out of the room. He didn't recognize the words or language, but there was a cadence to it that was familiar. Doc thought it was reminiscent of the inflection used in certain spells Erasmus had told him about. Spells of summoning and conjuration.

He was so absorbed in eavesdropping he nearly yelled when a small voice spoke to him.

"Mister?"

Doc bit back a startled scream and looked for the source of the voice. A few feet behind him was what he at first thought was a vent or grate, one of several that lined the wall at knee level. But the more he looked at it the more clearly he could see that it wasn't a grate – the bars, horrifyingly, were like jagged teeth in a half-closed smile, forming a small cage. Inside the nearest one was the girl from the missing poster.

Doc put a finger to his lips to quiet the child and searched the next-closest mouth-cage. Inside, he saw bones, and old, graying clothing.

You can't save everyone, he thought. You can't save everyone.

He crouched down beside the cage the girl was locked in and examined the teeth. In the dim light it was hard to tell if they were simply carved to look like fangs, or if they were organic; the coloration looked like bone, though, and the stone the fangs were embedded in were a glistening, raw red.

"I'm going to get you out of here," he said. "What's your name?"

"Carmen," the girl said.

"Okay, Carmen. I'm Doc. Let's find a way to get you out of this cage. Was there a key?"

She shook her head.

"It just opened on its own," she said. "Then the bad man threw me inside and it closed."

Doc tried to let the gut-wrenching terror he felt at that description not show on his face, but he could tell from Carmen's expression that he failed miserably.

"That's okay. We can fix this," he said. He tried pulling on one of the teeth, but it held fast, and then thought about kicking it, but worried he'd make too much noise.

Magic it is, then, Doc thought. He called to mind the language of word-magic Erasmus taught him, and, in that lilting, eerie tongue, asked the cage to open.

Nothing happened. Doc nodded, both irritated and curious. Erasmus had taught him that most things would do as you asked if you knew their name and made the request the right way. A locked window, a cloud blocking the sun, a fire burning too bright. But sometimes you had to be more forceful. You had to change your request to show the named thing who you were.

"I asked you once," Doc said in the language of magic. "And now I command you. Open your gates and let this child out."

He felt a pulse of pain in his mind, a sharp pushback from the cage, like a willful refusal. Doc asked again, this time more forcefully. He added a twist to the spell that implied a threat, that there would be consequences if the door did not comply.

A few seconds later, the toothy gateway opened, more mouth than doorway. Doc's breath came short as he reached his hand inside to Carmen, half-expecting the teeth to snap shut, either clamping down onto his wrist and taking his hand, or lacerating the child as she stepped out. Neither happened, though, and the gate remained open even after Carmen was free. For some reason, Doc spoke a word of thanks to the cage, as if to reward it for fulfilling his command.

And then he noticed the chanting had stopped.

Doc carefully stood up to his full height and then felt a sharp pain explode in his shoulder. He spun around and fell backward onto the ground. Beside him, Carmen screamed in fear. Looming over him was what at first he thought some kind of demon, but he quickly realized it was a man in a grotesque mask. Antlers jutted from the mask's forehead eerily like bony, broken fingers.

"The great ones must be fed," the man said, and raised his weapon above his head. It was a knife, comically ornate, with a wavy, pointed blade. He prepared to jab it downward into Doc's half-prone body. "The great ones are hungry."

Without thinking, Doc made three quick gestures with his left hand—a point, a clench, a twist—and a faintly greenish burst of arcane force shot from his closed fist. This struck the knife-wielding man in the chest, knocking him off his feet. Doc struggled back to kneeling position and watched as the masked man stubbled, tripped, and then fell backward ten feet from him. It would have been a comical site, Doc thought, except for the horrific cracking noise he heard as the man struck the cavern floor.

When do I get to learn how to cast a fireball? Doc had complained to Erasmus for months as he'd taught him the simple telekinetic spell he'd used on the man. But the old wizard was adamant. *Trust me,* he'd said. *A good hard shove will save your life a lot more often than pyromania.*

The man with the dagger didn't get back up. Doc winced, half with worry he'd just killed a man, half at the worrisome dampness on his back he knew was his own blood. He looked down at Carmen as if to apologize, but she was looking past him and pointing.

"What are you..." Doc started to say, but then reflexively spun around and cast another spell, a sort of inversion of the one he'd used to push his attack away. This time, a nearly translucent wall, not unlike a soap bubble, spread out from the palm of his hand, just in time to deflect another blade – this one aimed at his neck. Another masked man stood to Doc's right, reversing his grip on his knife to go for another stab.

"You don't know what you've done," the creeping knife-wielder said. "The great ones cannot go hungry. If they are not fed, they grow so angry..."

Doc felt his head swim and realized he could feel the trickle of blood from his shoulder all the way down into the small of his back, pooling here and growing sticky and cold. Don't you dare pass out, he thought, gritting his teeth less at the pain and more at the growing weakness of blood loss. He took a step back protectively toward Carmen and then glanced past his oncoming attacker. Doc spotted a loose rock, nearly the size of a cantaloupe, resting on the ground behind him. He reached out an open hand for it.

"Come to me," he said to the rock in the secret language of magic. It leapt to the air with brutal speed and rocketed toward his outstretched hand. The masked attacker seemed to notice its approach only at the last minute, turning to investigate just in time to take the rock full in the face. His mask shattered, horns splintering and falling to the ground like splintered branches. Doc caught the stone, covered in blood and too heavy for him to hold in one hand without the aid of magic, and then tossed it aside.

I've got to get this kid out of here, he thought. But then he looked past the body of the first masked man, where the chanting had been coming from. He could hear a pulsing noise from within, like a heartbeat.

"Did you see any other kids here?" Doc asked Carmen, who stared at him with horrified wonder. Doc turned back to the tunnel from which he'd arrived, and then once again to the alcove where the pulsing noise was emanating from.

I have to be sure, he thought.

"Stay right there," he said, inching toward the deeper opening in the cavern. I'll just look, Doc said. I won't let the kid out of my sight. If it's bad, I'll run. I just need to make sure there isn't some other child waiting to be eaten by whatever these great ones are. I'll never forgive myself if I just walk out.

As quietly as he could be, going weak in the knees from blood loss, he walked up to the entrance and listened. The closer he got, the more it truly did sound like a heartbeat. Ba-dump. Ba-dump. Ba-dump.

The room beyond was dark, lit only by the faintest of torches. A stone bier, too finely carved to be some improvised table, rested in the center of the room, mercifully empty of victims. Standing over that bier nearly stole Doc's bladder control. A twelve-foot-tall humanoid shape, hunched and big-belled, with huge eyes glittering red and a mouth like a toad. Wings sprouted from its back, bat-like and comically small for the creature's bulk. Doc held his breath for longer than he realized, waiting for the creature to move, before convincing himself that it was, in fact, just a statue.

And then the statue blinked.

Doc turned tail and ran, then, forgetting the pain in his back and shoulder, the cloudiness in his head replaced by the sharp clarity of adrenaline. He scooped up Carmen as he ran by her, the child wrapping her arms tightly around his neck, and he bolted back down the original tunnel.

"Close your eyes, Carmen," he said, unsure if he shouted it or whispered. "Don't look back. Just keep your eyes closed till I tell you we're safe."

She said nothing, clinging even more tightly.

For a heart-stopping moment Doc thought he was lost, until instinct or memory took over and he tore left into the narrow hallway leading to the break in the sewer pipe. He almost fell over as his boots struck the slimy muck coating the pipe, but he stayed on his feet, and kept running, faster than he'd ever thought he could. The cool river air hit his face like a cleansing rain, the opening of the drainpipe feeling like an oncoming train before him.

"Something's coming!" Carmen wailed in his year, but Doc didn't look back, afraid that if he did he'd lock up, or trip and fall, and no spell shield or telekinetic push was going to save them from that. He didn't hear footsteps behind him, no thunderous creature in hot pursuit, and somehow the quiet made it worse. If he could hear its claws scrabbling on the concrete it would give a home to his fear, rather than this nebulous, surreal terror.

Finally he burst out into the daylight, nearly falling headlong into the river. He turned left again, not slowing down, worried he'd slip and fall and take the child with him, but his boots somehow maintained their grip on the wet concrete. The sun was still shining down on them, a mid-afternoon glow that would have been beautiful in any other circumstance. Finally, he came across an iron ladder leading up to the street level.

"Hold on tight," he said, needing both hands to haul himself and Carmen back up the ten or fifteen feet back to the real world. And now, he thought, he had to look, had to be sure if they were being followed. He started to climb and, teeth clenched so hard his gums began to bleed, he turned to face where they'd come from.

He saw only the river, passively flowing toward the ocean, golden sunlight breaking across its surface. No unearthly creature slouching toward them to devour them.

Doc wasn't ready to feel safe yet, though. He dragged them

both up the ladder, landing in a dead-end road where locals would park to walk along the river. He half-expected along, reptilian arm to explode from the river and drag them to their deaths below, but nothing came. He carried Carmen another block, then set her down and took her hand so he could walk with him. They found a bench on a busier street, a place where they could sit and be seen by other people but not overheard, and Doc tried to catch his breath.

"You're hurt," Carmen said.

"I think a little bit," Doc said. "It's okay. Are you okay?"

"I don't know," she said.

"Hey," he said, reaching into his pocket and pulling out the missing poster. He handed the poster to her. "Your family is looking for you. Want to go home?"

"Yeah," she said. "Can I go home now?"

***

In hindsight, he should have called for a taxi. But instead, Doc limped across town to the apartment building listed on the missing poster, on the opposite end of town from where he'd grown up himself. He used a simple illusion spell to hide his injury and make them both look more inconspicuous rather than covered in muck and blood. They talked the whole way, about her siblings – an older sister, a baby brother – about her mom and dad, and her grandmother who lived upstairs. She asked him his real name and he told her he couldn't remember it anymore, but his new name was Doc Silence, which she said was very silly.

He said he thought so too.

They arrived at the apartment building, and Doc asked the door to the foyer to open, which it did, and then Doc asked her which number she lived in, and she told him, so Doc scooped Carmen up so she could push the call button herself and talk into the speaker.

"Mama," she said through a smile. "It's me."

Doc could hear her mother growing hysterical on the other end, telling her to stay put and she'd be right down, could hear a young girl's voice crying in the background, her sister's Doc assumed. He sat Carmen down on a small countertop covered in mail and flyers and told her to wait here, and her mother would there soon.

"Will you stay and meet her?" she asked.

Doc shook his head.

"It's better if I don't," Doc said. Too many questions, he knew, the sort of questions that only had answers that caused more questions, and Erasmus had warned him over and over again that most people don't need to know about the things that wait for them in the darkest of places. The world is hard enough without knowing monsters exist.

"Can I tell her you saved me?" Carmen asked. Doc heard a door bang deeper in the building somewhere upstairs. Her family rushing to her rescue. Time to go.

"Sure," Doc said. It's probably fine, he thought. I'm not real anymore anyway. She might as well tell him one of Santa's elves saved her.

Unsure what to do, he put a hand on her hair and smiled.

"You stay safe, okay? You'll be fine. I'll make sure those people never take anyone else ever again."

"Okay," she said. "You'll be safe too?"

"Sure," he lied. And then he stepped back out the front door, turned up the collar on his ruined jacket, and walked away, casting another illusion to hide himself from her family. He could hear crying and fussing, Carmen talking and then bursting into tears, even the sound of an older woman, her grandmother Doc figured, who could barely contain herself.

Doc nodded to himself and smiled.

And then he went back to the river.

***

Erasmus found Doc sitting on a bench directly across the river from the pipe where he'd found Carmen. Doc had been there for hour hours, waiting and watching to see if anyone came or went from the tunnel, human or otherwise. He wasn't sure what he'd do about it if he had, but he wanted to be sure. But night was falling, and his back hurt like hell, and his eyes were growing heavy.

The old man grunted as he sat down next to him.

"You look like garbage," Erasmus said.

"Yeah," Doc said.

"So I understand you saved one today," Erasmus said.

"I think there were probably a lot more before her I didn't save," Doc said.

Erasmus nodded.

"There's so much darkness in the world, kid," he said. "You have to pick the battles you can win."

"Did I win this one?"

"You're breathing," Erasmus said. "The child is home with her parents. You won."

"That thing is still in there," Doc said.

"Maybe," Erasmus said. "But with no one to feed it, it'll go back to sleep for another century or more, and no one will be dragged into the darkness."

"Can we kill it?"

Erasmus shook his head.

"It'll just come back in another form," he said "At least now we know here it's hiding. That's another win."

"I know I can't save everyone," Doc said. "But I'd like to try."

"We all do at first," Erasmus said. "I won't try to stop you."

"Erasmus," Doc said.

"Yeah?"

"I want to be able to cast a fireball," he said.

"We can do that."

"I also want a sword."

"A sword."

"Yeah," Doc said.

"What are you doing, pretending to be Gandalf?"

"I killed a man with a rock today. I think a sword would be less

49

horrific."

"Ever stabbed someone with a sword?" Erasmus said.

"No."

"I'll get you a sword and you can decide if it's less horrific than a rock."

"Fair enough."

"Now let's get that shoulder looked at, hero," Erasmus said. "And then we'll work on a fireball."

The old wizard grunted again as he got to his feet, and offered a hand to help Doc up, which Doc realized in that moment he actually needed. And together they walked home, wreathed in magic to make the world forget them.

Neither saw the thing slither from the pipe. It stared up at the night sky for a moment, searching the cosmos for some unknown answer. And then it left, in search of prey.

Chapter 8: A litany of cost

Erasmus had been right about one thing: the second enchanted tattoo didn't hurt nearly as much as the first one. Doc sat in the same chair in the same tattoo parlor in Dublin, the same artist, red-faced and exhausted, working her needle into his forearm. This would be one of two arcane sigils painted into his skin today: this one for war, conjuring a weapon should he need it, and the other for protection against harm. Doc had learned to cast both spells first by memory and then by instinct before Erasmus would take him back to Dublin, and now, with these mystic icons on his body, he could weave the spells even easier, even faster, without eating away at his own reserves.

"You have to master the spell before you can cheat a little," Erasmus said. "It's nothing but trouble, skipping ahead. I've seen men torn apart by their own ink, trying to control spells they didn't fully understand. Happened a lot during the war."

"Which war?" Doc asked.

Erasmus had to pause and think about it before answering.

"A few of them, if I'm being honest," Erasmus said. "Though I was specifically thinking about World War II. There was a particularly aggressive rash of fools who tried their hand at magics they didn't understand during that conflict."

Doc closed his eyes and listened to the buzzing of the tattoo needle, its bee-sting burn causing his heart to race.

"What kind of magic did the men in the sewers use?" Doc asked. "It wasn't like anything you've taught me."

"And it's not a kind of magic I intend to teach you," Erasmus said sternly.

"So it's not like ours," Doc said.

The tattoo artist, Bláithín, stopped working, and Doc opened his eyes to see her staring at Erasmus, who shrugged and sighed. The artist went back to work.

"No, it's not like ours," Erasmus said. "I've told you there are different kinds of magic."

"I'd like to know more about the other kinds," Doc said.

Erasmus fixed a grim expression on him.

"How am I supposed to fight it if I don't know what it is?" Doc asked.

"There's the quandary," Erasmus said. "I can't send you out into the world blind, of course. But magicians are, by and large, idiots. We can't keep our hands out of the cookie jar. We learn about a new kind of magic and we want to try it, to control it. And that is why there are so many dead magicians."

"I'm not an idiot."

"You walked into a sewer alone and were almost sacrificed to a star spawn for dinner. I'd say that makes you a Mensa candidate."

"You told me to go out and get into trouble!"

"Color me impressed by your ability to so easily find more trouble than you could feasibly handle," Erasmus said. "Fine. Fine. Ask your questions, and I'll answer the ones I decide won't lead you to getting yourself killed."

Doc winced as the artist wiped away ink weeping from his arm. That was the worst part, he'd decided, wiping away the ink and blood. The needle itself hurt less than the scraping of a paper towel against a fresh tattoo.

"Okay. What are the other kinds of magic?" Doc said. "What kind of magic is 'feeding kids to monsters' magic?'"

Erasmus rolled his eyes.

"The bad kind," he said. "I've been teaching you what I consider the… cleanest of magic. Magic is a litany of cost, and our magic pays in balance. We ask reality to change, and we must consider that change and how it impacts the world around it. The cost of word magic is that you must learn it. You must speak its tongue, and ask when you can, and demand when you must, and you must always be aware of the difference. If you demand too much to warp this world, the world will take the cost from you."

"Which is why you say we ask first," Doc said.

"Exactly. Word magic is a polite art."

"Art?" Doc asked.

"Don't let the movies fool you. Or other magicians, who might one day tell you otherwise. There's very little science to magic. You don't dole out change in mathematical equations. You must be creative. When you ask the world to change itself for you, you tell a story of what you want it to be, and that story must be convincing. The more artistic your skill, the stranger and more beautiful the magic you can create."

"So we're artists, not scientists," Doc said.

"In a way," Erasmus said. "Not that we don't share similarities with scientists. We're always searching for the undiscovered thing. We share what we learn, and hoard what we know."

Doc glanced down at the tattoo on his arm. He knew it was the first letter of the name of a war god, the symbol a letter in a forgotten language.

"What about the symbols in our tattoos?" Doc asked. "Are those also word magic?"

"Sister to it," the artist said softly. Doc turned to face her, and she looked at Erasmus questioningly. The old magician nodded to go on. "Spoken magic is transient. It ebbs and flows. If you commit magic to writing, it becomes something else. An anchor for the impossible in this world. It's why magic books are so valuable. Why certain runes and sigils are frowned upon, if not entirely forbidden. They share a lot of similarities, but written magic and spoken magic aren't the same, though they do work side by side."

"You've been teaching me how to use written symbols in some of my spells," Doc said.

"For things you want to be less transient," Erasmus said. "Bindings and summonings. Warnings and defenses."

"And neither of these make you nervous, at least teaching me," Doc said.

Erasmus shook his head.

"Teaching anyone magic makes me nervous, but I can live with the cost these spells will wield over you," Erasmus said. "Plus they're my specialty. I'm best suited to teach these to you."

The artist wiped his arm again, this time with a clear, healing gel of some kind. It burned, and then cooled, and Doc felt a strange, chilly energy creep down his forearm.

"Okay then," Doc said. "Tell me about the kind of magic I shouldn't learn."

Erasmus cocked his head at him.

"I'm serious," Doc said. "This isn't me trying to tell you to tempt me to try something stupid. I want to know what bear traps to not step in."

Erasmus weighed his thoughts for a moment, then nodded.

"Fine," he said. "There is word magic, written magic; these are old, and take time to master, but if you control them, you are self-sufficient, able to call upon the energy around you as you will. But other magicians are impatient. Or they aren't happy with their mastery of these slower magics, so they look for short cuts. One of those shortcuts, for example, is blood magic."

The artist paused in her work to make a warding symbol in the air with a black-gloved finger, then went back to her art.

"Blood magic is exactly what it sounds like—you shed blood and take the life energy from your victims. It's barbaric work," Erasmus said. "Some practitioners keep their sacrifices small, bleeding animals for example. You might have heard old stories of witches or shaman reading entrails of an animal. That's minor blood magic, and not the worst in the world, but the cost for true blood magic escalates quickly."

"I don't know," Doc said. "Killing a goat for a spell sounds pretty awful to me."

"Oh, I don't like it at all," Erasmus said. "I'm a vegetarian. I don't even like sacrificing a turkey for a sandwich, let alone a spell. But you understand what I'm saying. The greater the sacrifice, the more powerful the magic."

"Is that what the men in the sewers were doing, then?" Doc said. "Human sacrifice?"

"Maybe," Erasmus said. Doc saw the old magician catch a questioning look from the artist. "No, no, not here. This was on the other side of the Atlantic."

The artist shrugged grumpily and went back to work.

"If it wasn't blood magic, what was it?" Doc asked.

Erasmus scratched at his short silver beard.

"I'd suspect it was a pact with the creature," he said.

"A pact," Doc repeated.

"Some magicians bypass learning magic at all," Erasmus said. "Why spend years learning proper magic when you can go right to the source? They make deals with demons or other immortal creatures from beyond in exchange for power. For some, this is playing with fire while covered in gasoline. For others, it is the high art of deal-making. I've met some incredibly powerful spellcasters who juggled pacts and deals with any number of entities, trading in favors or information or worse. Some are even brokers of that power and pass the cost of their spells onto unwitting victims, middle-men of mystical."

"At least that doesn't sound as bad as blood magic," Doc said.

"Oh, gods, that is absolutely wrong," Erasmus said. The tattoo artist chuckled softly. "I'd rather have you dabbling your little hands in blood magic than even think about some sort of deal-magic."

"Really?" Doc asked.

"Yes," Erasmus said. "At least with blood magic you pay the cost on the spot. With pacts, you trade away future harm for immediate power. It's the worst kind of compact."

"So maybe those men were paying their cost by giving the monster children," Doc said.

"Maybe," Erasmus said. "More likely though, the cost of the power they'd obtained was the damnation of becoming monsters themselves. For many of the undying things who make deals with mortals, giving away a bit of magical ability is nothing compared to the benefit of corrupting living creatures and turning them into monsters, agents of evil among humanity. It's hard to tell, though. Immortal denizens of other planes are almost impossible to truly understand. It's why you'd be an idiot to make a deal like that. You'll never know what was in the fine print."

"Is that a literal statement or are you being metaphorical?" Doc asked.

"About the fine print?" Erasmus said. "Both, honestly. Sometimes there really is fine print. A lot of demons become lawyers if they stick around the mortal plane long enough."

Doc sighed, not sure if Erasmus was joking or not, and the fact that the artist laughed didn't help clarify.

"So there's word magic, blood magic, bargaining magic... do they all do the same thing?"

Erasmus half-nodded, half-shook his head, a perfect pantomime of noncommittal.

"Like I said, magic is art. What you do with it depends on how creative you can be with it. But all of these let you tap into that font of change you need to sculpt your art."

The artist cleaned off the tattoo one more time, sprinkling a silvery powder on it which Doc knew to be arcane in some way, which was absorbed into the ink on contact. She covered the wound carefully in plastic wrap, which then taped down. Doc took a sip of some water and sat up in the chair a bit.

"Any other terribly dangerous types of magic I should avoid

being tempted by?" he asked.

"Just know what you're getting into before you try anything," Erasmus said. "Fae magic is dangerous because it's seductive and charming, but the fae are all con artists and you can't trust a thing any of them say."

"That sounds like you're making a generalization," Doc said.

"Talk to a couple of faeries and get back to me on that," Erasmus said. "And of course be wary of any natural spellcasters. It's not that they're bad, per se—it's that if they're born into a magical aptitude and nobody helps them learn to control it, they're basically time bombs."

"People can be born knowing magic?" Doc said.

"Less 'knowing' and more naturally able to tap into the magic all around them," Erasmus said. "It's rare, but it happens, and I'd say about a quarter of the natural disasters that have happened in human history have been because someone didn't get to them first."

"Human time bombs," Doc said. "Got it."

"Also, be wary of true believers," Erasmus said. "They tend to have no idea what they're doing either."

"Like, religious magicians?" Doc asked.

"Not exactly," Erasmus said. "It's like this: the magic is out there, untapped potential. And if someone believes they can do something hard enough... sometimes they can get lucky and tap into that mystical energy."

"Which they then attribute to what they believe in," Doc half-said, half-asked.

"Like bloody Peter Pan," the tattoo artist said, prepping her inks for Doc's next tattoo.

"What?" Doc asked.

"I do believe in fairies, I do, I do, I do," Bláithín said. "Flying around like he owns the place."

"Wait, Peter Pan is real?" Doc asked.

"I should know," the artist said. "I inked him. He lost a bet and had to get 'Wendy' on his rump."

Doc looked at Erasmus for confirmation, and the old magician just smirked.

"I can't tell if you're both putting me on," Doc said.

"Ah, sarcasm," Erasmus said. "That is its own kind of magic entirely."

Chapter 9: The leaving

In his later years, Doc would tell you, if you asked, that he left the City in search of adventure. He'd tell you that he grew tired of a one man fight against strange cultists who lived beneath the City, or that he grew bored of one place. He might tell you he left when Erasmus disappeared for a while without explanation, which is partially true, though not the whole story.

The reason he left, which Doc would never tell anyone, not for many, many years, was he saw his father on the street, and his father looked right through him.

The City is a massive place, with a population large enough it's not impossible to go months without seeing a familiar face. This is doubly true if your familiar faces are from the suburban outskirts of the City, away from the bustle and action of the downtown. And truth be told, Doc didn't spend much time out in public anyway. He was off practicing spellcraft with Erasmus, or teleporting to strange locations where the old magician would teach him about leylines, or hidden libraries, or monsters humanity thought were just myth and legend.

But on this particular day, Doc stopped for a cup of coffee, politely holding the door for someone walking out with a cardboard tray of drinks, and that person turned out to be his father.

Doc felt his heart break, but smiled as kindly as he could, and his father nodded back as if he were a stranger. He got into a car outside, where their cheerful family dog, a mutt who had been just a few years old when Doc gave away his name and his life, sat in the front seat, mouth open as if the aging dog were smiling. The dog looked right at Doc, though, and Doc realized he knew him. The spell didn't work on him, Doc thought, biting his inner cheek to fight back tears. I never existed for my family because of that spell, but for my dog, I just left one day and never came home.

Doc bought his coffee, threw most of it away, and went home to start packing.

***

Erasmus wasn't there when Doc left, but the old wizard had prepared him to break out on his own already anyway. By this time Doc's upper body was half-covered in mystic tattoos, runes of protection and teleportation, sigils of fire and ice and air, words in dead languages evoking or warding off spirits and shadows.

Erasmus had also taught him what he referred to as common sense magic, and somehow, Doc was more uncomfortable with this sort of sorcery than conjuring fire or turning stone to water.

For example: Erasmus taught Doc how to create money.

"I'm not really sure this is legal," Doc said the first time Erasmus showed him the trick. It was easy, alarmingly simple, really. The magician could coax actual currency from bank machines if he wanted—"machines are terribly vulnerable to magic," Erasmus said, "as they run on pure logic and can't adjust to chaos." Or he would use his preferred trick, which was to turn strips of paper into money. He would hold the paper like playing cards and whisper to it, and suddenly spread out in his hands like a fan would be dollar bills in whatever denomination he requested.

"How do you not get arrested?" Doc said.

"Look, kid, money isn't real," Erasmus said. "Money is a mental construct just like magic, only it's boring. Someone shakes a bit of cloth with someone's face on it and tells you it can be turned into bread, or a coat, or a car. All we're doing is tweaking the mythology of currency."

"This feels kind of... I don't know," Doc said.

"Gauche?" Erasmus offered.

"Y'know, I wasn't going to use that word, but that might be the one I was looking for," Doc said.

"Oh, it's gauche. It's trashy. It's boring," Erasmus said "But magicians for thousands of years have conjured the means they need to survive. If a magician must spend all his waking hours toiling for something like money, when will he have time to practice his art? In fact, you're doing the world a service by conjuring your own money."

"You realize you sound like you're making excuses," Doc said.

"Look, if I turn this," he said, wagging a stack of Post-It notes, "into twenty dollar bills, whoever I give them to can spend them, and nobody gets hurt. I happen to know at least three magicians who manipulate the stock market, and frankly, I have no guilt about what I do compared to harm those sleaze bags do."

"I still don't like it," Doc said.

"You don't have to," Erasmus said. "But some day, you'll need a train ticket, and you'll turn a brochure about a local museum into what you need, and you'll be happy for it."

As Doc stood in the train station holding, in fact, a brochure for a local museum, he wondered momentarily if Erasmus had somehow looked into the future. In this case, though, Doc did not turn the brochure into money. He spoke words of transformation and words of luck, and across the room, a seat on the train disappeared from the computer system, and a ticket for that very seat appeared in his hand where the brochure once rested. This was a trick Erasmus had taught him only when Doc had demanded to learn how to cut out the middle man. He was more comfortable manipulating probability or seat numbers than he was turning lead to gold, or paper to a cotton/linen blend.

He took his newly minted ticket, hefted his backpack, and headed for the train, heading south for places he'd never been.

In his bag he carried a notebook. One of many, actually—the bag was enchanted, another project assigned to him by Erasmus, so that it would be both bigger on the inside and resistant to theft by ordinary means, and so it carried far more books than it should have. But one notebook in particular contained a list of places. Places where weird things happened that scared people, or made them doubt their eyes. A map of strange places where magic might be needed. Where Doc might learn something, or do some good, or maybe even both.

And so he sat in his seat, the train car mostly empty, a sad indication that Doc had committed petty magical theft for no reason, really, and he watched the City, the place where he was born and grew up, disappear behind him. He felt a heady combination of emotions, relief and anxiety, nostalgia and excitement, regret and anticipation. He broke open his notebook, and he began to plan.

***

It would be a year before he heard from Erasmus again. In that time, he'd fought zombies in a graveyard in Tennessee, was nearly gutted by a lycanthropic wild boar in Georgia; he rescued a man who had been stolen away by Puk-Wudjie in Delaware, and nearly lost his life to a will o' wisp on a Florida swamp.

He also found that often, darkness had nothing to do with magic, and he tried to help there, as well. Spells could be used to find missing children stolen away by ordinary evil men as readily as they could be used to find grim, back-alley sorcerers.

After a while, he stopped feeling guilty about things like conjuring train tickets or turning scrap paper to money. He never asked for payment for his services, never asked for anything, really, and he knew he could do this because he didn't need anything. Magic had freed him to do something few people could do: to help without needing help in return. Sometimes his reasons were selfish. Yes, the will o'wisps were dangerous, but they were beautiful, and strange, and Doc Silence could be greedy in his desire to see new things and unlock the mysteries of the world. Satisfied curiosity was the payment he took from the stranger cases he solved. He'd trade these secrets for arcane tattoos, or for tools he could use in his travels. Sometimes he'd come across artifacts as well, charms or tomes from which magic wafted like perfume.

He was often afraid, and sometimes lonely. But it was an education. And he never felt like he had taken on a task he could not resolve himself. Not until the house in Louisiana, where the paintings moved, and the darkness knew his name.

Chapter 10: The house at the end of all worlds

There are an almost infinite number of haunted houses in Louisiana, Doc discovered, through story and experience. Haunted houses are mostly caused by pain, and any place marked by blood and sorrow will have more than its fair share. He learned early on to leave well enough alone, though. The restless dead were not within his rights to tell what to do or where to go. He would, particularly in his early years, occasionally be asked to exorcise an old manor, but mostly he would go, speak to the ghosts or spirits there, and ask if they needed anything. Once in a while there was some good he could do—bury a body left abandoned; replace a wedding ring stolen once even tormenting the apparition of a terrible man until he tore himself apart.

But he did not feel that this was his place, and often when he learned of a haunted building he would avoid it, because the dead, whether they wanted to be or not, were drawn inextricably to magicians, and even by twenty he was beginning to become worn down by the unquiet dead.

He was preparing to leave this haunted place and head north

again when he heard about the Marsh House.

A practitioner of street magic named Cassiopeia Jones mentioned it in passing as they traded secrets and shared a bottle, sitting on a balcony on a hot, quiet night. They'd been complaining, in a way, about the ghosts—not the ghosts themselves, but the endless pain and sadness of this place, the way it weighed you down, the fact that they felt like they could never fix all the suffering they encountered. Doc was ready to leave, but Cassiopeia was born there and felt as though the haunted places were her responsibility somehow.

"But not the Marsh House," she said, brushing long braids from her face. "I don't know what goes on there, and I don't care to. Whatever it is, haunted is the wrong word."

"What do you mean?" Doc said, trying to hide the curiosity in his voice. He failed, and Cassiopeia smirked at him.

"I hear that tone," she said. "I'd tell you not to go there, but telling a magician to not look for something is like telling a child to not stick a fork into an electrical socket."

"I'm not going to go there," Doc lied. "I'm just curious."

Cassiopeia shrugged.

"I like you well enough, Doc Silence, but if you want to disappear into the void, I won't stop you," she said. "It is said there are voices there, but not ghosts. That dark magic swirls around it, but not necromancy. That a shadow falls over it, but not a curse. And that it is far larger on the inside than outside."

"Sounds utterly boring," Doc said.

Cassiopeia laughed.

"If you go inside, let me say it has been a pleasure knowing you," she said. "May your death be swift and painless."

***

The Marsh House, which of course Doc decided to visit the next morning, was aptly named in more ways than one. It was, quite literally, on the precipice of a marsh, so close to the water that

Doc was surprised the structure still stood. And of course, it was once owned by a family known as Marsh, which, as metaphors went, felt a little too on the nose for Doc's liking.

Despite its location on what could be considered a death sentence for any home, the manor, a three-story mansion, once white but now spattered with green from age and moisture, seemed to be in relative good health. The windows had mostly remained intact, the door still on its hinges, and the encroaching wetlands had not yet eroded the foundation, though sharp swampy grass grew up all around the property, and drooping trees hung like spider webs everywhere.

Doc parked a rental car on a road of questionable quality at the edge of the property and started walking toward it. He cast a minor spell causing the local insect population to find him less delicious and uttered a set of phrases weaving transformation and divination magic and ran his thumbs over both eyes. When he opened them, he could see the faint glow of magic from within the house, a jumble of deep blue energy peppered with what looked like motes of starlight.

"Huh," Doc muttered to himself. He'd never seen anything quite like it; a unique pattern of mystic energy that felt both simple and inscrutable. He wondered briefly what Erasmus would make of it, checked to make sure he had the heavy flashlight and knife he carried just in case his spells didn't work, and walked up the path to the front door.

Doc assumed the door would be locked. Someone owned this building, he assumed, be it heirs of the Marshes or the bank who held its mortgage, and someone would claim responsibility for it and want to protect it. But the door opened with a simple turn of the knob. Doc nudged the door fully open with the toe of his boot and stepped inside, closing the door quietly behind him.

Within, he found himself in a narrow foyer, black and white tiles now stained with age slightly slippery below his feet. A staircase with an elegant bannister lead upstairs, with doorways left, right, and center ahead of him. He took a few strides toward the bannister and looked back, where he found the door not only closed behind him, but thirty or forty feet further away than he expected.

Bigger inside, he thought, grimacing and wondering what he'd gotten himself into.

His eyes still ensorcelled by the detection spell he'd cast on himself, he could see a glow from the doorway ahead to his left and made his way there. Turning the corner, he found a grand living room, a moldering couch near a cold fireplace, a great window looking out at what should have been the marsh.

The marsh was gone.

Doc stepped up to the window, which had a bench built in below it, and examined the world outside. Blackened ash or sand covered the ground, with bits of ember or flame bleeding up from below. The sky was a grim red in color, with dark mountains far in the distance.

"Terrible, isn't it," a woman's voice said to his right. Doc turned, feigning calm indifference as his heart leapt into his throat. He wasn't sure what he expected, a ghost, an apparition, some spectral presence, but instead he saw a painting on the wall, a woman in clothes better suited for a hundred years ago looking back at him.

"Doesn't look pleasant, no," Doc said to the painting. He placed his fingertips on the window and found it hot to the touch.

"It rarely changes," the painting said. "I've been looking at it for so long, and it almost never changes."

"Are you trapped in there?" Doc asked.

The woman smiled and looked appraisingly at the frame around her.

"No," she said. "How can someone be trapped in that which they are?"

"Metaphorically I'd say that's pretty common," Doc said, almost laughing at himself. "It's easy to be trapped by who you are. But I'm not sure about this."

The woman shrugged.

"It doesn't bother me," she said. "Is it still America outside?"

"It is," Doc said.

"Hm," the woman said, and Doc could not tell if she were pleased or displeased by his answer.

"Do you want to leave here?"

The woman shrugged apathetically.

"Hell is hell," she said. "At least I have a room with a view. You should talk to the others, though."

"Others?" Doc asked. The woman in the painting nodded.

"I wonder if you'll stay," she said. "I wonder what room they'll hang your painting in."

Doc nodded politely to her and started to walk away, toward a doorway at the back of the room.

"I guess we'll find out," he said.

This led him into a grand kitchen of sorts, more black and white tile, marble countertops covered in dust. There was no rotting food, something Doc had come to find was a staple of haunted houses, but pots, pans, plates, utensils, everything stood at the ready, as if phantom dinner guests might arrive at any moment. To his left, the kitchen opened up into a kind of glass conservatory, and outside, he saw a lush jungle, light rain pattering against the glass.

"I know you're watching me," Doc said out loud.

The tattoo on the nape of his neck, a stylized eye in blue-black ink, was noticeably hot, a warning sign he was being observed. Doc didn't turn around, but he flexed his left hand—the one that would summon the sword he could conjure with a quick spell—and made a slight gesture with his right hand, preparing a defensive spell should something lash out at him. He heard the faintest whisper of a disgruntled sigh, and nothing happened.

"That's fine, then," Doc said, though he found he could not relax either hand to release the spells he'd prepared. "We can talk when you're ready."

He turned around and cut through the kitchen into a hallway, framed in sturdy, dark wood. To his right, he could see the doorway he'd entered from—too far away given the distance he'd walked, but that was a problem for later—and to his left, what appeared to be a study or library. He went left.

Doc stood in the doorframe of the study for a moment, taking in the absurdity of what he saw through the massive windows dominating one wall of the room. An arctic tundra gleamed there, snow pristine, the sky barely a different shade of white. Unable to fight off the curiosity, he walked up to the window and touched the glass. It was freezing, the heat from his fingertips creating condensation as they pressed against the glass.

He scanned the walls, which were lined with books. Most were mundane copies of classics, though sometimes those classics deviated in strange ways. *Hamlet, a Play By Christopher Marlowe*, jumped out at him. Something called the *Daemonium Vulgate*. He was almost startled to see one book glowing, but then remembered he'd cast the divination spell on his eyes. He pulled the glowing book from the shelf and chuckled. It was titled *The Planar Guide to Forever*.

"I'm taking this," he said to the empty room, tucking the book into his coat. His tattoo was still burning, but nothing took the bait. "I guess we'll just carry on."

"Take it," another voice said, this one male, formal, a hint of old-timey-ness to it. "It does us no good."

Doc searched around until he found the source, a photo propped up on a desk in one corner of the study. He had a handlebar mustache, ruddy cheeks, a pinched nose.

"What would do you good?" Doc asked.

"To have lived a better life," the man said. "Time is fleeting, young man. Do not allow yourself to be beholden to regrets."

Doc bit his tongue as a line from a song slide through his mind, something about not reminding the singer of his failures, because he hadn't forgotten about them. Too late, he wanted to tell the painting, but he just nodded again.

"Is that why you're here? Because of regret?" he asked.

The painting shrugged.

"Being here is all I've known," the painting said.

Doc nodded and left the room and the painting behind. He walked back down the hallway toward the foyer. Counting his steps, it took two hundred paces, though he knew he was only perhaps forty feet into the house. He started to head up the stairs, his hand leaving a trail of cleanliness where the dust came away at his touch. At the top of the stairs, he found himself at a T intersection. He looked up and saw that part of the roof had a domelike design, transparent, made of many windows. Through it, he saw the night sky, though he knew it could not be later than noon, and he recognized without looking too deeply that the stars he saw in this night sky were not those he would see in the night sky outside the manor. He continued his series of left turns, and found himself in a hallway between a master bedroom and a nursery. The window in the master bedroom showed a cityscape outside; the nursery, a cold night sky lit by what appeared to be the Aurora Borealis.

"Hello, Doctor Silence," a voice purred from the shadows. Doc could not determine which room the voice came from, or even if it came from either at all. He waited and listened.

"No need to be so formal," he replied. "Just Doc is fine."

"It's been a long time," the voice said. It had a deep, resonant quality, as if it were coming from underwater.

"Has it?" Doc said. He could hear his heartbeat in his ears. Up until now he'd been standard-issue afraid, but hearing his own name come from a disembodied voice had turned his blood cold. "I don't remember meeting."

"We will meet many times over the years," the voice said. "This is just one of many first times we meet."

"So you're a time traveler?" Doc said. "Here I was thinking this was just an old house full of ghosts."

"I am neither," the voice said. "I am a Nexus. We are tied together, you and I."

"That's unfortunate," Doc said. "I really do try to keep my entanglements to a minimum. Are we enemies?"

"Sometimes," the voice said. "But there's no reason we can't be friends."

"Sure," Doc said. "Just a couple old buddies, a magician and a house."

Doc lurked just inside the master bedroom and saw a painting staring back at him, a full beard, receding hairline, clothing from a bygone era. This figure, unlike the others, did not speak, though he pressed his palm against the frame, begging to be let out.

"What happened to the man who built this house?" Doc asked. "Who was this Marsh?"

"Andrew Marsh. In truth, no one important," the shadow voice said. "A man who liked to play with geometry, who found a pattern he shouldn't have."

Now the painting had locked eyes with Doc, pleading, full of despair and fear. Doc tried to ignore him, but he felt those desperate eyes on him no matter where he looked.

"Did you kill him?" Doc asked.

"No, of course not," the voice said. "He's here, still. They are all here. Everyone who has ever come to live in this Nexus. Perfect guests, in perfect little boxes."

"Are you going to keep me here too?" Doc said.

"I don't want to keep you here," the voice said. "You have so many places to go."

Doc walked back out into the hallway, thought about skipping the nursery, but then decided he couldn't. He had to know.

He stepped inside and saw a small bed and a cradle. Don't look at the far wall, he told himself, don't look, but he did, and there, in a painting, was a young girl holding an infant, seeming as surprised to see him as he was to see them.

"Help us," she said, and Doc skittered back out into the hallway, too ashamed to reply.

He took a few deep breaths, trying to calm himself. His hands felt numb with fear, tingling at the fingertips.

"What do you mean by Nexus?" Doc said. "I don't know what you're talking about."

"Of course. You haven't been here before. Not this version of you," the voice said. "It's a place between. Where different versions of the world collide. That's what Marsh didn't realize he'd found, when he built his home here. A place where all worlds dance on the head of a pin."

Doc began turning the options over and over in his mind. The word that stuck out to him was geometry. Something was wrong with the geometry of this place. He walked into yet another bedroom, in which he saw a painting beside a four-post bed containing a sad teenaged girl scratching a dog behind the ear. She locked eyes with him, and before he could look away, she whispered: "Break this place. Please."

"How?" Doc blurted out, suddenly angry with himself at the thought the shadow voice could hear him.

And then something about the frame caught his eye. A very specific shape in each corner of the frame, a sort of gem-shaped pattern, faceted like a geodesic dome. It marked each of the four corners of the painting. All the frames are the same, he thought, remembering the frame in the living room, in the bedrooms. Where else have I seen that shape?

He tried to stop himself from running into the hall again, but it turned into something of an undignified half-jog. He looked straight up.

There, in the middle of the dome, was that same faceted pattern, the centerpiece at its apex.

Doc ran down the spells he knew in his arsenal. Fire, ice, electricity, all the tricks he knew to cause harm didn't seem appropriate for breaking a massive glass dome. He thought about word magic, of asking the dome to collapse, but he didn't know the protective magics it might have weaved into it, or the true name of the shape at its center.

Doc closed his eyes and thought of one of the simplest spells in his repertoire. He reached a hand up and tried to push at the shape, shoving it through the top of the dome, but it resisted, refusing to be moved.

"Ah, you're still at this stage," the voice said. "When every problem is something to be broken. I'd say it's disappointing, but you're new yet. We'll see a better you later."

"Maybe," Doc said, struggling with his focus on the spell. He could feel the weight of it through the spell, the heft holding it in place. "I tend to disappoint everyone though."

"You'll never lose that contrarian streak, though," the shadows said. "It's our favorite part of you."

Doc sighed, shook his head, and then started laughing.

"Contrarian it is," he said.

And he reversed the spell to push down, working with gravity rather than against it.

He heard the breaking of moorings before he saw the geometric centerpiece shift, and started to run just as he heard the crack of wood, a wine of bending metal, and finally a deafening shattering of glass. He started running down the stairs, shocked and horrified to see the staircase had somehow stretched to three times its original length or more. There was a child crying in the distance somewhere, a man's voice shouting, a dog barking, and somewhere, a strong, confident voice chuckled.

"We'll find each other again," the shadow said, before the metal geodesic centerpiece slammed into the second-floor hallway and started to pursue Doc down the staircase, thumping along like a runaway boulder.

Doc's mind raced as he tried to reverse the same spell again, to perhaps divert the rolling semi-sphere, or push it back up the stairs, but he didn't have the focus or skill or strength. Instead he used that very same spell to shove the front door open at the foot of the stairs and ran for his life, diving out the doorway as the inanimate object chasing him crashed into the foyer and came to a halt.

Doc sprawled in the mud and rolled, tasting grimy water in his mouth as his shoulder slammed into an exposed rock. He struggled to his feet and tried to run, but he slipped in the mud again and went down on one knee.

And then he heard the voices again, not the taunting voice of the Nexus but the woman in the parlor, the children, the others trapped in the paintings throughout the house. He saw drifting, ghostly figures spiraling into the sky through the broken dome, some reaching out to take each other's hands before they disappeared from sight.

Doc stumbled back to his feet, holding his battered shoulder, and waited for something to emerge from the Marsh House, some shadow-beast or demon, but nothing did. The door swung in a light breeze. He thought about closing it, giving the old home some dignity, but he couldn't bring himself to place a single step on the property again.

Instead, he limped back to his car, and left the Marsh House where it stood, on the edge of forgotten swampland and memory.

***

Cassiopeia was surprised to see him that night and said so outright.

"Figured you'd disappear yourself in the old Marsh House," she said, handing him a cup of strong coffee. His body had been trembling the entire drive back to town despite the warm Louisiana air, and the hot coffee seemed to help a bit.

"I shouldn't have gone there," Doc said. He didn't mention that the eye tattoo on the nape of his neck had been burning most of the drive back, and still flickered with the heat of being observed every so often. He wondered if he had not returned alone. Whatever he'd broken with the dome had set those spirit-paintings free; had they also released the creature that called itself the Nexus? Was it here with him now?

"Tell me you got something out of it, at least," Cassiopeia said. He mentioned freeing the paintings, though he lied a little and simply referred to them as bound spirits or ghosts, and then he showed her the book.

"*The Planar Guide to Tomorrow*," Cassiopeia said, examining the cover, then thumbing through a few pages. "Sounds like New Age garbage to me, but people like us know full well how often you can find truths woven into lies. Maybe it was worth the trip."

"Maybe," Doc said.

"You leaving town for real this time?" Cassiopeia said, handing the book back to Doc.

"Yeah," Doc said. "I think I should leave speaking with ghosts to people who know better."

"You know where to find me if you come back down this way," Cassiopeia said. "Stay weird."

Doc found a bus headed north and took it, unsure where exactly he might go next. As he tried and failed to sleep, he wondered what would become of the Marsh House.

And somewhere on the water's edge, the door to the manor swung closed. Glass rose into the air, reforming the dome, the massive centerpiece drifting slowly back into place. The paintings remained silent and empty, but outside each window, a strange new landscape awaited, unseen by human eyes.

Chapter 11: Interlude – Wizards don't need passports

Doc sat leaning back in the tattooist's chair, one arm draped over his head in an undignified pose. Bláithín was working on a design, something she said was in the Atlantean alphabet, which Doc had requested after a recent run-in with a water spirit that nearly drowned him in a pond. He knew spells to help him breathe underwater, but he panicked and forgot the motions, and wanted something to help him cheat on the spell should he ever find himself unable to breathe again.

"Still no word from the boss, eh?" Bláithín said, not looking up from her work.

Doc shook his head – very, very slowly, so as not to upset the needle's mark.

"I'm starting to get used to the idea of Erasmus not coming back," he said. "It's been over a year."

Bláithín grunted, though in agreement or disagreement was unclear.

"You never know," she said. "Time is a funny thing. Could be he's someplace where it feels as though he's been gone a week."

"Would've been nice of him to say where he went," Doc muttered. He found himself in a sort of daze, his breathing measured and careful as he tried to stay still for Bláithín's needle. "I have a question for you."

"Ah, sure, go on," Bláithín said.

"You know the money Erasmus paid you with was conjured, right?" he said. "It's not real cash. I don't understand why that's not a problem."

The artist laughed, shaking her head, pausing to check the head of her tattoo gun.

"Of course I know it's magic money. You think I'm an eejit?"

"No," Doc said.

"It still spends, though, right?"

"Sure."

"And I can't do that kind of magic," Bláithín said. "I can do this kind of magic, the magic of images and runes. That's my purview, that's my specialty. I'm awful at things like turning Kleenex into Euros. But can you do what I do?"

"Absolutely not," Doc said. He'd been in her chair dozens of times already, his upper body becoming a tapestry of black and blue ink, each one tied to different arcane abilities or spells. She somehow turned something that should have been as close to mundane as magic could get into an elegant art.

"And did you believe I figured you had a job at Tesco's or whatever, saving up for your next tattoo?"

"I hadn't thought about that."

"So you see, it's not really a cash transaction then, is it?" she said. "It's a trade. You trade the magic you can do, that conjuration or transmutation or whatever you do to make that happen, and I in trade provide the service of ink magic, skin magic. You're not buying my art with paper money. You're trading magic you can't do for magic I can't do. It's how magic has always worked. It's what's kept magicians from killing each other for centuries—trading favors."

Doc nodded, then winced as Bláithín went back to work.

"So then," she said. "Where do you go next, if your boss man is still in absentia?"

"No idea," Doc said. "I was thinking I'd travel, but I don't have a passport. I'm pretty sure I don't really exist, not since I gave my name away. Pretty sure social security numbers and all that go with it when you stop being you."

"That's not an inaccurate statement," Bláithín said. "It's a bit more twisty than that, but it's close enough."

"Plus I can make money, but I don't know if making money will work to buy a plane ticket," Doc said. "Like, it's one thing to use it to buy lunch, but a plane ticket feels a little more official."

Bláithín stopped tattooing and stared at him. Doc stared back, questioning.

"Where are you right now," she asked.

"Here, in your tattoo parlor, in your chair," Doc said, suddenly worried he'd offended her.

"And where is that," Bláithín asked.

"Dublin?" Doc said.

"And how did you get here?"

"Huh?"

"Did you take an Aer Lingus flight? Go through customs? Pick up your baggage at the carousel?"

"No," Doc said. "I teleported here. Oh!"

"Right. Did you need a bleedin' passport to come here?"

"I did not," Doc said, a smirk growing on his face.

"You're a feckin' magician, Doc Silence," Bláithín said. "Wizards don't need passports. You go where you want to go, when you want to go there. Magic is a burden, magic bears a cost, but the fringe benefits of magic is if you want to go to Paris, you go to Paris and nobody can stop you."

"I'm an eejit," Doc said, mimicking Bláithín's words.

"Sure, but you're cute," she said. "Makes up for a lot of your flaws."

Doc laughed, hard enough Bláithín had to stop tattooing until his ribs stopped moving.

"Okay, though, one more question," he said. "What about not speaking the language?"

"If Erasmus left you here and didn't teach you a translation spell he should be sanctioned for negligence."

"No, he taught me one, but I have to keep casting it over and over again," Doc said. "It'll fade midway through a conversation, and it gets awkward."

Bláithín cocked her head and grinned.

"You want the mark of tongues, then?"

"The what of which?"

She tapped a small, thus-far unmarred spot on his neck, halfway between his clavicle and his ear.

"Simple mark. I can do it for you today, if you want. Touch it and make the right gesture, and you can understand languages you hear, and your words can be understood by those you want to hear them, if you wish them to."

"And I can give you more magical money for this?" Doc asked.

"Tell you what," Bláithín said. "I'll do the mark of tongues for free if it means you'll actually go see the world and get yourself out of America for a while."

"I guess my only question is: where do I go first?" he said, and settled back in to let Bláithín finish her work.

Chapter 12: The demon of the opera

Doc spent some time darting across the globe, visiting places he'd only read about in books or seen in movies. With a few simple spells and the tattoo Bláithín had given him he could listen to conversations in any language, and tried to come to understand as much as he could about the places he traveled to. The longer he was away from home, the less it felt like home, but he never truly found a home anywhere else, either. He knew, even early on, that he would forever be the on the outside looking in. And while he wasn't happy about that, exactly, he was resigned to it, and he learned to identify other outsiders and connect with them, fellow wanderers without a place to call their own.

Wherever he went, he sought out mediums or witches, shamans or ghost hunters, anyone who might, in some way, have a connection to the weird. And there was always someone, especially in the old cities, where ghosts built up like the wreckage of time, where mysteries were as much a part of these places as cobblestone sidewalks. He met few true wizards, though, which he had been warned about long ago by Erasmus, and while expected, it made him feel lonely, a solitary magician among those who only half-understood the shadows they explored or fought.

Once in a while, he'd try his hand at normalcy. He'd befriend people who weren't a part of the underbelly of the arcane, ordinary folks who had no idea the things that lurked in sewers and shadows. He found these people at first alien and uncomfortable, but later charming in the things they did not know; and after a while, he came to realize that the reason they did not know that monsters existed was that arcanists like Doc himself existed, holding the line against encroaching evil.

More than once, Doc wished he could be like them, to give back all the terrible knowledge he now possessed, but then he'd remember the thrill of spellcasting, the joy of twisting reality with your mind, and he'd know he preferred not live in ignorance, even if it meant looking at the world through a grim and unblinking lens.

Doc was describing this convergence of worlds to a friend from the stranger side at a café in Paris. Doc never found himself at ease in Paris, as though the expectations of cinema and history felt above or beyond him; his friend, a Jesuit priest twenty years his senior, currently dressed as a civilian and drinking a tiny cup of black coffee, looked as though he had always belonged here, though he was born a thousand miles away in Spain. They'd met at an exorcism in Malaga a while back, a bad exorcism, in fact, where amateurs with archaic beliefs were brutalizing an unwell man without a demon or devil within him, which both Doc and Father Arturo had arrived to intervene in. They worked together to save the young man, who was not possessed by spirits but by a glimmer of magical ability, just a hint of the ability to read thoughts, and struck up a strange friendship, the apprentice wizard without a teacher and a middle-aged man of the cloth who had learned that magic was real and that he had some small talent for it himself. They didn't travel together but would bump into each other in the places the world didn't feel quite right. Or, in this case, on a busy street in Paris, as tourists, lost between jobs chasing shadows.

"What brings you back to Paris, then, my young magician

friend," Father Arturo said. He seemed particularly relaxed, which, Doc had come to learn, usually meant his actual employers had no idea where he was.

Doc shrugged. He didn't want to talk about the real reason, that he'd just come from Sevilla where he'd pretended to be normal for a while, and found himself too restless and bored to spend any more time with the friends he'd made there, and had up and left one morning, claiming he was needed for work elsewhere. His friends were medical students, and they had no idea what Doc did for a living. He felt vaguely bad about lying about it, but felt worse about how relieved he'd been to walk away.

"Why are you here?" Doc asked, ignoring Arturo's question. The priest took note of Doc's avoidance, raised an eyebrow, smiled warmly, and ignored him dodging the question.

"I'd heard that an opera house had appeared out of nowhere, and that dark magic emanated from it. I was curious to see this place myself," he said. He ordered another coffee in perfect but charmingly accented French, and then gestured for another coffee for Doc as well.

"Did you find it?" Doc asked.

Arturo's otherwise lighthearted demeanor darkened.

"It's in a place in between," he said. "It is here, but not here. A shadow of a real place. I did not like it, so I did not go inside."

"Where is it?" Doc said, marginally attempting to hide his curiosity and failing entirely.

"I told you I did not like it," Father Arturo warned. "It has an abyssal stench to it. I would not go inside, and I would recommend you do not either."

"Abyssal?" Doc asked.

"Something from beyond," Arturo said, thanking the waiter as he returned with coffees. "The place stank of hellfire. I want nothing to do with it."

"How does an opera house just appear in Paris?" Doc asked, gesturing around him at the bustle and crowds. "Did it take the place of something else?"

Arturo shook his head.

"Sometimes there is space where space is not, room where there is no room."

"Sometimes the phone booth is bigger on the inside," Doc said.

"You say that with a smile, but you know it to be true," Arturo said. "I found it in an alleyway. Perhaps it is an opera house from a different Paris. Perhaps it is a trap. All I know is it had a shadow across it, and if you were smarter, you would not look for it. But you are not smarter, are you."

Doc grinned and asked for the address.

"If it's dangerous, shouldn't we lock it away so no one can be hurt by it?" Doc asked.

"There is a fine line between fool and hero, my young friend," Father Arturo said. "I fear you have not yet committed that line to memory."

***

In the end, Father Arturo refused to give Doc the address, but by now Doc had learned a bit of divining magic for secrets the world didn't want to share, and a bit of practical investigative skills for things that did not require a magician's touch.

He threw a few runes, talked to the bellhop at a haunted hotel, and chatted with a pigeon who was once the familiar to a wizard named Vincent Noir, and eventually he found the place. It was easy to miss for anyone not looking for it, half-shrouded in illusion magic, wedged between a bakery and grocer. But if you looked down that alley out of the corner of your eye, there it was, a magnificent entrance to an old, forgotten opera house.

Doc knew instantly why Father Arturo had warned him off. There are dark places, and there are places that feel corrupt, and this was by far more the latter. He could sense waves of corruption emanating from it even as he walked up the short stairway to the double doors. But Doc had not yet learned caution, and stepped confidently inside.

The foyer was empty. A box office, something from a bygone era, waited for an audience that would never come. Blood-red velvet ropes were ready for an opening night crowd, but only Doc was there to see it, and he skipped the queue anyway. He half-expected some spectral ticket taker to ask him to pay an entrance fee, but he strolled inside unmolested into a grand, opulent theater.

It was no small theater, with seats, Doc estimated, to hold a crowd of maybe 1,500 attendees. The seats were small, in that old-fashioned way, built for an age when men and women were just a bit smaller, uncomfortable for modern audiences. He'd been to shows in New York and Boston in theaters like this in his travels, though he hadn't taken in any live performances in Europe, which felt somewhat wasteful and more than a little wrong.

Spotlights illuminated the stage, which made Doc question who might be here acting as stage crew. A massive, sumptuous red curtain hid the bulk of the stage, and motes of dust, like lost and forgotten memories, danced in the blades of light that slashed over the empty seats.

Doc walked softly, placing his booted feet gently against the carpeted lane between rows of chairs. The room was so silent he nearly jumped out of his skin when a voice spoke. It was rich, sonorous, inviting, but with just a hint of malice.

"Welcome to my theater, little wizard," the voice said. "I'm afraid there's no show today. But perhaps you are here to audition."

"Just passing through," Doc said, running a few fingertips across the back of one seat, coming away gray with dust.

"No, you're not," the voice said. Doc knew it was coming from just behind the curtain, despite the way it echoed around the hall in a disembodied way. An easy trick, he thought. Almost mundane. But no one who could conjure a theater in an alleyway in Paris was a mundane spellcaster. "The bane of magicians everywhere— you're always looking for something."

"Well," Doc said, walking slowly toward the curtain, mentally preparing which spells he may need next. "Isn't that the defining characteristic of magicians? Curiosity?"

"In a way," the voice said. "At least the bookish types, like you. I can see the words writ all over your body, little wizard. Doesn't it feel limiting? Relying on scribbles on your flesh to grant you power?"

Ah, Doc thought. There's a tell. He's from another philosophy of magic. One of the ones Erasmus warned me about, most likely.

"Maybe I just like how they look," Doc said. He reached the short set of stairs that would take him up onto the stage, but hesitated. Something didn't feel quite right; the old theater smells of mold and dust were cut through but something else, like smoke, and sulfur, and the barest hint of something predatory and dangerous.

"What if there was an easier way, though," the voice said. The curtain moved slightly. Doc took an involuntary step back. It took him a few seconds to realize his heart was pounding in his chest. It felt strange to be so afraid, he thought. He'd seen so many terrible things in recent years that a mystery voice behind a curtain shouldn't kick off his fight or flight reflex. But he had, nevertheless, an overwhelming desire to run.

He inhaled slowly before speaking again, trying to keep his voice steady.

"I suppose you're going to offer me an easier way," he said.

"Why not?" the voice said. "From what I understand about you, Doc Silence, you came to magic involuntarily in the first place. Why work so hard? Why make it more difficult to achieve the greatness and powers you are capable of? Why struggle so, when the keys to great power are there for the grasping?"

"So you know my name," Doc said.

"I do," the creature said. "Perhaps I know both of them."

This statement made Doc's veins grow cold. Could he know my real name? Doc thought. No one could, that was part of his indoctrination into magic. He had to be bluffing.

"You almost had my attention until you started lying," Doc said. "And here I was thinking we were having a real conversation."

"I know you have a brother," the voice said. "And I know what magicians like you give up to learn their art. What if I told you I could give you your family back."

Doc felt a rage well up inside him, but he wasn't sure where to direct it. Am I mad at this voice for offering me something he can't give me? Or am I mad at Erasmus for telling me this was an immutable part of the craft, for taking something from me to better manipulate me? No, Doc thought, this is some dark being offering a bargain, trying to turn me against what I've learned. Erasmus helped me save my brother. All magic has a cost. Whatever he's offering me, Doc thought, that has a cost too.

And so he asked him.

"What do I give you in exchange for my family back?" Doc asked, trying to keep the rage from his voice and failing. He strode up onto the stage, suddenly unafraid of the being hearing his footfalls. He clenched and unclenched his fists, resisting the urge to summon his sword to his hand.

The curtain moved again, and this time, a set of long, red fingers, tipped with sharp black claws, reached around the felt and began to pull it back. They were unnaturally high in the air, too tall to be a human.

"Just a soul per person I restore to you," the voice said, and the curtain drew back fully, revealing a massive, masculine figure, skin a deep red, eyes glowing yellow-orange. Long black horns swept back from his forehead, elegant, like gazelle horns, and when he smiled he had white, sharp teeth. His face seemed to shift and change, never settling on a precise appearance, as though his facial structure shifted to suit his very thoughts. "It doesn't have to include your soul. Any soul of quality will do."

The creature strode forward onto the stage, black-hooved feet clopping on the wooden floor, and his massive wings followed, veined and knobbed with old scars.

Doc could feel a part of him drawn toward the demonic creature, his scalp tingling with nervous, fearful energy. He resisted the urge to draw a weapon, and instead called to mind the protective wards inked onto his collarbone. They burned against his skin as he muttered a simple spell quietly.

"What is a soul of quality?" Doc said.

"You know it when you see it," the demon said. "Some souls are just worth more. It depends on what happens when you take the soul away, you see. You can change the whole world by taking one soul, or change nothing by taking a thousand."

"Am I a soul of quality, then?" Doc said. His scalp, his face, his whole body had a heat to it now, somewhere between embarrassment and bladder-loosening terror.

"We've looked into your futures, Doc Silence," the demon said. "And we'd love to have yours. But I do understand it can be hard to give up. We are open to negotiation."

"We? There's more than one of you?" Doc said.

"As many of us as the stars," the demon said. "But they aren't here right now. You're dealing with just me."

"And who are you?" Doc asked, his skin burning more than before, a trickle of sweat running from his hairline down into his left eye.

"He is Ahnloch, a tempter," the strong, reassuring voice of Father Arturo said, echoing through the theater. "And he is no one of importance, Doc Silence."

Doc didn't look over his shoulder at Arturo, keeping his eye steadily on the demon, who smirked and broke eye contact to look out at the priest.

"Ah, the failure of God," Ahnloch said. "You were once a soul of quality too, but your light has dimmed so quickly. You know your superiors know of your moonlighting. They watch your every move, your sacrilege, your betrayal."

"My failures are my own problem, demon," Father Arturo said. "And I am far too aware of them to have your petty jabs cause me any pain."

The demon shrugged.

"I don't want to cause anyone any pain," Ahnloch said. "I was just having a conversation with our young friend here. Perhaps to save him from being a withered old waste of potential like you."

"You're quick to insult my friend," Doc said. "Did you save no malice for me?"

The demon laughed, and it was a sound Doc would take to his grave; a rumble of thunder the screams of the tortured damned, wrapped in an almost charming smile.

"Why would I insult you? You have nothing but potential, and have done nothing to cause me to think less of you. Unlike the old liar over there, wearing charms of a faith he no longer believes in."

"I believe what I believe in," Arturo said. Doc could hear stress in Arturo's voice, fear, a heaviness in his breathing.

Doc could think of only one spell that might be of use here, one he'd only used on minor terrors to send them back to where they came from. The idea of dismissing a full-fledged bargain demon from this reality felt like lifting a house with a tire iron. He stole a glance at Arturo; the priest looked older now, sweat gathered around his eyes, his jaw set as though to keep himself from screaming.

Doc had no tattoos to help with this spell, no charms, no tools. It was not something he ever though he'd need in a moment like this. But while the demon's focus turned back to Arturo, gleaming yellow eyes mirthful and almost pitying, Doc chased a symbol in the air with his forefinger, creating a sort of compass of pale blue light that stayed behind where he drew. He grabbed hold of that floating sigil and spun it like a ship's wheel.

"I send you back to where you came from, Ahnloch," Doc said in the steadiest voice he could muster. "You are not welcome here anymore."

The demon whipped his head back toward Doc, realizing his mistake. The circle expanded, runes and sigils floating within it like dancers, and Doc pushed it forward, sending it arcing toward Ahnloch. The demon began casting a spell of his own, but Doc and Arturo together muttered the words to the same spell, tearing apart the weave of Ahnloch's spell like burning paper.

"We'll speak again, Doc Silence," Ahnloch said, just as the blue circle passed over him. He disappeared instantly as it struck, leaving only empty air where the demon once stood. Doc dropped the spell immediately, the arcane circle evaporating in the blink of an eye. Doc fell to one knee, hands and legs shaking with effort and panic.

And then the theater began to rumble.

"Out!" Arturo yelled, and Doc jumped to his feet and leapt off the stage, almost landing on his face as his feet hit the now-shaking ground. Arturo grabbed his arm, steadying him, and the pair began to run toward the exit. The theater contracted around them, growing smaller and smaller, the seats rising up the walls and ceilings as though the hall itself were closing like the iris of a camera. Doc could feel his clothes tearing, pulled back toward the contracting building, sensed Arturo lose his footing and helped the priest stay on his feet, and side by side. They crashed out the front door, tripping over each other and rolling down the red-carpeted stairs into the Parisian alley.

With a resonant popping noise, the theater disappeared, leaving them laying on the filthy ground of the alley, gasping for air.

"I told you," the priest said, catching his breath. "I told you to not come here."

"You knew I'd come here if you told me about it," Doc said, not bothering to get up off the ground. His whole body was shaking now, from adrenaline, from fear, from something else.

Father Arturo started laughing.

"I... suppose I did, in my heart," he said. "Maybe I knew I couldn't banish the demon alone. You, though. You, my young friend, continue to impress me. It's good to know you had it in you."

"He sounded like he knew you," Doc said, starting to push himself to his knees. He glanced over and saw Arturo doing the same, though more slowly.

"I've seen Ahnloch before," Arturo said. "But I'm not a tempting enough target for him, I suppose."

Now that they were mostly upright, Doc noticed Arturo staring at Doc with an odd expression.

"What," Doc asked.

"You... you are changed, my friend," Arturo said.

Doc's stomach flip-flopped in panic.

"What did he do to me?"

"I think... I think it was you who did it. You cast a spell more powerful than I think you were ready for. You did it well, but..."

"But all magic has a cost," Doc said. He touched his face. Everything felt like it was as it should be. No horns, no fangs, no keloid points on his face like a demon's. He finished staggering to his feet, and Arturo offered him a shoulder to lean on. Doc did not refuse.

"Here, I will show you," Arturo said, leading him out of the alley to the street. He turned Doc to face the window of the bakery, closed now, the dark interior allowing the window to be reflective, like a mirror.

"Huh," Doc said.

"Magic has a cost, but I do not think it's a terrible look for you," Arturo said. The priest ruffled Doc's now blue-white hair with a friendly gesture, then clapped him on the shoulder. "It looks almost as though it were meant to be."

Doc could see new gray on Arturo's temples as well, a salting of silver that was not there that morning. They both paid a cost inside the opera house, he thought. He ran a hand through his own changed hair, brushing it out of his face, which still looked young and unchanged.

"Maybe you'll stop calling me your young friend now," Doc said.

Arturo laughed.

"With that baby face, Doctor, I think not," he said. His face grew more serious then. "Do you feel different?"

"I feel tired, Arturo," Doc said.

"I would be worried if you felt otherwise," the priest said. "Let me buy you something to eat. Get your strength back, yeah?"

Doc nodded, keeping one hand on Arturo's shoulder to keep his feet under him.

"He said he could give me my family back," Doc said softly.

Arturo turned a grim eye toward Doc then, as serious a look the priest had ever given him.

"They always offer the things we want most," he said.

"Could he have given me my brother back? My parents?"

"Do you want the easy lie, or the hard truth?" Arturo said.

"The truth."

"Yes," Arturo said grimly. "He could have. But would your family love the man you became to restore them to you?"

Doc's throat grew tight, his eyes hot and itchy. He shook off the glimmer of melancholy and just shook his head.

"All magic has a cost," he repeated.

"And the quicker the path, the greater that cost," Arturo said. "You were brave to say no."

"I didn't really say no."

"Ah, but you quite literally told him to go to hell," Arturo said, and even Doc had to smile at that. "You should be proud. I am proud of you."

Doc nodded, let out a small laugh, and thanked the priest. They walked together to a restaurant Arturo had long loved, and had a dinner together, talking nothing of magic and only of the things that made the world worth saving. A woman in the restaurant complimented Doc's hair. Arturo roared laughing when she did.

But hours later, Doc wondered if the demon would return. And if he did, if he could say no a second time.

Chapter 13: Elephant and Castle

Doc had been enjoying his trip to London until he got stabbed by a gremlin.

The trip hadn't been intended for pleasure. Doc had gotten wind of a few rumors about the whereabout of Erasmus and clues pointed him to London where he spent a few days talking to local practitioners of various magical arts. A diviner who claimed to have once been related to a landed family told him that the old magician was no longer on this plane of reality, which didn't give Doc much to go on, but at least narrowed down his search parameters. And a witch who spent time between shifts at a local pub reading cards and signs told him that if he stuck around London long enough, he'd discover something that would set him on the right path.

And so he did.

He was a city boy, through and through, and there are few cities more city than London. He loved the feral energy of it, the old buildings alongside new technology, the bustle, the noise. The noise, he realized, made him feel safer—silence, despite the name he had chosen for himself, made him anxious, as though he needed a hum of sound to shroud his own thoughts from himself. He went sightseeing, and listened to old men telling tales in bars or at bus stops. He heard rumors, muttered between mundane observations, of the hidden parts of London, where the mystical seeped into the modern, and he investigated those, too. Haunted houses and churches, places where demonic symbols were hidden in architecture, found tracks of creatures not of this world pressed into debris in dark alleys.

And it was in one such alley he startled the gremlin who stabbed him, the little creature crying out in fear and malice as it jammed a broken bottle into Doc's side.

It happened too fast for him to react with a protective spell, and he knew it was bad the moment he felt the sharp glass bite into his flesh. The creature dropped the bottle and ran, clearly uninterested in seeing if its handiwork proved to be fatal or not.

Doc stumbled out of the alley, shocked to find the sidewalk empty of pedestrians, and somewhat relieved as well, not knowing what anyone would make of a bleeding American with blue-white hair staggering around in the street. He decided, perhaps irrationally, to try to get back to his hotel room to patch himself up, and headed for the nearest Underground station. Wobbling on his feet, his shirt and pants soaking through with blood, he made it to the top of the stairs at the closest station, Elephant and Castle, and made it exactly three steps down before he lost his footing and fell the rest of the way.

The colorful walls of the underground made for a brilliant kaleidoscope of color and confusion as he rolled, striking his head at least once on the steps before coming to a hard, angry stop at the bottom. He tried to groan in pain, but he'd had the wind knocked out of him by the fall, so he only managed a tight, squeaking wheeze as he got up to one knee, and then back to his feet. Will they let me on the train? He thought, balling up part of his coat into the ragged wound in his side. He'd seen worse on an American subway, but he hadn't been here long enough to know if they'd just ignore him the way a bleeding man could be overlooked in New York or Boston by uncaring commuters.

He tilted to the left, his shoulder against the tiled wall, and then sunk to the ground, his vision growing dim.

"What the hell happened to you?" a woman's voice said from somewhere nearby. Perhaps nearer than Doc knew, he realized, as everything now sounded echoing and distant. He felt a hand on his shoulder, and then on his face, lifting his chin to make eye contact. A woman, dark-haired, lips pursed in a stern, almost angry expression, pulled his left eye completely open, as though looking for signs of life.

"A gremlin stabbed me," Doc said. He words sounded muddy and slurred in his ears.

"Fine, don't tell me the truth," the woman said. She opened up a bag and pulled on a pair of rubber gloves and lifted Doc's shirt. "Well, something stabbed you, that's for sure. We have to get you to the hospital."

Somewhere in his fading consciousness, Doc realized that going to any environment where he might be documented might not be in his best interest while he was unable to weave enough magic to keep himself out of trouble, so he started to protest.

"I'm fine, I'm fine, it's okay, I'll just catch the next train," he said.

And then he blacked out.

***

Doc woke on a couch he'd never seen before in a flat he didn't recognize. The lights were on, but dim; outside, the London streets were filled with the din of early evening. He moved his limbs gingerly to make sure they all still worked and was pleased to find that was the case. His head felt as though it had been used as a basketball, and his breathing was short and ragged, but he was alive, and, to his relief, he was not in a hospital room.

He turned his head slightly and saw a small kitchenette to the left, better lit than the living area he was in. A woman had her back to him, long hair pulled in a messy side ponytail, and she appeared to be reading through something, which, Doc realized with a start, was the spell book he'd had in his coat pocket. He started coughing involuntarily and then tried to pretend to be asleep as she turned to look at him.

"Please don't compound the stupidest thing I've ever done in my life by thinking I'm naïve enough think you're actually asleep," she said, sighing irritably. "I'm nearly a doctor. I can tell if you're faking it."

Doc gave her a weak smile and tried to sit up. It was not as easy as he hoped it would be.

"You helped me," he said.

"I did, because that's what I suppose I'm being trained to do," she said. She had his spell book in her hand, her forefinger holding the page she'd been reading. "I should have brought you to the hospital."

"I'm glad you didn't," he said.

"Yes, I'd like to talk about that, actually," she said. "What's your name, by the way? No passport, no wallet, you sound American though I suppose I could give you the benefit of the doubt and hope you're Canadian."

"American," Doc said. "You're a doctor?"

"A med student," she said. "I should finish this year, provided they don't kick me out for sheltering a fugitive. Name? Please."

Doc started laughing. His side hurt so much he saw florets of white light in his vision.

"What's so funny? Don't have a name?"

"It's just… my friends call me Doc," he said. "I'm sorry, it's the truth."

"Not a medical doctor, though."

"Nope."

"Advanced degree then? You strike me as a professorial type, despite being a blood-soaked mess."

"Just a nickname," Doc said. "I'm too dimwitted to be a real doctor. Like how sometimes people will call a really big man Tiny to be ironic."

She let out a short, hard laugh and then opened his spell book.

"Could have told me you were some sort or archeologist or cryptographer with this," she said, holding up the book. "It looks like half-art, half-cypher from a spy movie."

"That's a more accurate description of what you're holding in your hand than you know," Doc said, finally finding the strength to push himself up onto his elbows to look her in the eyes properly. "You know my name. What's yours?"

"I don't think I properly know your name," she said. "Doc isn't enough to go on, not for a man without any kind of identification. All you had on you was this book and a stack of cash, which is not even remotely sketchy, I'd say."

Doc studied her face for a moment, the hard lines of her cheekbones, the unflinching, scientific way she looked at him. He thought about the lies he might tell, the glamour spells he could cast to fool her properly, to even make her forget he existed. But he hadn't had a proper conversation with someone in so long. And she saved my life, he thought. The least I can do is tell her the truth.

"What if I told you I'm a magician," he said.

"Like, on stage? Vegas-like?"

"No. Like real."

"Okay, Gandalf," she said. "If I'd known I'd saved a mental patient I would have called for help hours ago."

Doc made gentle, twisting motion with his hand and his spell book pulled from her grasp and drifted across the room gently to him. He plucked it from the air, then placed it down on the couch beside him.

"I did not just see that," she said. "That was a trick. You've got a string or something I didn't notice."

Doc shook his head. Another simple gesture, and a small globe of white light appeared in the palm of his hand. He let it roll off his fingertips and drift toward her. It danced around her like a pixie for a few seconds. She reached out to touch it, and the globe burst in with a pop of soft, sparkling light.

"Show me more," she said.

Doc found himself smiling in spite of himself. He'd been using magic to survive since he was a pre-teen. It was a tool, a weapon, a survival skill. He had never, not once, used it in front of anyone who had looked upon it with a sense of wonder. And here he was, watching a clearly brilliant young woman watching the simplest of spells with unabashed wonder. Something clicked in his chest right then, something he'd avoided ever since he gave up his true name. I'd like to know more about this person, he thought.

"Can I know your name?" he asked.

She looked away from the lights and grinned lopsidedly at him, something else people rarely did in his life. He couldn't remember the last time someone smiled playfully in his direction.

"You know you said you were stabbed by a gremlin when I found you."

"I think it might have been a redcap, the more I think about it," Doc said. "Stabbing is more of a redcap thing."

"Sure," she said, shaking her head. "You ask for my name, but I still don't think you've properly told me yours, and I've asked more than once now."

"I don't have one," he said. He paused, and then shook his head and looked at his hands. "I had to give my real name away. Doc's all I have."

"I don't know if I truly believe you," she said. "But for now, Doc will do. I'm Imogen. Now show me another one of these tricks of yours. Prove magic is real."

And he did.

***

For the first time in his life since becoming a magician, Doc realized, he found something nearly resembling normal.

He began spending more time in London than anywhere else. He still traveled the world through magical means, but London—

or more accurately, Imogen—became where he started to think of as home. She told him about school, and the struggles of nearing the end of it, and Doc found her stories, which she decried as boring complaints about the mundanities of study and school, enrapturing. He hadn't realized how living in this strange bubble of arcane and mystic had stolen away the ability to just be in the world. He found that he'd almost forgotten how to just go out to a restaurant and have dinner, having not had a real meal with anyone who wasn't a practicing spellcaster in ten years. They went to the movies together, which was a mind-blowing experience for Doc, who had forgotten how much he absolutely adored the movies growing up. Somehow the silver screen had lost its luster when he knew magic was real. Movie magic wasn't quite the same when you could do the real thing.

And sometimes they traveled the world together. Imogen never quite got comfortable with it, stepping through a portal and arriving in Mexico or New Zealand, and often spent large parts of the trip anxiously waiting for the authorities to ask how she got there. Doc learned he'd become almost too at ease with it, existing between the lines, being a ghost to the real world. He had nothing to lose no matter where he went; Imogen would soon be a licensed physician, with a real life, and real responsibilities. Something Doc was painfully aware he would never have.

There were nights he'd wander Imogen's apartment long after she'd fallen asleep, wondering if being in her life put her in any kind of danger—not of monsters, not of demons, but of falling into this space between the veils of reality, where only magicians and other shadows could exist.

The monsters scared both of them, though, the real ones Doc continued to encounter when he wasn't with Imogen. He'd come back from a trip somewhere on the other side of the world, lacerated and battered, and Imogen would put him back together again, using real, hard-earned skill to patch him up. She did this with grace and calm, but Doc knew it bothered her. He could see the look in her eyes as she stitched up claw marks across his chest, and her expression hung somewhere between worry, fear, and a growing sense of judgement.

Doc, who had stared down demons from the abyss, who had by this time faced vampires and unnamed beings from beyond the stars without fear, was afraid to ask her about that judgement, though. His stomach filled with acid at the very thought of discussing it, because he knew if they talked about it, they'd address it, and perhaps, perhaps, he would lose this one treasured tether to the real world.

There was one day, when they were having lunch in Manhattan—one of the cities so busy Imogen never really got nervous in, assuming she'd never be noticed in the crowd—when she finally brought it up.

"There are days I look at what you do and what I do and I think they're completely at odds," she said, sipping a cup of coffee and watching the world walk by in the sort of shambling chaos only New York could offer.

Doc hesitated before he said anything.

"What do you mean?" he said softly.

"I'm a doctor. I'm a scientist," she said. She didn't make eye contact as she spoke, which was just as well to Doc, who didn't particularly want to make eye contact in that moment either. "And you break reality. You prove everything I understand is wrong."

"Not wrong," Doc said. "Flexible. And what you know is true really is true. It's just that a handful of people can bend the rules."

"Right, but even a handful of people, Doc," she said. "Even a handful of people. That means the rules don't apply to everyone. And I'm not some sort of obsessive, hardline person who needs rules. I'm okay if they break or bend. Except…"

"Except what you are needs those rules," Doc said.

Imogen shrugged.

"Medicine is called a science, but it's really an art," she said. "Diagnosing symptoms, treating patients, we're winging it more than anyone in my profession wants to admit. But there are still laws of reality. And you, you don't exist in that reality."

"I'm here now," Doc said.

Imogen smiled, but there was a sadness to it, a profound longing Doc couldn't put a definition to.

"I know. I love you, you know. You stupid, strange wizard. I love a magician," she said. "We're like a joke. That one about the doctor who loves a wizard."

"I love you too," Doc said. I have since the moment you looked at me like a real person, he thought. Ten years and nobody ever looked at me like a real person. The rules of reality don't apply to me; but I would break the entire world for you if you asked.

"I know," she said. "But knowing what I know now, knowing what I learned from you, do you know what that does to me as someone who believes in science?"

"I can imagine," Doc said. "I'm not like you, I'm not educated, or trained, but I used to be a person who thought magic was a story, too, and then one day it wasn't, and nothing was ever the same. I had my grip on reality dashed on the ground when I was twelve. In a way I envy you, because you got the chance to understand how the world really works. I was so young I never really got to see the world as it should be. Only as magic treats it."

"And there are days I wish I could have my old worldview back," Imogen said.

Doc felt his stomach go cold, his hands numb. She's leaving, he thought.

"Do you wish we never met?" he said. And a little part of his mind, a rogue element of self-destructiveness, knew: I could make that happen. I could take away her memories of me if that would make her happy. It's not impossible. Maybe a life without ever having known me would be better for her. Maybe it's what she deserves. A life free of magic.

"No, I'm glad we met," she said, smiling at him with a radiant warmth that stole the breath from Doc's chest. "I just wish knowing you didn't come with the baggage of knowing the world makes no sense."

***

Imogen had a real life, real work to do, real goals to achieve, so they weren't always together. Doc's goals were more esoteric, but still more than enough to keep him busy full-time.

He searched for clues about the whereabouts of Erasmus; he continued to research magic, meet with other practitioners, and expand his mind; and as he always had, he tried to solve problems of the mystical and arcane when he encountered them.

Nearly a year after Doc and Imogen first met, he got wind of a series of disappearances in London, not far from Imogen's flat. They weren't the sort of missing persons reports that the authorities investigated; rather, he heard about them through the magicians' word of mouth, in the gossipy way magicians talk. Something strange was happening in an old, run-down neighborhood, they said, and folks were going missing who weren't missed by many people, and there was a hint of darkness to it that smelled worse than the usual crimes humanity was capable of all on its own.

I can get there without even using magic, Doc thought. It's my job to check it out.

And so he did.

Doc had, by now, become a half-decent investigator. Not the sort who could get a job with the local precinct, he knew, but he'd learned how to observe and listen, who to ask questions of and how to spot a lie or omission. He started with shopkeepers in the area, asking about strange occurrences, people they hadn't seen in a while, but he quickly knew that he needed to look just a little below the surface to get the answers he'd need. He sat for a while talking to a pair of homeless men, who provided great detail about some of their missing companions, though they said that folks like them disappeared all the time so they didn't think too much of it. He turned a sheaf of discarded flyers into pound notes and gave them to the men, for whatever purposes would help them get through the night.

And then Doc talked to a few of the neighborhood children. These were careful conversations, roundabout questions, but he knew that no one saw through the veil as easily as children, not even adults who lived on the edge of reality themselves, and no one could so readily pick up on a sense of palpable dread and threat like a child could. He remembered it well, the last time he saw his brother, before he gave his name away, how they knew, despite being taught that monsters were not real, that they'd been in the presence of something truly malignant, truly terrifying.

A couple of boys told him about an abandoned warehouse where they used to go to throw rocks at bottles.

"We don't go there anymore," one boy said. He was feigning toughness, but Doc hard the hard, icy edge of fear in his voice easily.

"Why not?" Doc asked.

"The building screams," the other boy said. The first shot him a filthy, belligerent glare, but the latter continued anyway. "You can hear it if you listen closely. It sounds like laughing, but then it doesn't, and then we ran away."

"Good man," Doc said. "Those were good instincts."

"And it smelled," the first boy said, almost defensively, as though he were jealous his friend told more of the story.

"How so?" Doc asked. "Like garbage?"

"Like rotten meat," the first boy said. Then he started to walk away. "You're not gonna go there, are you?"

"Thinking about it," Doc said.

The boy turned to his friend.

"Told you adults aren't smarter than us," he said, and together they hopped on their bikes and rode off.

It wasn't hard to find the building once he had those clues, a combination of asking around and a little bit of basic divination magic. Doc soon found himself outside stumpy brick warehouse, its metal door sporting a warning to keep out while being warped and partially open. A circular window above the door hinted at a life when the building was once more stylish or at least more functional, but now, it was a desiccated, crumbling structure long out of use.

He nudged the door open with his foot and stepped inside. The boys were right—the place stank something awful, a combination of old rot and new. The first level was mostly open space, shattered glass and graffiti everywhere. Doc whispered a simple spell and his footsteps ceased to make a sound as he placed his booted foot on the debris.

He easily found evidence of vandalism, both playful and malicious, and at least two places set up like tents where it appeared squatters had settled in for shelter. Neither tent was occupied, however, and both looked hastily abandoned.

Toward the back and in the corner, contrasting with the fading white and gray walls of the rest of the open space, he saw what looked like a small red brick hut, with a doorway and window, some kind of foreman's station or office. Doc stepped inside cautiously. Another door, partially closed, waited inside, just beyond a desk covered in soggy, partially burned paperwork.

It's always a dark, creepy door, Doc thought. Why can't it be a wide-open space, where I can see what's beyond? He thought about summoning the sword bound to the tattoo on his left wrist, but decided it would be better to not walk in with a medieval weapon in-hand if it were just another squatter inside. So he pulled the door open, waited for his eyes to adjust, and stepped within.

He was instantly assaulted by the smell. Rot, yes, but other, more distinctive, more horrifying scents—the heavy, threatening stench of a predatory animal, which made his heart race instinctively in his chest; the metallic tang of blood; and worse smells, latrine smells, as though he's walked into a big cat's enclosure at a zoo.

Now he summoned his sword, and the blade materialized in his hand, the weight reassuring as he tightened his grip upon it. Doc thought about calling up a magical light source, but thought better of it, instead uttering a quiet incantation and running the fingers of his free hand across his eyes, lightening the shadows of the room with hints of grayscale.

At the end of the hallway he found a hatch in the floor, lifted up and propped open, with a ladder leading down into the darkness. He stood staring down into that pit for a full minute before deciding to scale the ladder. I've done stupider things, he thought, remembering the rumors of disappearances, the sense of dread washing over him here telling him that someone had to fix what was wrong with this place. It might as well be me, he thought.

He reached the foot of the ladder and found himself in another lightless hallway. This one was rougher than above, the brick walls possessing an almost subway, subterranean feel to them. The smell was worse here, too, and the air uncomfortably still, a lifeless place, like a tomb. He started down the corridor, seeing no other path before him, and involuntarily tightened his grip on his sword.

He walked ten more steps into the darkened corridor before he saw the human finger on the floor.

A few years back, the sight would have pulled the air from his lungs; but the things he'd seen, especially since Erasmus' disappearance, turned what should have been a gurgled scream into a tired, almost frustrated sigh. Here there be monsters, he thought. Again.

And then he looked up and saw a monster looking directly at him.

This time, Doc let loose a small squeak of surprise. The creature looked human-sized, though with its hunched posture and long limbs, it was hard to tell if it were larger or smaller than he was from where he stood. It was nearly naked, a ragged, filthy cloth around its waist, pale-skinned, with knobs of bone showing through at the joints, ribs prominent and hungry. Its head was like a hairless dog's, with long, sharp teeth dripping with saliva.

The creature made no sound, did not move, and somehow the stillness was worse than had it lunged at him. And then Doc knew that the creature could not possibly be alone.

Doc heard a scratching noise from above him and looked up in time to see another such creature dropping from the ceiling, long, filthy, clawed fingers reaching for him. Without hesitation he swung his sword in an upward arc and felt hot, rancid blood rain down on him. The dog-headed creature cried out in pain and here the similarities to a canine disappeared—it was a human voice that cried out, squealing as the blade split its collarbone and dug into its lungs. The monster who had been in front of him took advantage of the distraction to lunge forward, and Doc tried to backtrack out into the open warehouse space where he could fight more freely, but slammed painfully into another body, that of a third creature, whose claws raked down his back, tearing his coat and flesh. He heard thumping footsteps and the first creature leapt onto him, knocking him to the ground, his sword clattering on the stone floor.

Cursing, Doc pulled a fistful of white powder from a pouch within his coat and slapped his palm against the floor. He blurted out a messy incantation just as he felt filthy teeth clamp down on his shoulder, the pressure blinding and the pain piercing, but he finished his spell, angrily roaring out the last few words. There was hiss and a thump and the entire corridor exploded in flames, sending the monstrous creatures sprawling and screeching in pain. Doc coughed as smoke burned his lungs. He snatched up his sword from the ground and pinwheeled around, not truly caring if he struck anything or not, half blind from the soot kicked up by his own spell.

He could see eyes glowing in the smoke and darkness now, gleaming, predatory eyes, moving in closer, the low rumble of growls that sounded more like empty stomach noises. One charged forward and Doc cut the creature down clumsily, taking off its arm at the elbow, but another charged and Doc's sword got caught in its torso, enabling another to lash out across the magician's stomach. Doc felt his own blood soaking his clothes, hot and coppery, as he pulled his sword free and bashed the nearest dog-faced creature in the moth with the hilt. He could see more coming for him now down the narrowed corridor, from deeper within, fighting with each other to get their turn at tearing him apart.

I can't win this fight, not this way, he thought, and looked up at the stone ceiling above the pressing onslaught of beast-men. He reached out a hand toward the stonework and, in the language of earth and stone, said two simple words.

"Please. Fall."

A brick came loose, and then another, and then two more, and suddenly the roof of the hallway was collapsing, peppering the monstrous, pale bodies with loud, brutal smacks and thumps. Doc ran backward toward the ladder and began to climb, reaching out to the ceiling once more and this time grabbing the air as if to pull the rooftop down with his gesture, pantomiming yanking the entire ceiling down upon the beasts, and as he did, he felt a pull and pop in his shoulder, a strain of real weight, and the ceiling did collapse, pulling thousands of pounds of building down onto the onrushing creatures. Doc scrambled up the ladder, nearly hauling himself out onto the floor, but felt a searing pain across his calf as something clamped down on it. He turned to see a surviving dog-faced abomination gnawing at him and Doc, desperate and angry and afraid, wove a spell with his hands, letting his sword drop and disappear back into its secret place from where he summoned it so he could mime with both hands a violent telekinetic pull. He envisioned two powerful hands, invisible, unstoppable, and the hands grabbed hold of the creature's jaws and opened them so violently the lower jaw came unhinged, purple tongue lolling uselessly. Doc kicked the terrible devourer between the eyes once, twice, until it fell away, plummeting back down into the darkness below.

He could still hear the stonework collapsing underground as he tried to get to his feet, his right leg giving out from under him. His boot was filling up with blood, and it felt as if his guts were an open hydrant of blood pouring down the front of his clothes. His vision went foggy and he could feel his heartbeat in his skull.

"No you don't," he said out loud, crawling for the door. "Not like this, not here, not this way."

Doc reached into his coat once again and produced an old,

cheap pocket watch. He flipped it open, dropped it to the ground, and picked up a loose brick from the floor nearby, smashing it down upon the watch and sending gears and glass flying.

"Die slower, you idiot," he said to himself. "Now's not the time. Die later."

He felt his heartbeat slow, and the pain in his wounds dull, not disappear, but fade into the background, enabling him to stagger back to his feet. He checked behind him to make sure none of the creatures were following him, and then wove his way back toward the entrance to the warehouse. Once he got outside, he slammed the door angrily behind him and retched. The daylight was fading fast, and Doc was both relieved for the cover it provided and fearful that it would protect any surviving creatures as well, but none exited the warehouse as he waited, his blood dripping slowly on the pavement below. As he watched, he removed a small envelope from his pocket and took out a thick green leaf and began to chew on it, the pain fading as he swallowed. He thought about lifting his shirt or pulling at his pant leg to check the damage, but didn't think he could stomach the carnage. Instead, he cast a simple illusion, enough to make him passable in public and not look as though he'd survived a near-fatal car crash.

And then he started stagging for the nearest roadway to find a cab ride to the only place he felt safe.

***

Doc awoke in Imogen's bathtub, his clothes cut from his body, Imogen leaning over his chest with a needle and thread in hand, cursing his name.

"I'm so tired of this," she said, before realizing he was awake. They locked eyes, and then she looked back down at the wound she was stitching, finishing up her work. She tied off the stitch and leaned back, stripping rubber gloves from her hands.

"I'm sorry," Doc said. "I took on more than I could handle."

"You do that more than is healthy, you know," she said. She ran a hand through his hair, turned his head side to side, checking his eyes for signs of a concussion. "What did you take for the pain?"

"I didn't take any medication," Doc said.

"You took something, medication or not," Imogen said. "Your breath smells like crushed mint and you never flinched when I stitched you up like a Christmas ham."

"Just a plant, an alchemical thing," Doc said. He went to reach into his pocket to show her the plastic bag he kept the small green leaves in, forgetting he wasn't wearing his coat. Or anything else, for that matter. He looked down over his chest and stomach and saw black lines of stitching and splotches of blood and bruising.

"What did you find?" she asked, not making eye contact.

"I'm not sure what they were," Doc said, the room feeling hazy and distant. "I think they were some kind of ghoul. Cannibals or man-eaters. They were taking people from the streets, dragging them underground. The children in the area were afraid. I had to step in. You know I had do something, right? It's my job to help."

Imogen stared off into space for a long moment, then exhaled.

"I love you, you know."

"I love you too," Doc said.

"And because of that, I want to ask why this is your job. But I know why it's your job. I mean I don't fully understand it. It sounds like make believe to me, and you've taken us to the other side of the world with hand gesture and a nonsense poem. But I want to know why you're the one who has to come home looking like you've been through a meat grinder."

"Someone has to do it," Doc said. He leaned up slowly, the pain from his injuries starting to seep back in as the leaf's numbing effects began to fade. "And there's so few people like me who can. And... Imogen, I can't do anything else. Does that make any sense? I don't exist. Not in any meaningful way."

"You exist to me," she said. "That matters to you, right?"

"Of course it does," Doc said. His skin felt cold now, less because of his nakedness but rather a draining fear in his guts. He'd just crawled his way from beneath a ruined building with monsters chewing on his limbs, but he was more afraid of what Imogen was about to say.

"Goddammit," she said. Imogen put her face in her hands and let out one single, heartbreaking sob, then steadied herself and took her hands away. "I can't watch you do this, Doc."

Doc opened his mouth to speak, but Imogen cut him off.

"I can't. And I can't ask you to stop doing it. You scare me. And I don't mean I'm afraid of you. I'm afraid for you, every time you're not here, because you go places people aren't meant to go, and I'm afraid they'll eat you alive. But then that makes me think: are you... are you really a human being? Or are you something else? I don't think you're a monster. I just don't think you're a part of the real world, and I am, I am so much part of the real world, Doc. I'm here, up to my elbows in it, helping sick people, trying to leave the world better than I found it."

"I'm trying to leave the world better than I found it, too," Doc said softly.

"And that's why I can't ask you to stop doing what you do," she said. "I've seen what you can do. God, am I the only regular, ordinary person who knows? Does anyone else know what you are?"

"No," Doc answered. "Other magicians know me. Other people like me. But no one..."

"No one ordinary."

"You are the most extraordinary person I have ever met in my life," Doc said.

Imogen laughed. It was a real laugh, but laced with sadness, and Doc saw the tip of her nose turning pink, the rims of her eyes.

"I just wish you could, I don't know. Leave it to the police, or the army or something. Why are you fighting monsters all by yourself in the dark when someone else could do it."

"There are things they can do, and things they can't," Doc said. "I think it's always been that way. We hear stories about scary witches on the edge of a swamp, or the wizard in a tower, or shaman on the hill, looking down over a village that doesn't understand them. And through all this time, Imogen, they've been there for a reason. They're out there on the outskirts where the veil is thin, and they tell the monsters they are not welcome here. That's what I became when I gave up my real name. I'm the shaman on the hill. The wizard in the tower. I'm the witch at the edge of the swamp. Watching for monsters."

Imogen chewed on her lip, shook her head, picked up a washcloth, stained pink with blood, and washed away some of the grime from his skin. She set the washcloth aside again and touched his face.

"Doc, you know what all those witches and wizards and shaman have in common?"

Doc felt his eye sting with tears. He tried to remember the last time he was sad, the last time he wanted to cry. He'd been afraid, he'd been in pain, he'd been lonely. But he hadn't cried since he gave up his name, since his brother looked at him like a stranger on the streets of their hometown, since he knew, truly and unequivocally, he could never go home again.

"People are afraid of them," Imogen said. "And they're all alone."

Doc sniffled, and nodded, and rubbed his eyes with a blood-stained hand.

"When I gave up my name, I knew I would give up the people I loved to keep them safe," Doc said. "And I did it, so that they could be safe, even though I knew they'd forget me. I didn't know that I'd be giving up anyone I'd ever love to keep them safe too."

"We probably never would have met if you hadn't given up your name," Imogen said.

"I feel like I should apologize for that," he said. "You know all sorts of things about the world you shouldn't have to carry with you. All I gave you was a burden."

Imogen shook her head, eyes glassy and filled with tears waiting to fall.

"I got to see behind the veil for a little while," she said. "And I got to see that there's someone brave, stupidly brave, who keeps the monsters away. I think that makes it worth the burden."

She studied his face for a moment, then closed her eyes, a single tear falling down her cheek.

"You have to go back there, don't you," she said.

"I have to make sure I finished the job. So no one else has to get hurt."

Imogen nodded, slid back along the edge of the tub to give him space, wiped her hands on her jeans.

"If you're ever truly in trouble. If you ever need someone to put you back together again," she said.

"I can't ask you do to that."

"You keep the monsters away," she said. "That's your job. Mine is keeping death itself away. We all have a purpose in this world, Doc Silence. Let me do my job."

"I will," Doc said.

She stood up to leave, patting a set of clean clothes she'd brought in for him and had placed next to the bathtub.

"For you," she said, and turned to leave. She paused and looked back at him. Her mouth twisted with ferocious emotion, then she calmed herself and spoke. "Will I forget you when you're gone?"

"I wish I could say you would," Doc said. "But I think that only happens once. You're stuck with the burden of remembering me."

"Good," she said, a true smile cutting through the melancholy air. "That's not a burden. That's a gift."

***

She walked him to the train station, neither willing to simply close a door, and down into the tunnels beneath Elephant and Castle. They said nothing as they parted ways, but both Doc and Imogen turned back to look at each other, twenty paces apart, walking in opposite directions, knowing, understanding, that they may never see each other again.

Doc could not read her emotions from across the empty subway tunnel, but felt a frigid, resigned emptiness within himself he struggled to hide. He nodded, and she raised a hand in goodbye, and together they walked away, Doc slowing his pace until he could no longer hear her footsteps.

He had every intention of leaving London, perhaps forever, but first, he had to finish his work. If he was not allowed to find happiness, he could at least know it was for a reason, he told himself unconvincingly.

It was well into the night when he found himself once again outside the warehouse, a bloody handprint on the door he knew was his own. On the way, he'd picked up six bottles of cheap spirits, the clerk asking him if he were throwing a party. Doc said "in a way," and meant it, sincerely.

He picked up a broken piece of wood that looked as though it might once have been part of a broom handle and banged on the metal door three times.

"Wake up, you vicious bastards," he said. He set the cardboard box the liquor shop had given him to carry his booze in down next to his feet, and poured a line of silvery powder across the front door, speaking an ancient, gargling spell as he did. He stepped back as he heard yipping and growling from within. There was a clatter of claws, heavy, animalistic breathing, and then the metal door flew open and one of the dog-faced creatures lunged at him. It stopped mid-air as though it struck an invisible wall trying to cross the threshold, falling back into its fellows behind. The gathering crowd of ghoulish monstrosities drooled and growled and whined as they watched him hungrily.

"We all here, then?" Doc said. "Good. I don't believe in murder. Let's make that clear. But I know what you are, and I know this world does not belong to you. You should walk among the dead. You are intruders in this place."

One of the creatures pushed its way to the front of the crowd and pulled back its canine lips, revealing yellowed, blood-stained fangs.

"You... talk... too much," the monster said. "We will lick the marrow from your bones."

"Maybe you will," Doc said. "But not here. This is my world, not yours. Go back to where you came from."

"Weak… scared…" the leader said.

And then Doc pulled one of the bottles from the cardboard box, its neck stuffed with cloth. He snapped his fingers and a small flame appeared between his thumb and forefinger. He used this flame to light the cloth.

"Yes," Doc said. "You are."

He threw the makeshift Molotov cocktail into the warehouse, sailing it over the head of the lead ghoul, and heard it smash. He smelled smoke and burning rotted flesh, heard cries not in pain but in frustration and hate. He picked up another bottle and lit the fuse.

"Leave this place and never come back," Doc said, tossing the second bottle, this time an overhand pitch right at the chest of the lead creature. It smashed and smeared him in burning alcohol. The ghoul stepped back, flesh blackening and cracking, but the monster did not cry out in pain. He stepped back, setting some of his fellows on fire as he walked by them. Doc lit and threw another incendiary, and another, until the interior of the building was lit up like a Jack-o'-lantern. The monsters screamed, and roared and chanted and growled, and eventually grew silent.

Doc heard sirens in the distance. He waited a few moments, watching for signs of life, or undeath, from within, observing the dancing flame, the curling smoke, the stench of burning corpses.

The sirens were too close for comfort now, and so Doc turned, tracing his fore and middle fingers across the tattoo to assist in teleportation, and stepped through a thin ripple in reality before him. He paid no attention to where the portal went. He only knew his time in Elephant and Castle was over.

Chapter 14: The Thinning Veil

After Imogen and Doc went their separate ways, Doc disengaged with what he'd begun to think of as the "real" world. There was the world of mortals, who walked among shadows never questioning the depths of their darkness, and there were the wizards and monsters on the other side of the veil. Perhaps, Doc thought, as he made his way into the Australian outback on foot like a fool, the two sides of the veil were never meant to meet. I am not a part of their world, and they are not a part of mine, and that is simply the way of things.

As a distraction from his aching heart, though he would never admit it, Doc threw himself more fully into his search for Erasmus. He'd been told time and time again by the old wizard's allies that he'd either come back when he was ready, or else never come back at all, because, on this side of the veil, sometimes wizards just disappear.

But rumors still spread, and Doc heard whispers that his mentor had been seen entering a cave in the Australian outback to deal with a beast, a living nightmare, that had stepped across the worlds and built a nest there.

And so Doc tracked down the name of the mining town someone had said they last saw Erasmus Hawksmith, and he teleported to his teacher's last known location, or so he hoped. That was two days ago. He spoke to some of the locals, a few of whom remembered a man with a foreign accent and gray hair passing through, though no one had a meaningful conversation with him, which was Erasmus' way in towns he didn't want to cause a fuss in. He asked about caves and caverns, too, and those questions received more accurate answers. Old mining caves, abandoned and not; natural rock formations; and one, a deep well in the earth, which the locals had long abandoned. Doc even managed to find a few men who had, as teenagers, went out to that very well, but they said they felt as though they were being watched the entire time and never went back.

That seemed to be the common theme of the cave. If you approached it, you never repeated the endeavor. The men told Doc about local stories of people entering the cave and never coming out, though they had themselves never knew of anyone who entered and not returned.

Doc had the men mark the location on a map, and the men were concerned that this American with strange blue hair intended to walk out into the wilderness alone, but he reassured them he was better prepared than he looked, folded up his map, and made his preparations.

Doc Silence was a child of the City, and he learned his craft in cities across the world, but he was no fool. He knew spells to conjure water and food, to block the heat of the sun, to regulate his body temperature to guard against extreme heat or cold. If his magic failed him he'd likely die out there in the wilds, but so far, Doc thought, the only thing that hadn't failed him in his life was magic. Everything else about him was a disaster, but his spellcraft he could count on.

The next morning he walked north, the sun blazing down on him with a vengeful glare, a backpack of supplies slung across his shoulders as a precaution, because he was confident in his abilities, but not overconfident. The sky felt too big here, too wide, too empty, and it made him anxious and agoraphobic in ways he had never experienced before. But he ran a hand across his eyes, a mixture of soot and blood on his fingertips to reveal the hidden pathways of the world as he brushed the red-black paste onto his eyelids.

The world began to sing.

There were old stories of the outback of course, of its connections to dreams, and Doc had heard both the messy, misrepresentative, appropriated stories of European travelers alongside those who grew up here and the tales of the things they'd seen. Magic was strong here, he sensed, that much was true, but magic was always strong in places where mankind had not clenched its iron fist down hard enough to crush the whimsy from the world, spaces where the magic roamed wild and unbridled and uninhibited.

Midday, he knelt down in the heat of the sun, his skin raw and head aching. Doc wanted to cast a protective spell to take the edge off the heat, but for his next step, he needed as little distraction as possible. He closed his eyes, touched the ground with his fingertips, and reached out for any sign of his mentor.

Were you here, you old bastard? Doc thought. Did you walk into the Outback and get yourself killed by some monster, or did you just abandon me like an unwanted house pet?

Footsteps began to appear in the earth, booted, slow. They led further north, walking slower than Doc had been moving, but steadily, determined, with a slight limp Doc recognized immediately. He had been here, Doc knew. Whether this was where Erasmus died or disappeared was uncertain, but at least he'd found a stop along the old wizard's way.

Doc got back to his feet and cast a minor spell that cooled his clothing, and another that shaded the sun from his face, and a third that took away the aching in his feet. Part of him thought he should challenge himself to survive the outback on his own physical strength, but he knew he needed to conserve his energy should he encounter whatever it was Erasmus was looking for here.

He followed the footprints in the dirt for miles, watching them disappear behind him as he passed each set. Getting home is the easy part, he told himself, brushing a few fingertips across the teleportation tattoo. Provided whatever Erasmus encountered doesn't kill me first, I guess.

Doc was almost disappointed when he finally found the cave. He might be a child of the City, but in his time with Erasmus and after, he'd seen his fair share of caves, places where monsters and mysteries lurked and waited. This one opened up like a giant divot in the earth, a scoop of ground with ugly, spikey plant growth around its mouth like a bad shave on a tired man's face. Doc sighed and stepped forward slowly, casting a different spell on his eyes this time, a phosphorescent powder assisting him to see in the darkness below as he crested the lip of the cavern's mouth.

It looked almost man-made, Doc thought, with a reasonable, easy-to-navigate slope to the floor leading deeper into the shadows. The floor of the cave was remarkably even, almost tidy.

Erasmus' footprints disappeared into the darkness. They did not turn around and lead back out into the daylight.

Doc took note of the position of the sun, beating down at him from past its zenith, but still early in the day. For some reason he preferred the idea of exploring the cave in the daytime rather than waiting until nightfall, though it would still be dark inside no matter what, and his spells would undo any disadvantage he might have with his vision. Creatures in caves like the nighttime, he knew. He'd faced enough vampires and lycanthropes and worse to know that the night belonged to them, not him.

He considered summoning his sword, but then hesitated. If something lived in this tunnel, he thought, perhaps I can negotiate with it. Better to walk in empty-handed than with bared steel. And truly, no magician is ever unarmed or empty-handed.

Doc entered the cave and hoped for the best.

The first thing he noticed was the smell. Not a bad smell, exactly; but rich, overwhelming, like raw spices, or something else more unusual and otherworldly. It grew stronger the deeper he went into the cave, and the air grew cooler, at first comfortable compared to the surface temperature, but then too cool, a chill running down his back where his shirt clung to his skin with sweat.

And then he saw the lights.

At first they looked like a set of closely packed holes through which blue-white light filtered out. Doc, not inclined to trypophobia, squinted and hugged a wall as he drew closer to get a better look. But the further he worked his way into the cave, the better his view of the glowing, misshapen spheres became. And he saw that they were moving. Moving, and blinking.

Eyes. They were eyes.

I should summon my sword, he thought, regretting his decision to start with the peaceful solution first. But still, he'd encountered more terrifying things than many-eyed creatures, and not all were dangerous or violent. Let's have a conversation, he thought. Yes, a conversation with the creature in the cave where Erasmus disappeared.

I should summon my sword, he thought again, and he did, quick, making the twisting hand motion to bring the weapon into his grip. He kept the blade pointed toward the ground, though, casually, Doc thought. I'm just casually carrying a sword as I walk into some alien creature's nest.

The eyes eventually coalesced into an asymmetrical head, chitinous, the color of old, dry bone, but fleshy, almost rubbery on the surface. Below the eyes, a wet, many-fanged mouth hung open, dripping a fluid that hissed and sizzled as it struck the cavern floor. Doc put his hand on the wall to steady himself, but found the stone to be too smooth, too soft, too damp. He looked at his hand, and then followed the surface he'd touched, a long, cylindrical spire that curved up to the ceiling and all the way to the massive mounded back of the creature in front of him. It was a leg, a long, segmented, insectoid leg, ending in a spiked, callused barb just inches from Doc's foot. Doc felt the leg begin to move beneath his hand.

And then the creature screamed.

The arthropod-like leg rose up and shot back down at Doc, trying to pin him to the ground. He spun out of the way, casting a spell with automatic, trained practice to let him move faster than his mortal legs could carry him. He darted across the inner cavern, dodging two more massive, spiked legs, which kicked up earth and stone in his wake.

"I come in peace, come on!" Doc yelled, diving to the floor and rolling under a scythe-like mandible he hadn't noticed before. "I'm looking for my friend, have you seen him?"

The creature screamed again, spitting acidic globules toward Doc, who threw up a protective shield of magic to save it from pitting his skin. The saliva hissed as it slid, green and viscous, onto the ground.

Doc could see all of the creature now as it stomped and twisted to engage him. Three massive, bulbous body segments, like a spider's, a long, curved hook of bone protruding from a twisting, obscene tail. The tail sought him out, swinging and slashing, and Doc had no choice. He brought up his sword reflexively and felt it bite into the carapace, cracking and splitting the creature's exoskeleton, exposing pus-colored meat beneath.

"I would rather just talk!" he yelled again, earnestly hoping this was some misunderstanding. Erasmus was as capable of hubris as any wizard, but even he wouldn't deliberately upset a creature like this, Doc knew, and if he had, his magic would have been more than enough to handle one monster. The old man wouldn't have been running around like headless poultry trying to avoid being gutted by it. Did this creature really kill Erasmus? Doc thought as he side-stepped a burbling puddle of spittle and swung the flat of his blade around to smash it into the creature's eyes, trying to distract or disrupt it.

He tried to be clever and duck underneath creature's mouth, but he was knocked back, gasping in horror as his jacket began to melt. Ripping the jacket off, he threw it at the monster's mouth, watching as the great beast worried and chewed the fabric until it was little more than melting tissue. He tried to deke left and run right, but the creature wasn't fooled, and as the massive mandibles reached for him, Doc threw his sword, point-first, directly into the beast's gullet. The sword embedded itself in the softer flesh of the creature's throat and tongue. Doc heard the metal squeal as it gave way under the acrid virulence of the acid.

"Gonna need a new sword, I guess," Doc said, slapping his hands together and throwing a fistful of peppery powder underneath the monster's belly. The powder exploded in a white-hot ball of flame, cooking the creature from below. It lashed out then not with a physical attack but a psychic one. Doc's mind filled with searing pain, and also images, sights and sounds of another world: violet skies filled with blood-red stars; a landscape of cracked and razor-sharp obsidian; creatures like this one hunting across a nightmare landscape, though hunting what Doc could not tell. He saw the creature—somehow he knew he was watching not just a creature like this, but this exact one—slither and squirm through a gap in the obsidian ground, skittering on long, sharp legs across a star-scape woven of eternity, and stepping through a black space between those stars into this cave. Here, in this reality, waiting, watching, hungry, and hunting.

"I'd send you home if I knew that's where you wanted to go," Doc said out loud, the uncountable, uneven blue-white eyes staring at him not with hate but with the patience of an old god.

This isn't a cave, Doc realized, seeing the alien intelligence, the hunger, the hatred in those pale, hypnotic eyes. This is a trap.

Doc reached up into the air above him, speaking words in a language only a handful of living people had ever heard, and he called down lightning. Not from the ether, not from thin air, but from the sky itself. The stone of the cavern split, sending rock and dirt and debris down not just onto the creature's back but onto Doc as well, a shard of rock cutting the wizard's face like a dull razor. Blue-violet electricity cascaded down through the crack in the cave, spearing the nightmare being in the back, the air humming with power, a deafening crack of stone and chitin. The lightning tore through everything in its path until it grounded itself in the cave floor. The creature—not a beast, Doc, knew, a thinking, planning being, malevolent, wanting—made one last attempt to devour the magician. But Doc, more by accident than skill, slipped from his perch against the cavern wall and beneath the snapping, needle-like teeth of this alien being's dripping maw. Doc staggered away, watching with pity as its great legs stomped and stumbled, its guts, partially cooked and blackened by the lightning bolt, spilling onto the floor like burnt cottage cheese. It cried out a terrible death wail, a squealing, piercing scream, and then it fell to the floor, and fell still.

Doc stayed very still for a while, watching and waiting for the creature to rise back up from the floor. But it remained still. When he walked cautiously over to its face, he saw the light had gone out in its eyes, which were now empty and clear, like balls of glass. He stepped over acidic puddles and deeper into the cavern, ignoring the half-melted sword he saw smoking on the ground.

He desperately hoped the extraplanar creature was alone here, and after a few minutes, his fears abated. No other alien spider-beings waited for him in the deeper reaches of the cave. Neither, he found, did Erasmus.

Instead, Doc Silence found windows.

They were like slivers in the veil, places the walls between worlds had grown very thin. Each window held a keyhole view into another place. He saw the obsidian-sharp home world of the spider he'd fought. He saw a place that was like his own, but upside down, with cities hanging like fruit from trees in the sky. He saw a landscape made of candy, and another in sepia tones, like an old movie. Some were like peepholes; others large enough for a man to pass through, if they wanted. There were dozens, if not more. World after world, portal after portal to places made of dreams and nightmares.

"I wonder which one Erasmus went through," Doc muttered

aloud. And why, he thought silently. Did Erasmus Hawksmith run into one of these dream-windows to escape the nightmare spider? Or did his curiosity get the better of him? Did he find a window he couldn't resist crawling through, leaving a half-trained apprentice behind to fend for himself?

Doc recast the spell that led him here, looking for Erasmus' footprints in the earth. It took him hours to find the trail again, obscured as it was by the monster's tracks and the destruction Doc had, himself, wrought. But finally, he located the prints in the earth. They led to a low-hanging doorway, to a desert made of silver sand, a pink sky warm and inviting above.

"Where did you go, old man?" Doc said.

He considered going through the window, to see what tempted Erasmus from this mortal plane. But he knew he wasn't ready, and perhaps he wouldn't like what he found on the other side. But he marked his maps, and drew a sigil on the wall of the cave to help him find his way back some day, a binding between places to bring him here again.

"I'm not done with you yet, Erasmus Hawksmith," Doc said, preparing the spell that would bring him home. "I just need to be ready in case neither one of us can come back from wherever you are."

Doc brushed the teleportation tattoo and felt himself yanked across space and time once more, away from this place where the veil was thin, translucent, and waiting to be passed through.

Chapter 15: The crone

The old seer lived somewhere in Eastern Europe, in a place where the lines between nations blurred and the rules of the mortal world were less important than the old ways. He got directions to her house from a Russian werewolf for the price of three rounds at a grimy roadside bar. It wasn't so much that the werewolf wanted to be paid for the information, but rather he needed a few drinks in him before he was willing to give up the information.

"I don't know what you want to talk to her for," he told Doc, scratching at a dense, jet-black beard. "The old woman terrifies me. You're a strange man, seeking her out."

"Why does anyone go looking for a seer?" Doc said, placing the money for another round on the top of the scarred, ancient wooden bar. "She has answers I need and can't get from anyone else."

"You know who she really is, though, yeah?" the werewolf, who had introduced himself as Timofey, said. "What she is?"

"I've heard rumors."

"The rumors are true," Timofey said. "She doesn't call herself by name, but she is exactly who the rumors say she is. And that is why you should stay away from her."

"And also why she might be the only person who can tell me what I need to know," Doc said.

"Crazy wizards," the werewolf said, throwing one hand up dismissively while tossing back the contents of his glass with the other. "You're all crazy. They say werewolves are dangerous, but at least we have a sense of self-preservation."

"And it's served you well. Self-preservation is why the real world thinks you're all just folklore and myth," Doc said. "I appreciate that you and yours are willing to speak with me about these things."

Timofey shrugged grumpily.

"Sometimes, it is good to have a wizard in your corner," he said. "Favors come back around. I know you're good for it, just like the old man was."

"I am. I promise."

"Where is the old man? He hasn't been by in years."

"That is exactly what I need to talk to the old woman about, Timofey," Doc said. "I can't find him."

"Probably dead, then," the werewolf said. "Got himself killed asking the wrong questions and talking to the wrong old women. Wizards are always getting killed by their curiosity."

"If I find him, I'll tell him you asked after him," Doc said.

Timofey laughed and ordered another round.

"Don't put my name in that old magician's head," he said. "It's bad luck to have a wizard thinking about you. In fact, put me right out of mind as soon as I finish this drink."

***

The old seer lived in a farm house twenty miles outside of the nearest town. Doc rented a car from a repair shop, which almost turned him down when Doc said where he was going. The owner gave him the worst car on the lot, muttering about how he didn't expect to ever see it again. The exchange left Doc vaguely hopeful he was headed to the right place, and less vaguely concerned about what he'd find there.

A thin, gray blanket of snow covered the landscape, with low grumpy hills standing sentinel in the distance. The sun never felt as though it fully reached its zenith, but felt rather like a perpetual late afternoon, the sky a hazy, unwelcoming yellow tinge. Beyond the hills, dark trees waited like a veil hiding secrets in an old fairy tale.

Doc saw the smoke before the farm, an almost welcoming trail of gray from an old-fashioned chimney. As it came into view, the house looked oddly placed, leaning a bit to one side as if it were tired. Doc pulled into a dirt driveway that let up from the ghostly, near-empty road. He pulled off to one side onto the dirt a few hundred feet from the farm and walked the rest of the way. He was soon set upon by curious chickens, hefty hens clucking and preening, a single rooster standing on a gray fencepost watching him with a warrior's gaze. Beyond the fence, Doc could see a handful of wiry goats chewing on blighted brush. The goats raised their heads to watch him curiously before returning to their meal.

Doc carried a small satchel with him as he walked calmly up to the farmhouse door. He politely knocked three times, then waited.

A few minutes went by. Rather than knock again, he turned away and started back toward the rental car.

"Now hang on," a woman's voice said. "You can't just knock on someone's door and expect them to answer, especially at my age. I need some time to get myself sorted."

Doc looked back over his shoulder and was honestly surprised by what he saw. By all accounts, the old seer had been described as a terrifying sight, but the woman in the doorway looked middle-aged, healthy, with high cheekbones, a prominent nose, dark hair with a distinctive white streak curling from her forehead and tucked behind her right ear. She was dressed simply, in earth tones, and held the battered screen door to her home open with a long-fingered hand.

"I don't want to be a nuisance," Doc said. "When you didn't

answer, I thought you must be busy."

"I'm always busy," she said. "But visitors are rare these days, and you have the look of a young man who has seen things. Come inside. Have some tea."

Doc accepted the invitation, following the woman into her home, which immediately felt cramped and uncomfortable in its layout. She seemed almost too tall for the interior, though it felt as though the house changed to suit her stature, while ignoring Doc's discomfort. On the other hand, the building smelled wonderful, and welcoming, a blend of sweet candy and a hearty dinner cooking somewhere within. She led him to a tiny kitchen, where Doc noticed there was not, in fact, a meal in process, the oven cold, the stovetop empty save for a small kettle which had just begun to whistle. She removed the kettle from the flame and poured steaming water into two small ceramic cups, arranged as though she were expecting company.

Perhaps she's always expecting company, Doc thought.

"There are those who come to my farm by accident, and those who come here with a purpose," the woman said, taking a seat at a small table, folding her limbs in casually. She reminded Doc of a spider. She gestured to the seat across form her, and Doc complied. "Which are you?"

"I've heard much about you," Doc said. "I came here with a purpose."

"Seeking answers, then," the woman said. "Normally I chase uninvited guests away, but my chickens told me you had a kind demeanor about you. The goats said you were dangerous, but goats are simple in that way; they do not understand that one can be both kind and dangerous."

"I don't know if I am kind," Doc said. "I want to be."

"And dangerous?"

"Unequivocally, though not to you," Doc said. "I suspect no one is dangerous to you."

The woman shrugged one slender, delicate shoulder dismissively, making a small, almost charming sneer with her lips.

"No creature is without natural predators," she said. "But I know you aren't here to harm me. Drink your tea, and tell me your name."

Doc sipped at the tea, which was smokey and slightly sweet, which caught him off-guard. He wondered briefly which laws of magic applied here, if breaking bread with this being would ensure his protection, or if he would end up in a cage to be fattened up for dinner. Well, I'm here now, he thought. No turning back.

"I'm called Doc Silence," he said, placing the tea carefully on the table.

"A false name," she said. "You are no physician, and you are certainly not silent. A sorcerer's name, too, if I'm not mistaken. You have the cast of a man who has thrown his true name away."

"You're not wrong," Doc said. The tea was warm in his belly, pleasant and calming.

"What brings you to my farm, then, Doctor Silence?" she said. "You came a long way, judging by your accent. Yes, I can hear it beneath the spell you are using to speak Russian. I see the mark on your neck there too, a rune of understanding. And I appreciate the effort, but there is no language I can't speak, and the spell isn't hard to hear through."

"Should I speak plainly, then?" Doc said.

"Speak however you choose, and I'll understand."

Doc smiled at her, and she smiled back. The warm feeling in Doc's belly from the tea twisted with a nervousness he hadn't had before, an awareness, suddenly, of how powerful the entity across the table from him truly was.

"Is there something I should call you? I have heard you called many names, but I don't want to offend," Doc said.

The woman chuckled and waved a hand around.

"Anything but Grandmother," she said. "I hate that. Makes me feel old. What names have you heard?"

"Jezda," Doc said. "Jezibaba. Iaga."

"I haven't heard Jezda in some time," she said. "Call me that today. I may change my mind later."

Doc nodded.

"Jezda, I am looking for a man."

"Your master."

"My teacher."

"Is there a difference?" she said.

"I'd like to think there is," Doc said. "But maybe I'm wrong. His name was Erasmus Hawksmith. I believe he was known to you."

Jezda grinned wickedly and nodded.

"Another sorcerer. Another dangerous man. Another name that was not his own. The real Hawksmith was not born in this world, you know. Erasmus stole the name because he thought it suited him, and because he thought it suitably dramatic for a wizard. Not wrong, in either case."

"Erasmus has been missing for a long while," Doc said.

"And you want to find him," Jezda said. "I can help you with this, but we must first bargain. Answers always have a cost."

Doc shook his head slowly, and Jezda raised an eyebrow.

"Are you refusing to bargain?" she said. Her voice purred, but there was an underlying threat to her tone.

"Not at all," Doc said. "But I'm seeking a different answer. I am happy to keep searching for the old man on my own. I'm learning much from my own investigations, and I wonder, in some ways, if Erasmus abandoned me specifically so I would investigate, so I would teach myself, without him there to guide me."

"Wizards are terrible teachers," Jezda said.

"They truly are," Doc said, and they both laughed together, an honest laugh that felt so genuine it made Doc's hair stand on end, the idea of a mortal and an endless being finding common ground mocking the flaws of magicians.

"So you don't want my help finding him," Jezda said. "You have surprised me, Doctor Silence, and now I must hear your question."

"I only wish to know if he wants to be found," Doc said.

Again, Jezda laughed, a real laugh, from her belly.

"You want to know if you're wasting your time," she said.

"Perhaps," Doc said.

"Do you care if he's alive or dead, if he's happy or miserable, if he's in this world or the next?" Jezda said.

"No," Doc said. "That's his business, not mine. Just if he's waiting."

"If your master has abandoned you like an unwanted puppy on the side of the road."

"Something like that."

"I've seen abandoned dogs," Jezda said. "It makes me angry. I like dogs better than people, you know. They don't lie. They just love. When I see humans abandon creatures who only know love, I want to punish the people who leave them behind."

Doc felt his eyes sting ever so slightly, the barest hint of a tear working its way to the edge of his right eye. For the life of him, he wasn't sure if he felt sad for abandoned creatures, or if he felt abandoned himself. He sipped his tea to hide the tightness in his throat.

"What do you have to offer me for this knowledge?" Jezda said softly.

Doc placed the satchel he carried on the table. It clinked like glass as he set it down. Doc opened the flap and pulled out a crystal sphere the size of an orange and placed it on the table.

"What is this, little magician?" Jezda asked, though Doc suspected she knew exactly what it was the moment she looked at it.

"It's a nightmare's eye," Doc said. "I have a dozen of them in this bag."

"Where did you acquire the eyes of a nightmare?" she said, picking up the sphere in one long-fingered hand and rolling it around in her palm, weighing it.

"The nightmare didn't need them anymore," Doc said.

"Did you kill it yourself?" Jezda said.

"I did."

"You truly have seen much in your master's absence," she said.

"Where was this?"

"In the Australian outback. A place where the walls were thin. I think it found the place by accident and set up a nest there."

Jezda held the eye up to her own and looked through it, distorting her green-gray iris.

"A dozen, you say," she said. "Are these all of the creature's eyes?"

"I kept one for myself," Doc said. "But if you'd like the thirteenth…"

"No, no, it's good you keep one. I like the idea of you keeping the thirteenth eye. That means something. That puts a thought out into the world, where it can take shape."

"So you accept my payment?" Doc said.

Jezda rolled the eye back to him, which he then placed in the satchel.

"Almost," she said. "I have one more caveat, before I answer. One more request of you, my abandoned puppy."

"Do I agree to it before you tell me?" Doc said, knowing this would be a breach of protocol.

"No, no, of course not. Do you take me for a cheat?"

"I only know that some say you invented the bargain," Doc said.

"That's a lie," Jezda said. "Someone older than me created the first bargain. The rest of us just make better use of it. My request, Doctor Silence, is that when you find abandoned dogs, you protect them, and you avenge them. I see a future in which this matters, where there will be strays who will need you. I think this is something you would do anyway, but I want you to do it in my name. So that I might receive payment for your good deeds."

"That seems a fair deal," Doc said, knowing full well somehow he would receive the short end of the bargain. It was an unbalanced deal he could live with, though, and it tied him to her, so she would speak to him again when he needed her.

"Then I will tell you that your master is waiting for you," Jezda said. She grinned, her lips and teeth taking on a predatory cast.

"Whether you think he's worth finding is up to you, though. A bit of free advice – I don't think you need him. Let him wait. You're not a dog to be abandoned, and your love is better given elsewhere."

Doc closed his eyes and nodded, unsure if he was relieved or angry, if he felt betrayed or challenged. He slid the satchel gently across the table, the gemlike eyes of the nightmare tinkling inside like icicles. Jezda picked up the bag and placed it beneath the table.

"I'm disappointed," Jezda said. "I saw a young wizard on my steps and I thought I might devour you, and keep your soul as a porchlight. I was so looking forward to tearing you apart for my stewpot, but then you had to go and be reasonable. I might even like you, Doctor Silence."

Doc smiled and made to stand up, waiting for Jezda's permission, which she granted with a nod. They rose together, and she led him to the front door once again, taking his hand in hers and placing the other around his bicep guiding his steps.

It was fully dark when he emerged, and somehow Doc knew that much more time passed outside while he was within the house. The stars were bright and cold, the animals all gone, chickens clucking from a cozy henhouse along the side of the farm.

"Don't be a stranger, Doctor Silence," Jezda said, and she kissed him on the forehead, dizzyingly tall, much taller than she'd been just a moment before. "I think we will have many more conversations in your lifetime."

"I hope so," Doc said, tightening his hand around hers in a gentle gesture of goodbye. As he stepped down the steps, he stopped once more on his way to the car. He looked back and saw Jezda, and for a moment she was all things: a withered old woman, an iron-backed matron, a delicate young woman, her dark hair in a long plait down one shoulder. "If I may, could I ask one question?"

"Ask it and I will tell you if I deem you worthy of an answer," Jezda said, once more wearing the face she'd had in the farmhouse.

"Do you know where I might find a new magic sword?" Doc asked.

And Jezda's voice broke into laughter, echoing into the cold, dark night, drifting up into the waiting blanket of stars above.

Chapter 16: Faeries and dragons

The tree stood in the center of a ring of stones in the center of a pale, washed out field of yellow grass. It rose out of a hill, with knotted roots coiling below and breaking through the surface of the earth like serpents. It didn't look like much, this tree, but Doc didn't need to call upon any spellcraft to sense the magic here, and the locals had warned him about it when he said he was heading to this particular hill.

Beware the hill folk, they told him. Be respectful. Bring gifts, if you have to go, or stay away if you can. Whatever you do, they said, pleadingly, don't upset them. Because you'll leave, and we'll pay the consequences of your blundering actions for three generations.

The fae hold grudges, this was very well known throughout the world of magic. But Doc wasn't here to fight or upset them. He was here to ask after a sword.

He felt the eyes on him before he saw them, but that was to be expected. The fae folk don't let themselves be known unless they want to be. Doc kept his eyes on the tree for a moment, but straightened his back and set his shoulders to let the watcher see

Doc was aware of him.

"You have the look of mischief about you," a strange, ageless voice said. Doc turned, hands open and at his sides, to regard the owner of that voice, a thin man, in incredibly pale, with dark hair and bruised bags beneath his colorless eyes. He wore a dark cloak wrapped around his shoulders multiple times, hiding any sign of his bulk or body language.

"I hear that a lot," Doc said. "But it's not my intention."

"You also stink of magic."

"Probably."

"Haven't had one of your lot around here in a while. Mostly local dimwits and stupid travelers trying to catch a look at an elf or two."

"I'm neither of those," Doc said.

The newcomer squinted at him, studying his eyes and face.

"What are you, then. A Cunning Man? A witch?"

"A little of everything," Doc said. "I prefer word magic, but I'm not picky."

"Word magic, is it," the fae said. "Well, you have good taste, at least. There's good stock in word magic. Delicious stuff if you use it right. Looking for the names of things, are you? If you are, you'd best leave now. We don't like anyone knowing our names."

"I'd be a fool to ask one of the folk for their name."

"You're standing in front of a faerie fort, looking at it like you're sizing it up for timber. You're half a fool already, Cunning Man."

Doc smiled and held up a bag he'd been carrying.

"What if I bear gifts instead?"

The fae eyed him suspiciously, wrinkling his nose.

"Gifts, you say."

"Chocolate."

"I can get my own chocolate, wizard," the fae said.

"I'd heard you liked American chocolate, though," Doc said, offering the creature the bag with an outstretched hand.

The fae looked for a moment as though he might reject it, and

Doc began wondering if he knew any spells at all that could withstand a true faerie curse. But then the fae took three swift steps forward and snatched the bag from Doc's hand.

"I thought you talked funny," the fae said. "American chocolate. Hard to get here. They have American candy in town, but it tastes wrong. It's too fresh. American chocolate is a little sour, because their factories were so far from the farms, so the milk would turn. The sourness reminds me of the old days, when we'd be offered milk in windowsills, just slightly turned by the sun."

The fae opened the bag and pulled out a candy bar. He attempted to unwrap it slowly and casually, but his impatience got the better of him, and he shredded the wrapper and took an aggressive bite, sighing contentedly as he chewed.

"There's enough in there for the others, if you'd like," Doc said.

"Bah, if the others wanted American chocolate, they shouldn't have sent me to scare you away alone," he said, taking another bite. "Your gift is accepted, American hedge mage. We won't send ten years of bad luck to follow after you like bad gas. Now tell us why you're here, so we can decide if chocolate is sufficient to prevent us from pulling out your eyes."

Doc ran a hand through his pale blue hair and looked back at the tree.

"I heard there might be a magic sword around here somewhere no one was using," he said. "I was hoping I could borrow it for a bit."

The fae finished off the first candy bar with a gloriously gluttonous bite, took a long moment to chew, savor, and swallow, and then answered.

"Ah, sure. There's a pig sticker around here somewhere. Belonged to some beardy mortal man, a hero or something, whatever that means."

"That's the one I'm looking for."

The creature looked Doc up and down appraisingly.

"Don't look like much of a fighter, Cunning Man."

"I'm a bit of a dirty fighter, if I'm being honest," Doc said.

"I can respect that."

"It's why I need the magic sword," Doc said.

"Set yourself up with an advantage."

"Exactly."

"Well, my folk, we don't like face to face warfare either," the fae said. "If you can't beat 'em, scare 'em, if you can't scare 'em, make sure their grandchildren are cursing their names for a family history of the pox."

"I can respect that," Doc said.

"So you want a sword," the fae said.

"I do."

"I don't suppose you've got anything to wash this chocolate down, would you now."

Doc reached inside his coat pocket and drew out a bottle of whiskey, shaking it so the contents sloshed audibly.

The fae raised an eyebrow.

"You are a Cunning Man," he said.

"Not really," Doc said. "I just know how to make sure I can make my hosts glad I stopped by."

The fae took the bottle, uncorked it with a comical pop, and took a hefty swig. He handed the bottle back to Doc and nodded his chin at him.

"Go on, then. Seal the deal. Don't make me drink alone."

Doc matched the fae gulp for gulp, the alcohol burning in his belly. It was only then that he realized how much he was worried— he'd settled into such a natural rhythm with the creature that he hadn't noticed the acid and anxiety swirling in his guts.

"Alright, Cunning Man. Me and mine won't keep you from the sword."

"Is it in the tree?" Doc asked, worried he was about to be tricked into desecrating the faerie fort.

"No, no," the fae said. He pointed at a nearby rocky outcropping, just beyond the yellow field of grass. "The dragon has it. Go get it from him."

"I'm sorry—the dragon?"

The creature let loose a gleeful spray of laughter, echoing into the cool gray sky.

"Ha! Only so cunning, aren't you," he said. "But don't worry, shouldn't be hard for a smart boy like yourself. Just go on in and take it."

"From a dragon," Doc said.

"Well, you don't right well expect him to bring it out here to you, do you?" the fae said, throwing an arm around Doc's neck, his hot breath sweet and fiery with chocolate and alcohol.

***

Well, at least the mouth of the cave wasn't big enough for a dragon, Doc thought as he began his decent, realizing as soon as he mentally said the words that he had no idea how big a dragon actually was, and that he was walking into this cavern with nothing more than some magic tricks and what amounted to the barest amount of quick thinking.

He didn't like caves. After a few of his earlier battles in his career, the idea of being underground had begun to take on an automatic, uncomfortable association, and a reasonable one at that. Nothing good comes from casually strolling into a subterranean space that could double as your tomb, Doc thought. He almost summoned a sphere of light in his hand before catching himself. Sure, Doc, just let the dragon know you're coming, good idea. Instead touched a rune on his chest and then touched both eyes, turning the darkness into a purplish grayscale. It took a moment for his vision to adjust but soon, he got a better sense of his surroundings—rough-hewn walls, a low ceiling, the dripping of water. He listened specifically for breathing, or perhaps the absent shuffling of a great beast's feet, but he heard nothing more than the soft echoing scrape of his own footsteps, which made him cringe every time.

There was an unexpected smell in the cavern, a sort of dry, slightly rotten scent. Not unpleasant, Doc thought, just a bit stale, like a basement that had not been used in a long time, overlayed with earth and decaying plants.

The cavern grew brighter, surprisingly, causing Doc's mystically enhanced vision to flare slightly as he readjusted. He blinked away bright spots in his eyes and found he could dispel the enchantment and see unaided, and so he did. High above, a gaping hole in the ceiling of the cavern let in a shaft of silvery light from above. The gap was wide, and scored with savage scratches, as if a massive creature had crawled its way into the air through it. An underground pond gleamed below the opening, pinging with the sound of falling drops of water. Doc saw bones strewn about, some human, most not, and other, manmade items abandoned as well. Of particular interest were several shoes, singular or in pairs. Ancient leather boots and sandals lay alongside Chuck Taylors or modern hiking shoes.

And then Doc spotted the silhouette.

On the far side of the pond, a great skull, seven or eight feet long, lay resting its bony chin on the ground. Enormous horns swept back from its eyebrow ridges, The horns had an almost tree-branch quality to them, coiling of unevenly from the monster's forehead. Doc could see teeth gleaming in the darkness, curved bone longer than his forearm. Those teeth held within them the very obvious remains of a human, two skeletal legs hanging sloppily from the monstrous mouth like a child struggling to eat spaghetti.

The skull was still attached to the body, and Doc admired the scope of it, the arched, spined back, the outspread wings, ancient flesh and sinew holding it together like spider webs. Doc kept his distance, circling the corpse, to get a better look at the other side of its face and the remains of its final victim.

On the left-hand side, Doc saw the head, shoulders, and arms of the warrior, shredded armor hanging from the meatless bones. The human skull was still somehow attached, hanging pathetically at an awkward angle.

And then there it was, resting in the hollow eye socket of the dragon: the magic sword.

Everything else in the cavern looked and felt ancient, carried off by the passage of time. The sword, though, looked as if it were forged only yesterday. The blade, resting in a crack in the dragon's eye socket, was silver and without rust or degradation. A short crosspiece held the sword in place, with a hand-and-half grip and a simple, circular pommel.

Doc strode carefully up to the dragon and placed a hand on the skull's snout.

"Were you a monster? Or were you just misunderstood?" Doc asked. He looked at the human corpse draped in the dragon's jaws. "And you. Did you come here to kill this wonder to protect your own? Or were you here for glory? What were your stories?"

Doc examined the skull closer, how dense the bone was. It felt as though it could withstand the passage of eternity. The warrior did not have the same dignity, fading into a graying, forgotten mess.

With a sigh, Doc put a hand on the sword hilt, and lifted it free. The leather on the grip was all but gone, but that was the easy part to fix. The magic was still there in the metal. That's what mattered.

Doc examined the blade itself and saw old runes carved into it. Protection, courage, strength. An old blade, from a time when magic mattered more. It was a sword that belonged in a better hand than his, but his was the only one willing to carry it, and so, Doc thought, he would have to do.

"Sorry," he said to the sword. "You're stuck with me."

Doc thought about casting a spell and teleporting home, but doing so right here, in front of the dead, felt uncouth, disrespectful. He sat down on a nearby rock and observed the dragon, the way the hips and shoulders were formed, the length of its claws.

Myths once walked this earth, Doc thought. How much of it has passed into the ether now? Though he could transpose himself across the world through magic, it wasn't his power that made the world feel small—it was the frequency with which he feeling as though he were standing before the last of something's kind.

He spent some time with the dragon, and with the warrior, listening to the winds tell their stories. A great battle, a test of will and might, fought for nothing, and ending with the death of a myth, and the death of hero, but the birth of a legend of a dragon beneath the hill, and a sword thought lost forever. Nameless gods and monsters fighting over scraps of memory.

Eventually, Doc placed a hand once more on the dragon's skull in a gesture of goodbye, and of thanks. He rested the sword gently on his shoulder, looking back just once to feel for a final time the grandeur and scope of the dragon's skeletal remains.

Doc walked back into the light, to the faerie ring, and the living world.

Chapter 17: Howling at the moon

Doc Silence was a city boy through and through, and he knew it. He'd been in strange places all across the world, been to jungles and forests and mountains and deserts, but he never felt at home in his own skin unless he was in a city.

So tonight, as he hoofed it up an incline in an eerie forest on the U.S.-Canadian border, he could not enjoy the beauty of nature, because he could not tune out the bugs; he could not enjoy the fresh air, because nothing smelled familiar; and he could not enjoy the quiet, because he did not have the din of the streets to give him comfort.

But still, he was here for a reason, and he could tolerate the wilderness just fine. A simple spell kept him warm, and another kept the biting insects away, and a third let his eyes see in the dark like a cat. Which was how he saw the massive, red-furred wolf blocking his path up ahead, and the jet-black second wolf who joined him, eyes gleaming gold as they reflected the moonlight.

"Hi, fellas," Doc said, keeping his hands apart and away from his body. "I don't have an appointment, but I'm a friend of

Erasmus Hawksmith. Was hoping I could talk to you."

The red wolf looked over his shoulder at the black, who trotted off into the forest out of sight. A howl echoed out in the distance, and Doc wondered briefly if he was about to be eaten, but then the red wolf howled back, and with a human-like shrug of the shoulder that crossed the uncanny valley, gestured for Doc to follow.

The red wolf led him along a game path, where Doc soon saw a campfire dancing between the trees. The wolf didn't slow down, assuming Doc could keep pace, and Doc cursed under his breath as he kept catching his boots on roots or vines. When he emerged into the campsite, he saw the black wolf seated protectively in front of a woman in a diaphanous white gown.

"You're Hawksmith's latest project," she said. Her voice was soft but commanding, her face ageless, neck and wrists adorned with bangles upon which Doc easily saw arcane sigils and marks. Another spellcaster, he knew, though the way her eyes gleamed in the darkness, something else as well.

"I am," Doc said. "And I'm trying to find him. It's why I'm here."

The woman nodded and touched the black wolf on the shoulder.

"It's fine, Gabriel. He's one of Erasmus' students. He means no harm."

The wolf let out a low, doubtful growl and sidled off into the woods. The woman gestured for Doc to sit down by the fire on a log that had been dragged nearby.

"I'm Leto, but I'm sure you know that, if you've found us," she said. "The old man has gone missing?"

"He just left one day," Doc said. "I assumed he was off on doing research, but then weeks went by, and months…"

"Maybe he forgot the way home," Leto said. "What are you called, wizard?"

"Doc Silence," he said, suddenly self-conscious of the cartoonish moniker he'd chosen.

"Just once I'd like to meet a wizard who decides his new name is Brian or Steve," Leto said. "But I suppose most of you give up your names at an age when you have delusions of grandeur, and most wizards never get over those."

Doc wondered briefly, for the first time in a long while, what his given name was. Maybe he really was a Brian, or a Steve.

"I have some idea where he is, which is why I came to you," Doc said, trying to refocus the conversation. He heard a rustling from the forest, and two men, one short and pale with red hair graying on the sides, the other tall and dark with long, jet-black hair, emerged. They sat down side by side across the fire. The red-haired man never took his eyes off Doc, watching him distrustfully, while the dark-haired man scanned the woods, watching for threats.

"Finnigan, Gabriel, meet Doc Silence," Leto said.

"Stupidest name I've ever heard," the red-haired man, who had answered to Finnigan, said. "You don't seem too surprised by us, though."

"I've met others like you," Doc said. "I helped track down a moon-sick wolf in the South of France a while back."

"Helped who," Finnigan said.

"Another of your kind. It was her husband who was sick. She didn't want to…" Doc tapered off.

"Should've found one of us to help her, not some cub wizard," Finnigan said.

"Aren't enough of us left. Maybe she couldn't find anyone else," the dark-haired man, Gabriel, said, the first time he'd spoken. "I'm surprised you met one of us at all in Europe."

"She said something along those lines," Doc said.

"She mention her pack?" Finnigan said, less aggressive this time.

"No, and I didn't ask," Doc said. "Didn't feel like it was any of my business."

"Just as well," Finnigan said. "None of us are from the same pack. You run with who you can find."

Doc nodded, not fully understanding.

"You said you had an idea where he was," Leto interrupted.

"I fought a nightmare in the last place Erasmus was seen in this world," Doc said. "A fully-grown nightmare spider. I think Erasmus is in the Dreamless Lands."

Leto raised an eyebrow questioningly, and Finnigan scoffed.

"Do you think I'm wrong?" Doc said.

"No," Leto said. "I've known Erasmus for many years. I have no doubt in my mind he'd be foolish enough to go there."

"I'd like to go get him back," Doc said. "And I understand that you know the right paths to get there."

Leto looked up at the moon in silence. Doc thought he'd lost her, that she would tell him no. But Gabriel chimed in.

"I've been there, once," he said. "It's a strange place, magician. A place where dreams shape reality, and not the other way around. It can be hard to find your way home."

"Any advice, then?"

"Don't go," Gabriel said.

"Just leave Erasmus there," Finnigan said. "It's not worth it."

Leto shook her head gently.

"Don't listen to them," she said. "If you're destined to go, you'll go. If not, you'll stay here. But if you do go to the Dreamless Lands, remember to bring gifts. Remember the rules do not apply there. None of them. And most importantly, have a reason to wake up again and return home. The Dreamless Lands are tempting. They offer everything you want that this world cannot, or will not, give you."

"Will you help me find the path there?" Doc asked.

Leto pursed her lips, neither saying yes or no.

"I would ask a favor of you, Doc Silence," she said.

"I've been warned about entering bargains," Doc said.

"With Others. We are simpler than that," Leto said. "I'm not asking you to make a bargain—I'm asking you to fulfill a promise. Are promises important to you, wizard?"

"Of course."

Leto laughed lightly at his response.

"You say that as though magicians usually honor promises. But you're young. We'll see."

"What would you ask me to do?" Doc said.

Leto sighed and looked once more at the moon.

"As my companions have said, there aren't many of us left," Leto said softly. "There may come a time when there are none. But I'm the last of us alive who can teach the old ways, and I worry someday I will not be here to continue. I have a feeling about you, Doc Silence. I think you will be a different teacher than your own, abandoning you to the world. There's a kindness to you I haven't seen in many magicians. There may come a day when one of ours needs someone like you. I'd like you to take responsibility for them, should that happen."

"You want me to adopt a werewolf," Doc said.

"No, I want you to set a lost child on the right path, as was once done for you," Leto said. "Is this such a great ask?"

"It really isn't," Doc said. "You're asking me to do the right thing."

"That is a great ask for much of humanity," she said.

Doc shrugged, not arguing.

"I'll do it," Doc said. "Of course I'll do it."

"Then I will give you a map and teach you a few words. And I will hope that you find your way home from the Dreamless Lands, with or without Erasmus Hawksmith."

"Thank you," Doc said.

"And little wizard, there is something you should know," Leto said. "If you do something like this, there is a chance you will attract attention. Moving between the planes as a human... it leaves a mark."

"I feel like a lot of what I do leaves a mark," Doc said.

"Then I'm sure you'll be fine, kid," Finnigan said. "Good luck."

Chapter 18: The Dreamless Lands

Doc Silence stepped through a sliver of moonlight and into another world.

The map Leto gave him took him to a precise place, on a specific mountain, at a particular time on an exact day, and Doc waited for the moonlight to pass through a cleft in a rocky outcropping, a silver crease in reality. He said a few words, traced a symbol in the air, and a gleaming crescent of light opened in front of him.

Unhesitatingly, he stepped through.

He found himself beneath a violet sky, in a field of pale blue grass. Overhead, a whale drifted like a dirigible on gentle currents, butterfly wings where its fins should be, singing a slow, elegant, ancient song.

Doc swore, profusely, creatively, his stomach tightening up into a fiery knot of fear. I have no idea where I am, he thought. I have no idea where this place is.

He pushed his growing terror down, trying to ignore the vertigo he felt beneath this strange sky. To distract himself, he found a patch of clear dirt—the earth was silvery here, not brown, and glittered in the alien sunlight—and began tracing runes in the ground. A spell of finding. A spell of searching. He spoke the name of Erasmus Hawksmith, and the runes began to glow, and then evaporate, becoming a faint golden shimmer in the air, telling him which way to go.

Okay then, Doc thought. I don't know where I am, but I know where I need to head. He stood up, dusted the silvery dirt from his pants, and started walking.

***

The wind sings here, Doc thought, lost in his own mind. He could hear a faint song on the breeze, not an illusion but a true melody, distant strings punctuated by piano. He worried briefly that that song was attempting to pull him from his path, like a siren's call, but it seemed more like ambiance than a temptation. It made the slow, shuffling journey more pleasant, he thought, as he reached the top of a hill and looked down across a field of wildflowers.

Then he heard the whimpering, and the snarling.

Doc ran toward the noise, but slowed as he saw the arched back of a reptilian creature hunched over in the grass, the muscles on its spotted back twitching as if it were digging. The whimpering, a soft, mewling sound, like puppies would make, was emanating from just beyond the creature.

Am I doing this? Doc thought. I didn't travel across the planes of reality to interfere with nature's course. But then he heard a pathetic yelp and he couldn't stop himself.

"Hey! What are you doing?" he yelled, regretting it the moment the words left his mouth.

The reptilian thing turned to face him, its long, crocodilian snout stained with bluish blood. There was a feral intelligence to the creature's eyes, and for a moment Doc thought it might speak. Instead, it charged at him, on all fours, long, muscular arms pumping as it tore up the ground, clawed hands and feet thundering ahead.

Reflexively, Doc lashed out with a telekinetic spell and sent the beast sprawling violently backward. The creature staggered to its feet, roared at him angrily with a sound that was half-great cat, half-bird of prey, and then backed away, eyeing him cautiously, before running into the grass. Doc watched for a long, tense few minutes, waiting for the creature to return, but it did not, leaving Doc alone with the mewling sounds of whatever it was devouring.

With equal caution, Doc stepped toward the source of the little cries.

He found a carcass there, a lanky, strong body covered in short fur, a massive head, topped with curling horns, staring up at him with glassy, dead eyes, a long purple tongue lolling out. The blood staining the ground was the same color as that which had painted the reptilian monster's maw. Doc nudged the corpse with his foot, but it did not react. He peered just over its open ribcage, and finally found the source of the whimpering. Two tiny versions of the dead creature looked up at him, curled against the belly of the beast. They were nearly identical, with little nubbins where the horns would be. One started at him and let loose a sad little wail, and Doc couldn't tell if it was a cry for help or an attempt at intimidation. The other pup hopped up on its back legs and pushed at the body of its parent as if asking for attention.

"Hey, guys," Doc said. He knelt down beside them and held out a hand. The first pup sniffed it, then nudged it with its forehead; the sibling soon followed, chewing playfully on his fingers.

Doc stood up and searched the horizon, for what he wasn't sure. Another parent, perhaps. Or to see if the predator who had killed the adult hound was waiting to finish its meal. He looked down once more to find both pups staring up at him expectantly.

"I can't believe I'm doing this," Doc said.

He took off his coat and bundled both creatures inside, scooping them up gently. They both took up position resting on his forearm, side by side. One stared off into the distance; the other looked up at him, then thumped its square little head against his chest.

"I guess you're coming with me," Doc said, and picked up Erasmus' trail once more.

***

Doc walked for a few hours before he began to wonder what he would feed these little beasts, or more to the point, if he'd ever find what he was looking for. Worse, the sun hadn't moved in the sky, a permanent fixture staring down at him from above.

He was just beginning to feel like he'd made a mistake when he saw the walking carriage trudging along in the distance.

It was like a fairytale cart, a curved, pumpkin-like center bookended by a seat for a driver on the front, for guards on the back. It had no wheels; instead, huge, elephantine legs trundled relentlessly forward, slow, deliberate, steady, sure. On either side, a pair of outriders seemed to be acting as an honor guard. At first Doc thought they were men on horseback, but as he drew closer, he realized they were in fact centaurs, both armed with elegant and seemingly impractical polearms. One seemed to notice him and pointed in his direction, and the entire entourage changed their path to instead head straight for him.

"What do you think, fellas," Doc said to the puppies in his arms. "Friend or foe? Probably both. I guess we'll find out."

One of the centaurs cantered up to within shouting distance, resting the butt his weapon on the ground.

"What are you doing here, outlander," the centaur asked. He wore a breastplate made of a gleaming metal that looked like the night sky, full of stars.

"I'm looking for a friend," Doc said. "Erasmus Hawksmith. Do you know him?"

The centaur looked over his shoulder at the carriage, then back at Doc.

"And what are those," he asked, nodding at the puppies.

"I don't rightly know," Doc said. "But they were in danger, so I saved them. Not sure what I'm supposed to do with them."

The centaur wrinkled his brow, then trotted back to the side of the carriage, whispering something inside. It wasn't until now that Doc noticed the carriage driver, a humanoid with deer antlers and eyes like a goat's. The driver stared at him wordlessly. Doc noticed a crossbow on the seat beside him.

"Outlander," the centaur yelled, holding open the carriage door. "Our queen would speak with you."

"Queen?" Doc asked.

"Do you not have that word where you come from?"

"No, just... not dressed for royalty, I guess," Doc said, gesturing at his shabby clothes.

"Don't make her wait," the centaur said. "And bring the creatures."

Doc shrugged and made his way to the cart, gingerly climbing inside while wrangling the two small beasts in his arms. It took his eyes a moment to adjust, but when they did, the sights within took him completely by surprise.

The carriage was most certainly bigger on the inside, its walls smooth and dark, the ceiling a sea of stars. Sitting on a cushioned bench was a woman smirking at him. Her skin was pearlescent white, slashed with bioluminescent red stripes. Her hair was that same shade of red, spikey and messy. She wore a pale gown so thin it seemed almost pointless, and Doc found himself blushing, unsure where to aim his eyes. In his panic he settled on, of all things, her tail, a long, serpentine appendage curled up on the bench beside her.

"Sit, magician," the woman said. Her voice was young and old and ageless all at once, as if his ears, his brain were incapable of processing the sound appropriately. "I am Lady Dreamless. I understand you're looking for the Hawksmith."

Doc sat down across from her, struggling to keep the pups in his arms.

"I am," Doc said. "He's my mentor."

"Not much of one if you're walking across the Dreamless Lands on foot," she said. "Are those for me? It is customary to bring me gifts, you know."

"Gifts?"

"The little creatures giving you so much trouble over there," Lady Dreamless said.

"I... I honestly don't know," Doc said. "I think maybe I was meant to find them. And meant to bring them here."

One of the pups leaped from his arms and bounded clumsily across the carriage, jumping, with much effort, onto the bench and into the woman's lap. She made a small, delighted noise, scooping the creature up. The pup's brother made the same journey, and soon they were both with her on the couch. She cooed at them and spoke softly in a language Doc didn't understand, and for a moment this Lady Dreamless seemed very young, the façade of imperiousness fading.

"Do they have names?" she asked.

"I think they should," Doc said. "But not yet."

"You should name them, gift-bringer," she said. "You honor me with this gift. Demon hounds are impossible to train if you don't find them as infants, but if you do, they are eternally loyal, and eternally adoring."

"Demon hounds," Doc repeated. "Good to know."

"Name them, magician. You know the importance of names if you are a student of the Hawksmith. Three names for all things, though these little creatures need only one just now."

Doc watched the little pups frolic on the couch, play-wrestling, their weirdly muscular, doglike bodies so strong for such tiny things.

"There are two brothers in a myth from back home I enjoy," Doc said. "Maybe that would do. Castor and Pollux. Warriors. Brothers."

"Castor and Pollux. I like those names," Lady Dreamless said. "Myth has a place here in my lands, you know. Many myths are born here before they find a home in another world. And now that we know their names, I should ask you yours, wizard. Not your true name, of course, because I respect the rules of magic, but your chosen one."

"I gave up my true name," Doc said. "But I am called Doc Silence."

Lady Dreamless studied his face, puzzled.

"Magicians give up their birth name, not their true name. No one can give up their true name. It's impossible. Do you not know yours?"

"I'm still learning, I guess," Doc said, hoping he was hiding his confusion, and, he realized a growing panic. True name? Erasmus, you truly are a terrible teacher if you lied to me about my name.

Doc frowned and found himself staring at the little demon hounds. One—Pollux, Doc decided—stared at him sleepily.

"You look sad, magician. Perhaps this is a gift you were unwilling to give?" the woman said.

"No, I was just thinking they wouldn't be safe with me," Doc said. "I think maybe they were truly meant for you."

"Trouble does follow your kind like a shadow," she said. She leaned back, poured herself a glass of something clear, and filled a second glass, handing it to Doc. He sipped it, expecting water, but it tasted of citrus and burned like alcohol. "For this gift, I offer you safe passage in my lands. I like the look of you. Most magicians who pass through here are old and grim. You are grim, but the weight of time is light on your shoulders."

"Doesn't feel that way, but thank you," Doc said. "Could you tell me where Erasmus is?"

She smiled at him, and once again Doc found himself blushing. He glanced out the carriage window and happened to make eye contact with one of the centaurs, who was glaring at him with a look fit to kill.

"Better yet, I can take you to him. He's a bit stuck, your mentor," Lady Dreamless said.

"Stuck?"

"Yes. He dreamed something into being here, and when you dream a thing, you are forever bound to it. You cannot abandon dreams, or they grow feral and wild. Like gardens. Or children. They must be tended, and Erasmus Hawksmith tends a very powerful dream indeed."

***

The Lady Dreamless instructed her carriage to bring Doc Silence to Erasmus Hawksmith, and begrudgingly the driver and the centaur escort did as commanded. They took him to a tower set into a cliff made of glass, the stones making up the tower a shade of cobalt blue that reminded Doc of the sky just before twilight, when you might see the first hint of stars.

"Your teacher resides within," the Lady Dreamless said. She sat casually in her carriage, legs tucked up beneath her, her chin resting on the knuckles of one hand. The two demon hounds were napping on the cushion beside her. Castor was snoring.

"Thank you for your help, your highness," Doc said, hesitating before the title, unsure what the proper honorific for a queen of dreams might be. The Lady Dreamless took it in stride and did not correct him. "I owe you a debt."

"You brought me gifts," she said, stroking the top of Pollux's head gently. "Your debt is paid. But I would like to see you again, little magician. Would you come to my wedding?"

Doc opened his mouth, then snapped it shut. Something in the back of his mind told him there was some sort of double meaning in the invitation. And yet, after a brief pause, he nodded.

"I would be honored," he said. "Who is the lucky groom?"

The Lady Dreamless made a pouting face, teetering on a sneer. She looked out the window with faintly glowing eyes that narrowed with annoyance.

"They want me to marry the Nightmare King," she said. "I think it is a bad match, but our kingdoms think it will bring great prosperity and power."

"You would prefer not marry him?" Doc asked.

"I would prefer to marry someone of my choosing, if anyone at all," Lady Dreamless said. "We are the stuff of dreams; why should we be beholden to the laws of mortal and man?"

"I couldn't agree more," Doc said.

"Good," Lady Dreamless said, smiling at him with unnerving delight. "Then I will see you at the wedding. At the appointed time, a door will open, and you will walk through. You will find yourself appropriately dressed, and among gods and dreams and night terrors. You will have a seat reserved just for you."

"I look forward to it," Doc said, and was surprised that he meant it. After years of scrounging for magic in dark places in a world that did not want to believe in it, this place, this dreamscape, was awash in the pigments and watercolors of magic, and it terrified him, and brought him joy he did not know he was capable of feeling.

"Go get your master, then, and drag him back to your dreary world," the Lady Dreamless said. She touched Doc's cheek gently and made a small cooing noise.

"I have one last question, if I might impose," Doc said.

"Of course, little magician."

"Do you know the best way back home from here? Is there a path I should walk to stay clear of nightmares?"

She smiled again, and this time there was no mischief in it. Her nose wrinkled in a way that made Doc's stomach twist.

"Erasmus Hawksmith has a planar knife," she said. "Use it to cut your way home. And if I'm being blunt, Doctor Silence, I suggest you take the blade from him and keep it for yourself. He is old and wonder does not flow from him the way it does you. I think you deserve to walk the higher planes more than he does now."

"I will consider it," Doc said, trying to recall what he'd read about planar knives, and feeling a growing irritation that Erasmus hadn't told him about this one. "I look forward to seeing you again someday."

"Be safe, my kind little wizard," she said. "I fear you are too good for this world of yours. I hope I am wrong, but I will be disappointed if I am."

Doc felt heat in his cheeks, bowed his head slightly and stepped from the carriage. The centaurs eyed him suspiciously as his feet hit the ground, but Doc simply shrugged at them and started walking up the glass-like steps into the tower, ignoring their stares.

The interior was cool and dark, his footsteps echoing against the stone floor. Stairs led up to a second tier, and at the top of those stairs, Doc could just make out a silvery light glimmering. He found himself unconsciously trying to move stealthily up the stairs, unsure why he felt compelled to not make his presence known. This was Erasmus. His friend. His teacher. Not some monster, not his enemy. Perhaps the Lady Dreamless had led him astray, but really, would she have invited him to her wedding if she just meant to feed him to a creature in a tower?

Still, Doc placed each footstep gently, compelled to respectful quiet.

When he reached the top of the stairs, he saw a massive astrolabe spinning slowly in the center of a great chamber. The silver light cascaded from tall windows behind it, the light not matching that which existed outside the tower, cooler here, softer. A single figure sat in a chair in front of the astrolabe, swaddled in an oversized coat. His hair was wild, his beard overgrown, but Doc recognized the wizened face of Erasmus Hawksmith sitting there, watching the astrolabe turn and twist.

"Erasmus," Doc said.

Hawksmith startled, turning to face him, his eyes piercing and wild at first, then softening. A single tear ran down from the corner of his left eye and disappeared into his beard.

"Doc, my boy," he said. His voice as raspy and weak. "I knew you'd come."

"Erasmus, what are you doing here," Doc said. The older wizard crossed the room, limping slightly as if he had not walked in hours. He took Doc by the shoulders and drew him into a hug.

"Doc, I didn't mean to, but this place, I let my attention slip," he said. "I let my guard down, and I dreamed."

"What did you dream, Erasmus?" Doc kept one hand firmly around Hawksmith's bicep to steady him.

"Doc, I dreamed a school," Erasmus said. He gestured to one of the walls, a part of the chamber Doc hadn't examined yet. It was a map, but unlike any earthly map Doc had ever seen. He saw the names of planes, the spaces between worlds. Worlds that were spheres, or rings or islands floating in space. And on each of them, a sketch of an identical building stood.

"You dreamed a school," Doc said.

"I did. I didn't mean for it to become real, but it was just there, and then it grew, and I had to protect it, Doc, I had to keep it safe, I had to make sure it was remembered," Erasmus said.

"You had a student, waiting for you back home, but you dreamed a school into existence instead," Doc said. He felt betrayed, and the bitterness in his heart felt alien and uncomfortable.

"I knew you'd be fine," Erasmus said. "I taught you well. Doc, you were my best student. In all these years, in all these worlds, you were my best, my favorite, and I knew you'd be okay."

"I was a kid, Erasmus."

"You were a magician. I made sure you were a magician before I ever left you alone," Erasmus said.

He sounded so proud, Doc thought. So pleased. And I have been so alone for so long.

"I've been looking for you," Doc said. "You could have come home at any time."

"I couldn't, though," Erasmus said. "Can't you see? All these lives. All these points of light. Across the multiverse. Doc, I was waiting for you to come find me. Think of the things we could do together with this school. We could save magic. Magic is dying on Earth. You know this. You've seen it. This could bring it all back."

"Why isn't your school on Earth, then, Erasmus? I see schools across the universe up on that map. But none at home."

"It… it wouldn't take," Erasmus said. "It wouldn't take root. I tried, Doc. I tried. All this time. So I could go home. So we could teach together. But it just wouldn't take."

"Do you think maybe it's not meant to be?" Doc said. He scanned the chamber looking for the planar knife. Mystical trinkets were scattered all around, spell books and scrolls, wands and cloaks and magic rings. And one item, in a scabbard, blade flat and square like a razor, the handle made of stone the color of soap bubbles.

"Erasmus, what happens if you set the schools free?" Doc asked.

"I… I don't know," he said.

"You set me free," Doc said. "You let me grow. Without you."

"I did."

"Maybe it's time, old friend," Doc said. He put a hand on the side of Hawksmith's face and forced him to look him directly in the eyes. "Set your dream free and see where it goes."

"You've done so well, Doc," Erasmus said. "This place, it's so hard to let go of. The Dreamless Lands want you to stay."

"I think you're right," Doc said. "What do you say, Erasmus? Let's get you home. Let's get you right again."

Erasmus put his hand on top of Doc's and nodded once, fiercely, blinking tears from his eyes.

"I knew you'd come find me," Erasmus said. "My last apprentice. My best one."

"Is that the planar knife, Erasmus?" Doc said, nodding to the table where the blade lay. Erasmus nodded.

Doc crossed the room, cautiously as if he might startle the older wizard if he moved too fast. He picked up the knife, sliding it partway from it scabbard. The metal was so thin it seemed nearly translucent. A blade to cut reality, he thought. A dangerous thing. Mine now, I suppose. He examined some of the other items on the table and found a smaller, hand-drawn version of the map on the wall, which he rolled up and tucked into his coat, and a few small spell books that caught his eye. Doc turned back to Erasmus, who was watching the astrolabe spin.

"Dreams are a terrible thing, Doc," he said. "They give you what you want, but never what you need, and they evaporate like tears in the sun the moment you look away."

"We can come back here someday, if you want," Doc said.

"We could," Erasmus said, his voice clearer than it had been just moments before, like a man truly awakening from a deep and wild slumber. "But it won't be the same. Dreams are never the same when you return to them."

Doc held out a hand. Erasmus stared at it for a moment, then smiled and took it.

"I could have spent forever here, you know," he said.

"I know," Doc said.

"Thank you for reminding me who I am, Doc Silence," Erasmus said. "The world is yours now, I think. You've become a better teacher of yourself than I ever was to you."

"I don't know about that," Doc said. "But we can talk about that back home."

And with that, Doc drew the planar knife from the scabbard and deftly sliced through the air. Reality split like a paper cut; as it parted, he saw the City just beyond, the familiar sight of street and skyscraper, an overcast sky filled with rain and potential.

Together, Doc Silence and Erasmus stepped through time and space, and back into the lives they'd left behind.

Chapter 19: The truth about names

Doc Silence was intensely overdressed.

He sat across a small table at a small café overlooking a beach in Portugal. It was a beautiful day, a crystalline blue sky filled with radiant sunlight, but Doc squinted and sweated, half-tempted to cast a spell to regulate his body temperature but too uncomfortable to want to make the effort.

Across from him sat Father Arturo, looking infinitely more comfortable, dressed in slightly rumpled linen, a pair of sunglasses perched on his head. It was the first time they'd seen each other since Paris, the first time since Doc returned from the Dreamless Lands, a journey Arturo seemed almost hesitant to believe really happened.

"You found the old man, though," the Jesuit said. Doc nodded and smirked as he noticed the old priest catch himself looking at a young woman walking by, shaking his head at himself.

"I did. He's... different. But recovering."

"I always thought the Dreamless Lands were a myth," Arturo said, taking a sip of his beer and looking out over the water. He gestured at Doc with his chin. "You know, you could magic yourself up something more comfortable to wear."

"I know," Doc said, sweating through his black tee shirt, uncomfortable in his denim pants and steel-toed Doc Martens. He'd found that magicians tended to become more and more set in their ways as they got older, taking on a distinct look, like a personal brand. He wondered if that particular quirk were setting in early for him. He'd been through a lot in the past few years. He felt older than he was.

"Suit yourself," Arturo said. "You won't catch me dressed in my vestments here."

"I don't catch you dressed in your vestments much at all," Doc said. "Sometimes I wonder if you're lying about being a priest."

"Ask the Church. They wish I wasn't," he said. "But they're stuck with me, for now."

Doc ran a hand through his damp hair, wishing he wasn't so stubborn. It'd be a tiny transformation spell to just make his clothes lighter, turn his boots to deck shoes. But no, must be true to myself, he thought. He sighed and decided it was time to get around to asking the question he came here for.

"Arturo, I need to know about true names," Doc said. "I should have learned more about them from Erasmus, but he went off the map for so long. It feels like a dangerous gap in what I know."

"It is a dangerous gap, but fortunately, if you don't know your own true name, it's harder to steal it from you," Arturo said.

"I always thought I gave away my true name to become what I am now."

"You gave away a name, yes," Arturo said. He leaned in conspiratorially. "We all have many names. The one we're given, the one we choose for ourselves, the ones we earn. You gave away the one that gave you history. It's an important name. It's why the sacrifice means something."

"But that's not my true name."

"No, your true name…" Arturo made a vague hand gesture in

the air. "It's like an aura around you. You can hear it if you listen. It's hard to find, harder still to steal. Once you learn it, you should keep it secret. Never give it away. True names are power. The more people who know it, the more vulnerable you are."

"Do you know your true name?"

"I do," Arturo said. "And I'm not telling it to you."

"I wouldn't ask," Doc said, smiling. "But I want to know my own true name."

"As you should," Arturo said. "Frankly, I'm upset Erasmus didn't show you how to do this, but to be fair, name magic is his specialty. I'm sure he had a reason."

"Or he just forgot."

"Or that," Arturo said, smiling.

"So is there a spell I need to learn?" Doc said. "An incantation, some mythical animal part I need to sacrifice to an elder god or something to learn my name?"

Arturo chuckled and shook his head.

"You just need to listen, my friend. Find a place sacred to you. A place where you are your truest self. And just reach out into the ether, hold your palm out like you're trying to catch a hummingbird. It'll come to you, like a ghost."

"Is there any danger in learning my true name?"

"There's danger in everything we do," Arturo said. "But there's danger in not knowing, too. If you know it, you can protect it. If it's just out there in the cosmos, well, who knows."

Doc nodded, sipping at his drink, squinting out over the ocean.

"I should learn it."

"I agree."

Doc sighed.

"Arturo, sometimes I wish you'd found me instead of Erasmus."

The priest let out a barking laugh.

"Oh, no. No you don't. I never would have taken you in. It's too risky taking an apprentice. You got lucky. As angry as you might be with Erasmus, Doc, he taught you well. You're a better magician than wizards twice your age already. Part of that is who you are, but part of that is you were found by someone who knew the right kind of magic to open the universe to you, specifically. The two of you were meant to connect."

"You believe in fate now, Padre?"

"I believe that things happen for a reason, sometimes good, sometime bad. And I think you were found by the right wizard, and you were brave enough to incur the cost. I think because of that you will be important long after I'm dead and gone."

"That's morbid."

"And you're young. I'm just speaking mathematically," Arturo said, politely ordering another round with a gesture. "Do you know where you'll go to learn your name, my friend?"

Doc mulled it over. He thought about all the places he thought of has home, and none of them brought him peace.

"I have some options," Doc thought. "Does the resonance matter?"

"Resonance?"

"The emotions I feel there. Sadness. Joy."

Arturo rubbed his beard, pondering.

"I suppose it might matter," he said. "But I think I'd stay away from pain. Find a place where you feel safe."

"That narrows it down," Doc said.

"You know you're a great magician when few places feel safe," Arturo said. "But I think you'll do fine."

***

Doc bounced around the world like he was chasing his own memories.

He went first to the City—his City. Home. Where it all began. He stood on a rooftop and stared out over its messy glory, and it filled him with love, but also guilt, remembering the monsters he'd faced here, and how long he'd been away. He went down to the Fens after that, to where it all began, and found it full of ghosts and regret. His brother would be grown now, but Doc could only think of the child he knew, the brother he loved, the memories he'd traded so that his brother could grow up safe and happy without him.

As if pressing on a bruise, he went to London next, stood outside Imogen's old apartment, though he knew full well she'd long since moved on, living a life she deserved, without demons and magic, making the world better with her wonderful mind and her skilled hands. He wandered down to Elephant and Castle, though he did not expect to find his true name there. He simply wanted to revisit it, the place where his last attempt at a normal life had failed so spectacularly.

He went back to the dragon's cave, not because he felt attachment to it, but because he knew there was nothing there that could harm him, hidden behind fae magic and coiled in the embrace of a dead legend. He found solitude there, but not peace.

As he considered his options, he teleported to Dublin, and, on a whim, found himself in Bláithín's chair for a new tattoo. It was a minor enchantment he'd learned from a fox-spirit and con artist named Renard Todd a while back, something to help with petty illusions, a small symbol Bláithín wove into the other ink on his nearly covered right forearm. He told her about finding Erasmus, and the artist seemed slightly relieved but mostly amused that Erasmus would, for all intents and purposes, forget to come home because he was too busy imagining something, but she was glad they were both safe and looked froward to seeing them both again.

Doc stepped out into the night, a light mist falling down around his shoulders and he meandered to St. Stephen's Green. The park closed at dusk, but Doc passed through the fence as if it didn't exist and sat down on a bench looking out over the pond. It was quiet, and empty, but without bad memories or particularly good ones either. Just a place he knew, a place he returned to.

"Huh," Doc said. Perhaps the best I can do, he thought, is neutral ground.

He closed his eyes and listened. The rain picked up, and he was lost in the sound of it plunking into the pond, rustling through the vegetation. It plastered his hair to his head, but that felt appropriate and right. He could taste his own skin and sweat and soap as the rain ran down his face and into his mouth.

And soon, he heard a word.

It was unlike any word he knew, in any language he'd ever heard. It's a sturdy word, he thought, a reliable one. It gave him a sense of home, of self. It felt like everyone he'd ever loved calling out to him at once in a whisper.

My true name, Doc thought. He tried to commit it to memory, but realized he didn't have to – once heard, he could not forget it even if he wanted to. It lodged into his brain like a scar, like a soul. It was alien and familiar, beautiful and grotesque, ephemeral and earthly all at once.

Something clicked inside his heart, like a gear settling into place, and he knew, in this moment, something was forever changed in him. The magic in the air around him seemed closer, more tangible, more profound. He felt as though he'd found something he never knew he lost, and it made him feel whole, and right, and strong.

He remained in St. Stephen's Green until just before dawn, long after the rain relented, rising with the sun as it turned the sky a soft silvery pink.

Doc smiled to himself, and opened a portal in the air before him, and knew he would never be the same again.

Chapter 20: The duel

Doc first sensed he was being watched while talking to a ghost in Tokyo. He'd gone there because he'd learned of the spirit of a magician who had once spent a great deal of time in the Dreamless Lands, and Doc spent several hours walking and talking with the lonely apparition, whose memories of the higher planes were sharper than of the real world. But as they prepared to part company, Doc felt an electric tickle across his shoulders. He asked the spirit if he sensed it as well.

"I do, but it's not here for me," he said. "Tread carefully."

"Any idea what's watching me?" Doc asked.

"Darkness," the spirit said. "I don't want to be here when it finds you."

And with that, the ghost melted away into the late-night Tokyo crowd, leaving Doc alone and paranoid beneath beautiful neon light.

Not much in the mood for a confrontation, Doc opened a portal and stepped through it, nearly being run over by a car on a busy street in Ahmedabad. The temperature difference hit him as hard a car would have, though, and he immediately began to sweat in his heavy coat. Doc found a quiet corner—as quiet a corner as he could find in this area and scanned for his pursuer.

He felt those eyes on him still and gritted his teeth in annoyance. A teleporter of some kind then, something not bound by the laws of physics. Fine, Doc thought to himself. Let's make this a merry chase, then. He opened another portal, this time outside a bar he visited once in Reykjavik. His skin prickled once again at the temperature shift, almost dizzying as he dashed from one corner of the world to another. He began to walk casually down the street. It was morning here, and quiet, and the hum of the watcher's gaze was stronger and clearer. Doc ran through the map in his mind, of all the places he'd been, all the places he was willing to fight. A delay tactic, he leaped from Reykjavik to Berlin, and then Berlin to Athens. He stayed in Greece for only a few seconds before leaping to Sydney, and then to Los Angeles, to Martha's Vineyard to Malaga. The tattoo designed to help him with this teleportation spell began to itch and grow warm, as if warning him the limits of its benefit were rapidly approaching.

One last jump, then, Doc thought, and called to mind a stretch of desert in Arizona, a place where he once watched a phoenix egg hatch. As soon as he stepped through the portal he activated a half-dozen charms and talismans on his body, cast several protective spells, and brushed his hands across his eyes so he could see into the ethereal and shadowy mirrored layers that lay silently atop the material world.

When he turned to face his pursuer, he saw a man standing in the desert, swathed in a black, leathery cloak. His arms were hidden beneath the garment, unmoving. In fact, the only part of him visible was his face, an eerie pale, with glowing red eyes. Horns twisted from his forehead like an antelope's. Two fleshy tendrils hung from his chin like a beard. When he opened his mouth, oversized fangs became clearly visible.

"Clever boy," the man said. Doc knew he heard the words in English, but they were spoken in something else, a language from a lower plane, slimy and obscene. "If you can't set the rules of engagement, at least choose the place where you die. Didn't want to fight me in downtown Tokyo, did you."

"Engagement? Didn't realize I had marriage in my future," Doc said, his left hand prepared to summon forth his magic sword.

"I am a fan, actually," the demonic stranger said. "I don't visit every wizard. Just the ones who grow too strong."

"Too strong? I'm little more than a Vegas illusionist," Doc said.

"Oh, modesty is so boring," the stranger said. "You've accomplished so much so soon."

"Are you here to give me a reward?"

"I'm here to root you out before you grow too strong," the stranger said. "Nothing personal. It's just a way of balancing the scales. You killed my brethren in Paris, you see, and we've been watching you ever since. The world can't have too many Silver Mages in it, and the Eye of All Things is beginning to take notice of you."

"I have not a single clue what you're talking about," Doc said. "But I am too young to be this tired. Just tell me who you are so we can work this out or kill each other."

"I am Culler, the Mage Slayer."

"Not melodramatic at all, are you."

"You of all people know we don't choose all our names, Doctor Silence."

"True enough," Doc said. And then he cast a spell to tear the eyeballs from the Culler's skull.

Culler waved his hand in front of his face with a casual coolness that set Doc's nerves on edge. He felt the unseen mystical tethers of his spell snap like string as the Mage Slayer severed the arcane bindings. Doc took a step backward and, without hesitating, snapped his fingers and traced a circle in the air, summoning forth a ring of fire around the approaching creature.

Culler stepped through the flames as if they didn't exist.

"Mage Slayer, right," Doc said. "Regular tricks won't work—"

Culler shrugged his shoulders, and his leathery cloak unfurled, stretching out into enormous, black bat-like wings. Before Doc could even swear the creature leapt into the air and dove down on him like a bird of prey, his hands—each finger tipped with a vicious claw—reaching for Doc's neck. He snapped his hands up to cast a protective spell around himself, and heard those claws squeal against the soap bubble-like shield between them. Culler smiled, displaying a mouth of sharp, predatory teeth, and made a few quick motions with his hand. The protection spell shattered like thin glass and clattered to the ground.

As Culler reared back a clawed hand for another strike, Doc wove a quick telekinetic spell and yanked a large stone from the ground, catapulting it at the creature. The rock collided with a meaty thud as stone smashed into muscle and bone, and the impact was enough to drive the Mage Slayer back a few steps.

Thinking fast, Doc threw a hand up into the air and, with a single magic word, pulled a bolt of lightning from the sky. The blue-white electricity smashed down onto the demon's shoulders, lighting him up from the inside and filling the air with the smell of cooked meat. But the attack did not slow him; instead, still bitterly smiling, he advanced on Doc like a stalking cat.

"All sorts of little tricks, wizard," Culler said. "Creative, but they're still just tricks. I've seen worse, and I've seen better."

The two sparred in the desert sand, claws flashing and shattering shield after mystical shield as Doc struggled to stay on his feet. Aware he was outmatched, Doc tried to open a portal to escape through—maybe I can lead him on a merry chase, he thought—but he bit his tongue as the portal slammed shut before he could step through.

"Oh we've already done that, Doctor Silence," Culler said. "I'm not chasing you anymore."

The distraction was enough for Culler to slip in through Doc's defenses and rake his claws across the wizard's chest, shredding his shirt. Doc felt his own blood pooling along the waistband of his pants as it ran down his stomach.

"Why me," Doc asked. "There's magicians all over the world.

Why come after me?"

"I have my orders," Culler said. "You mean why don't I go kill some ancient old hag, or a failed Catholic priest, a magical tattoo artist, or some half-wit sorcerer selling potions out of the back of a van?"

"Not suggesting you do, but I'm just curious," Doc said, running through the options at his disposal in his mind.

"Because you stand a chance of changing things, and they don't," Culler said. "You've got the attention of the wrong people, and they don't like what they see you doing with the power you have in your hands."

"I'm barely more than a Vegas performer," Doc said. "A circus side show. What do they think I am, a superhero?"

Culler grinned wickedly.

"Interesting word choice," he said.

"And you, what, make sure there isn't too much magic in the world?"

"More like I make sure the magic in this world is in the hands of the right people," Culler said. "Magic is like an ecosystem. It needs to be observed, fostered at the right time, pruned at others. Your futures hold too much wild magic for some peoples' liking."

Doc pressed a hand against his chest, and his palm and fingers came back soaked with blood. He wondered briefly if the demon had perforated anything important inside.

"Did you say futures? Plural?"

"Maybe I did," Culler said.

"Just when I get used to multiple planes of reality, now I need to worry about different, what, timelines?"

"I wouldn't worry about that, little wizard," the demon said, flexing his claws, which seemed to grow even longer and sharper in the night, tipped with Doc's blood.

"Well, I can't just give up now," Doc said. "You gave me a whole new set of questions I'll need to find answers to."

Doc took a deep breath and called forth and summoned his sword into his hand, the ancient, dragon-blooded blade. If it was strong enough to kill a dragon, Doc thought, it should be good enough to wound this creature. Or so he hoped.

He slashed with the blade, which Culler parried easily with a sword of his own, a wide, ugly sword of black metal. The creature held the sword with a casualness that indicated just how comfortable he was with the weapon.

This really isn't my strong suit, Doc thought, calling up spells that would speed up his reflexes. He felt that magic flow through his veins, through his nerves, and the jitteriness became something else as his limbs became light and free.

Just in time, too, Doc realized, as Culler's heavy blade came crashing down on him. Doc was able to get his own sword up barely fast enough to keep from having his head split open. He twisted and jabbed with his own weapon, but the Mage Slayer batted him away like a child.

Doc bounced back and whispered another spell, this time bring up shards of ice like lances from the earth. The points pierced Culler's left calf and right thigh, but he flexed and splintered the ice, continuing forward unfettered.

"That almost hurt," the winged creature said. "Let's see how a practitioner of word magic does without his voice, shall we?"

Doc readied himself to counter whatever spell Culler would cast, but instead, the Mage Slayer pulled a vial from a chain around his neck and smashed it in the palm of his hand. Doc tried to curse out loud, but no sound came from his throat.

"That's better," Culler said, eyes flashing gold in the dark desert night. "I don't blame you for fighting, but it's really over more quickly and painlessly if you just give up."

Doc wished he had a witty retort—not like Culler would hear if I said it anyway, he thought—then started running through his options. His sword arm was already tiring as he blocked blow after blow, each one stronger than the last. The night sky was crystal clear and full of stars, and Doc wondered if this would be the last sky he'd ever see.

The blood on his palm grew tacky and cool, as if reminding

Doc of its presence, and of his waning life force. He remembered the early lessons Erasmus taught him. The different kinds of magic. The darker kinds, and the light.

Did I promise I'd never? Doc thought, reaching into his torn shirt and dredging his fingers through his own blood. Did I say I wouldn't? But I've learned about it. What's the point of learning about magic if you don't use it when you need it.

He balled up his bloody hand into a fist and willed the life force dripping from his fingertips to give up the power it contained. He traced one red finger across the sky and lashed out at Culler.

From nothing, a red whip appeared in the air and coiled itself around the demon's neck. No, not from nothing, Doc knew—from the blood he was sacrificing in place of the words he could not say. He pulled back with that hand violently and tightened the blood-whip's chokehold on Culler's throat. The creature gasped for a moment, eyes bulging, but then reached up and dug his claws into the red cable, which burst and split like a cut garden hose. The remaining strand loosened from Culler's neck and fell away, draped over his shoulder like a grotesque scarf.

"Blood magic," he said, his voice rougher than before. "Perhaps we misread you. Too bad we won't see how that thread turns out."

The Mage Slayer dashed forward again, more flying than running, and grabbed Doc by the throat, lifting him off his feet. Doc felt the clawed tips of his fingers digging into his skin.

"This should have been easier," Culler said. "I'd be impressed, but I hate having my time wasted—"

The creature's voice faded into a gurgle of pain as Doc jammed his sword into the creature's guts all the way to the hilt. The barely human face of the Mage Slayer turned truly bestial then, spikes growing out from the ridges of his eyebrows, a forked tongue sticking out in a rictus of pain and rage. He threw Doc aside like a toy, sending the magician sprawling in the sand, the sword still sticking out of the monster's stomach.

"You," Culler said, advancing on him with a hunched, horrifying gait. He never bothered to pull the sword from his belly, and Doc could see the blade, covered in purplish blood, jutting out from Culler's back. "You think some enchanted sword is enough to kill me? You are a child. You are a *corpse*."

Doc pushed himself up onto his elbows, and then to his knees. He looked down at his hands, the right one covered in his own red blood, the left in the purple blood of the demon, cuts and scrapes shredding the palms of both from rolling across the desert grit.

Doc traced the purple blood across his eyes like battle paint. His vision blurred, then snapped crystal clear. He reached out toward the advancing Culler with his left hand, and the sword tore itself from the creature's body with a violent spurt, the hilt smacking into Doc's waiting, purple-blooded palm. He slammed the point of the sword into the sand like a cross and made identical arcane movements with both hands, then aimed them at Culler.

The world became shades of purple, pink, and red as a magenta bolt of magical energy burst forth from Doc's hands, striking Culler right where a heart should be. Doc made two fists and pulled back toward himself, drawing the magenta energy into himself as well. There was a terrible rending noise, the Mage Slayer's wings went rigid as if to take flight, then flopped down, lifeless and rubbery.

Culler dropped to one knee, eyes flickering like old lightbulbs. His head began to shake and convulse. When he smiled again, his teeth were stained with his own purple blood.

"Well," he said, his voice rasping, choking. "This changes things. I'll see you soon, demon-blooded."

Culler, the Mage Slayer, slumped forward, a heavy, undignified fall. His dark blood stained the desert sand, and all around him, twisted, spiked plants began to immediately grow. Doc almost retched as the demon's body began to liquify in front of him, but he forced himself to hobble forward and examine it. The world swam as dizziness threatened to overtake him, but despite the unsteadiness, there was a sharpness to his vision. The world felt more alive, more present. The silence of the desert was instead filled with sounds he hadn't heard before.

He saw, in the slimy mass left behind by the Mage Slayer's body, a single golden pendant, with a sharp, red-black stone in the center of it. He picked the pendant up and stuffed it in his pocket clumsily and then tried to stand to his full height, but fell down, landing hard on his tailbone. He looked down at his chest, tried to assess his injuries, but there was too much blood, too much destruction, his wounds plugged with sand and stone. He tried to get back to his feet, but couldn't.

I won, and I'm still going to die here, Doc thought.

Doc lay down on his back and stared up at the stars. It was as good a place as any to die, he thought. He wondered if anyone would wonder what happened to him. Probably not. It was just as well. Magic seemed to devour people more than save them, anyway.

He closed his eyes, and the world was purple and dark. And his last thought was of home.

***

Doc woke up in a bed, head aching, the smell of antiseptics strong and clean. Not dead, he thought, because I'm in too much pain to be dead. He struggled to sit up and tried to take in his surroundings. Everything he looked at felt strange, as though he were seeing details he didn't want to notice.

This was a room in a clinic of some kind, he judged, by the walls and tiled floors. He scooted himself to the edge of the bed and dangled his feet over the side, wriggling his toes to make sure they all still worked. His torso and neck were bandaged.

"Hello?" he said, less to see if anyone was listening and more to see if his voice worked. Nevertheless, a familiar voice answered, and his heart cracked and broke like stone.

"Thought I'd never see you again," Imogen said, entering from the adjoining room, wearing medical scrubs. "But I walk out of the café with my breakfast and there you are, bleeding to death on the sidewalk. Like you'd never left."

"Imogen," Doc said. "I'm sorry. I was... I was dying in the desert."

"You were dying in Oxford," she said. "Knowing you though, I guess you could have been dying in two places at once."

Her tone was angry, but Doc knew her long enough to see it was half-hearted. She leaned against the doorframe and crossed her arms.

"I didn't mean for this to happen," Doc said. "It must've been a reflex."

"Dump yourself bleeding to death at the feet of your ex, sure," she said. "Are your eyes a reflex too, then? Or have you finally got the devil in you?"

"My eyes?" Doc said.

"Glad they were closed when I brought you in to the clinic. They think you were a victim of a stabbing but Lord knows what they'd think if you'd open your bloody eyes, Doc."

"I don't understand," Doc said.

Imogen nodded to a sink and mirror opposite the bed. Doc struggled to his feet. Imogen didn't offer to help, but he was glad she didn't. The pain of his injuries was being overwhelmed by a mortifying guilt that he'd intruded on her life at all, let alone needing to be put back together again like an eggman.

He staggered the few steps to the sink and looked at himself in the mirror. The face looking back at him was his own; but his eyes now glowed with blue-pink, with wisps of purple flame flickering from the corners. The flames trailed and drifted when he turned his head left and right. Gingerly, he ran his fingers through the fire to see if it gave off heat, but it did not, though the flames reacted to his touch, dancing and spinning around his fingertips.

"What the hell did I do," Doc said.

"Probably what you had to," Imogen said. She'd entered the room now, and closed the door behind her, standing behind him in the mirror so he could see her face. "Doc, when I was stitching you up, I could see your body putting itself back together again slowly. You really don't know what happened?"

Doc smiled bitterly and turned away from the mirror.

"I broke a promise so I could survive," Doc said. "I'm wondering now if that was a mistake."

"Well, what's done is done," she said. "And you're still in the world, and that's all that matters today. Figure the rest out tomorrow."

"I am so sorry I did this to you," Doc said.

"Like you said, a reflex," she said. "What was the last thing you remember?"

"Wondering if..."

"Wondering what," Imogen said.

"If anyone would wonder where I'd gone," Doc said.

"Some of us will always wonder, Doc Silence," Imogen said. "You're like a stray cat. I can't be the only one who figures someday you'll get in a fight you can't win."

"I think that myself sometimes."

Imogen looked over her shoulder toward the door. She ran a hand over her mouth, ran the back of her hand across her chin.

"The police should be here soon to look in on the stabbing victim," she said. "I didn't tell anyone I knew you."

"Thank you."

"Was it a lie?"

"I hope not,' Doc said. "It'd be easier for everyone if I'm gone when they get here."

"'It would."

Doc made a vague gesture with his hands, and the hospital johnny he'd been wearing transformed into a close enough approximation of his usual outfit. It was then that he realized Imogen had been holding something this whole time. She handed it to him.

"Here," she said. "Might help you be less obtrusive."

It was a pair of sunglasses, silver rimmed with red lenses. He felt a wave of nostalgia as he saw the red glass. These were expensive, and stylish, but he'd once held a child-sized pair not unlike them.

"What are these, Benetton?" he said, hiding the emotion in the back of his throat. "I can't take your sunglasses. These are really nice."

"I thought they were 'fashion,' but they make me look like a spaceman," Imogen said with self-effacing smirk. "They'll do you more good than me. Just take them."

Doc unfolded the glasses and put them on, looking once more in the mirror. They did a fair job of hiding the alien purple glow of his eyes, at least, though Imogen was right, they did belong on a spaceman. He stared at himself just a little too long.

"You okay, Doc?" Imogen asked. "You look... you look really sad. Sadder than usual."

"I once bought my little brother a pair of red-tinted glasses," Doc said. "It was the last time I spoke to him. Before..."

He made a resigned gesture at himself, shocked at how raw the shame felt.

"Before all this," he said.

"You never told me that story," Imogen said. "About the glasses."

"It was a small thing," Doc said. "Just a tiny detail. But thank you. For the glasses."

Imogen inhaled, words on tip of her tongue, but she was interrupted by sounds outside the room. They both turned as they heard muffled voices in the hall and exchanged a worried glance.

"Go on, do your disappearing act," Imogen said with a toss of her head.

Not enough time, Doc thought. Not enough time, not the right circumstances, never the right life. This is how it will always be, won't it. Alone except for brief moments that remind me what I gave up.

"Thank you," Doc said. "For everything. Again."

"Doc, I never want to see you in that state again," she said.

"I understand," Doc said. "I won't bother you anymore."

"I didn't say that," Imogen said. "Just look better than a corpse if we cross paths someday, okay? The world's better with you in it."

"People keep saying that," Doc said.

"Because it's true."

The voices in the hall grew closer. Imogen winked and tilted her chin. Doc put hand over his heart, and then cast a teleportation spell and watched the hospital room disappear. He didn't even care where the spell took him. He just wanted to leave. Before he couldn't.

Chapter 21: Interlude – Annie on the beach

For no particular reason, Doc found himself on a beach in Honolulu at twilight. It seemed like a decent place for a pity party, he supposed. Also, he could find a stretch of shoreline to be alone, which was a plus since he tried to avoid being around other human beings ever since the change to his eyes. They never returned to normal, and he was still too mad at Erasmus to ask him about it. He supposed he could talk to some of his other contacts, but he wasn't ready for that, yet. Doc wondered if he should tell the others about the attack, but the Mage Slayer had seemed so disinterested in any of Doc's friends and allies it felt almost insulting. Sorry, friends, I'm so much better at magic than you. Only that I was targeted for assassination by a killer demon.

Doc sat down on the sand and looked out at the ocean, wondering at first what might be out there in the darkness, and then about old stories he'd heard, of Atlantis, of ghost ships. There was magic wherever you looked in his world, he knew, but you had to know how to find it. He was so lost in thought that he didn't notice a woman approaching until she sat down about twenty feet from him. She had a shock of pink hair pared down into a pixie cut, an olive green tank top with a red star on it, and burgundy pleather pants tucked into combat boots.

Most strangely, though, she also wore red sunglasses.

Doc turned his full attention on her, and a long moment later, she noticed.

"Oh, hey Doc!" she said, and stood up, dusted herself off, and moved over to sit down next to him.

"I'm sorry, do we know each other?" Doc said.

The pink-haired woman laughed and pushed her sunglasses up onto the top of head. Her eyes were not, in fact, blazing arcane infernos, but instead a deep brown, that seemed to glitter with gold in the moonlight. Doc had missed earlier that the wristband she wore appeared to be a piece of technical hardware, with buttons and a screen, all dark.

"Oh, shoot. This is before we met. Sorry."

"Before we met?"

"In this timeline. I must have taken a wrong turn somewhere. I'll leave and come back later," the woman said, starting to stand up again.

"Wait. Just hang on," Doc said. "Did you say this timeline? As in there is more than one?"

"Yeah, babe," the pink-haired woman said. "Maybe this is supposed to be the first time we meet in this one. I might be remembering wrong."

"Just... let's start at the beginning. You are who?"

"Anarchy Annie. I'm your best friend," the woman said. "Or I will be. Trust me. It's inevitable. Happens in every timeline."

"I don't have friends," Doc said.

"Yet," Annie said. "Did that guy try to kill you yet?"

"Which guy."

"The one with the wings," Annie said.

"Yeah? I mean there have been a few."

"I mean you got your proper eyes now, right?"

"I wouldn't call them proper," Doc said. "Terrifying balls of fire, maybe."

"Yeah, no, if you survive that fight in this timeline you're good. That's an important day for you. It's a touchstone. We all have touchstones. If we miss the touchstone we screw up the timeline."

"You keep saying that word," Doc said. "I haven't come across any time magic. Probability, sure, magicians love tinkering with fate, but timelines are news to me."

"Well, I don't use magic, but I mean what's the old saying, any technology sufficiently advanced enough…"

"How?" Doc said. "How is this even possible?"

"I come from a long line of people for whom physics just don't work the same as they do for everyone else, okay?" Annie said. "I shouldn't say more than that because I don't want to create a rupture in the timeline. I'm already early and screwed that up."

"So you don't use magic. You just jump through time," Doc said.

"With a little help," Annie said, gesturing to her wrist cuff. "But it's mostly me. But it'll make more sense when you meet the others."

"The others," Doc said.

"*There are more things in Heaven and Earth, Horatio, than are dreamt of in your philosophy*," Annie said. "Bill Shakespeare said that. Weird guy. Met him once."

"Just… stop," Doc said. "What are you talking about?"

"Look, you have a path, and I shouldn't mess you up on it, okay?" Annie said. "But if you stay on the right path, you're going to do my ancestors a solid. You're actually going to help a lot of people, babe. I know you spend most of your life feeling like nothing makes sense, but just know there's hope."

"Is it worth it?" Doc asked. "You know the future, or you know some different futures. Is everything… Is it worth it?"

"Depends on who you ask," Annie said. "Time and fate are weird things. I think it is. But you're my best friend, Doc. And I have all of history to find a best friend. I could pick anyone. You're the one, pumpkin."

"I'm hallucinating, aren't I," Doc said. "I lost a lot of blood the other day. I haven't recovered."

"Sure," Annie said. "Tell yourself that. It'll make it more fun when we meet properly later."

"What's your last name?" Doc said. "You said I do your family a solid. How will I know?"

"You won't," Annie said, fiddling with her wrist device. "But that's the thing, Doc. Won't matter if you know it's the right time or not, or if they're my family or not. You have a heroic nature. It's one of the more charming things about you. But hey, I'll see you soon, okay?"

"Wait!" Doc said, but then Annie winked out of existence before his eyes, and, if it weren't for the print of her boots and butt in the sand, it would have been as though she never existed.

Doc closed his eyes tightly, removed his glasses, and rubbed the bridge of his nose.

"There are more things in Heaven and Earth," he repeated. "That is certainly the truth."

Chapter 22: The vampires of Memphis

Doc Silence had been all over the world, and he never felt like he belonged anywhere. But there were places he felt just a little less out of place, like perhaps the weirdness he gave off like a fog went a little less noticed. These places were most often big cities, where everything is weird and one odd magician with silver-blue hair was nothing to think twice about.

But more specifically, places that drew artists to it tended to also draw magic, and these were the spaces where Doc – who practiced magic based in words, a kind of endless and impenetrable poetry – truly felt as though he was welcome.

Memphis was one of these cities, with its lean and hungry musicians casting spells of sound and lyric. Music, Doc knew, was barely a step removed from actual magic, a primal thing torn from the depths of humanity in a way even those who created it barely understood. Music was older than history, older than time, and just moments older than magic itself.

So on this night, as he walked beneath the neon glow of Beale Street, he almost felt safe. Perhaps safe was the wrong word, but unnoticed is as close to safe as he'd ever get, and this was enough for tonight.

The bar he looked for was unknown to anyone not attached to the mystical. Ordinary folks would walk right by it, and it was listed on no touristry register, no real estate listing, no official document of the waking world. The music here wasn't just magic in theory but in practice, the sort of ancient magic that wove sound and spell, and if you strolled by unwittingly, you might hear something haunting, a voice or tune that reminded you of a place you forgot you'd been, a love you'd lost and hadn't thought of in years, a melancholy memory you never wanted to think of again.

The bar was called The Haunting Place and evoked all meanings of the word.

Doc Silence was in his shirtsleeves tonight, the strange sigils and runes scrawled across his skin not out of place in a rock and roll town, and even his red glasses barely elicited a second glance despite the late hour. He made his way to The Haunting Place slowly so that he could listen to the live music from the street, eavesdrop on the easy conversations of untroubled minds trading tales of joy and sorrow, the smell of cigarettes and alcohol and other delights. He wondered what it would be like to go to a city like this without the ability to see ghosts lurking on street corners. Without knowing that monsters walked among men everywhere. To just listen to music in peace.

He disentangled himself from the pedestrian crowd and into a muggy, darkened alley. A single light shone down on a simple, unmarked red door, and Doc walked in without hesitation.

The face on the other side of the door was ghastly pale, with slicked back hair and eyes tinged ever so slightly with red. He smiled at Doc with incisors that were unnaturally long and inhaled in a way that was overtly predatory, but then wrinkled his nose and took a step back.

"Sorry," he said, putting his hands up apologetically. "I didn't know."

"You usually size up everyone who walks in to see if they're dinner?" Doc asked, putting more edge in his voice than he intended.

"Just folk I don't know," the bouncer said. "We don't get many like you in here."

Doc decided to roll with it and slid his glasses down just enough to let the purple flames lick up over the rims.

"Innocent mistake," he said. "Is Charlie in?"

"The Baron?" the bouncer asked. "Yeah, he was playing earlier. Taking a break at the bar."

"Thanks," Doc said, and walked in without paying the cover.

If one were to cast a cursory glance across the bar, it might look like any other dive in Memphis; rows of bottles behind the counter; faces young and old; a band setting up on stage. But if one stopped to look closer, the little details would shine through: the tattoos weren't rockabilly but arcane; there were monsters hidden among the mortals, with skin of pearl or scale, or even translucent; the blue-white hue of ghosts; messenger bags were instead spell books; pocket knives were sacrificial blades.

Doc spotted who he was looking for easy enough. There was space around this individual, but just beyond that respectful distance, others were vying for his attention – hangers on, groupies, both mortal and not. Charlie, or the Baron Charlamagne Smythe, if using proper names, was shorter than his attitude hinted at, wearing tight jeans, expensive cowboy boots, a retro Western-style shirt open a few buttons too many, revealing a pale, hairless, muscled chest upon which rested a gleaming talisman on a leather loop. He was clean-shaven, clear-eyed, with hair cut close on the sides and back but with a foppish flop he kept parted to the right. He had a guitar with him, of course, which he rested against the bar while he sipped at whiskey with one hand, running the other through his hair to keep it from plastering to his forehead in the heat.

Doc pushed his way through the crowd, hearing himself cursed out by more than one groupie, and took the seat next to the Baron, ordering himself a drink.

"Well, look who it is," Charlie said, his voice silky and woven with a smooth southern affectation. He clapped a hand on Doc's shoulder and leaned in. "Been away a minute, Doc. We missed you."

The Baron waved a hand dismissively at the bartender.

"Doc here drinks on me," he said. "Bar full of posers and we got ourselves a bona fide wizard. How about that."

"How you been, Charlie," Doc asked, smiling and trying to match the Baron's friendly tone. He found code switching for the slow drawl of the Baron hard, his own mind calibrated for the sharp bark of the City and the northeast in general.

"Oh, you know. Living."

"Really?"

"Or un-living, if you want to be technical, which I don't care to be," the Baron said, throwing back a slug of whiskey. "What's with the shades, Doc? You gone all Hollywood on us?"

"Got a minute to talk private, Charlie?" Doc asked.

Baron Charlie hesitated, looked around the room, taking in the hangers-on with a sort of low-grade disgust, then nodded.

"Sure, Doc. Andy probably won't mind us using the back room for a quick minute, right, Andy?"

The bartender shrugged and indicated a door nearby. The Baron picked up his guitar and started heading that way, Doc following close behind. As several folks made disappointed noises, Charlie held up his free hand.

"Now, now, I'll be back in a minute. I just need to have a *private* chat with this here certified mage, okay?"

That seemed to assuage the crowd somewhat. Doc and Charlie entered the back room, closing the door behind them.

"Trying to get me alone, Doc? You know there are plenty of people who'd love to get me in the back room all by themselves," Charlie said.

"All business this time, Charlie, sorry to disappoint you," Doc said, and removed his red sunglasses. He took some pride in seeing actual shock on the Baron's face as the flames danced and cast purple shadows across the room. Charlie's mouth went from a shocked circle to a grin, revealing long, sharp incisors.

"Oh my dearest boy, what did you go and do to yourself," Charlie said.

"That's what I was hoping to ask you," Doc said. "Something tried to kill me, and nearly succeeded. I... used some of the tricks you taught me to get the upper hand, but then this happened."

"That is not the usual result of blood magic," Charlie said. He came closer and took Doc's jaw in one long-fingered hand, turning him side to side to get a better look at each eye. "I just explained blood magic to you. You never tried it on a practical level. How'd you do improvising during a duel?"

"Sloppy, but it worked," Doc said. "I didn't like it."

"Not many do. Got to have the disposition for it," Charlie said. He released Doc's face with a gentle grace of his fingers and stepped back. "Truth be told I wasn't fond of it until I became, well, what I am now. Sustaining one's self on the blood of the living makes you a tad less squeamish about things sanguine."

"This is not a result of blood magic, then," Doc said.

"No," Charlie said. "Well, no but maybe yes. What were you fighting, hon?"

"I have some guesses," Doc said. "He called himself a Mage Slayer."

"But that's a title. That's not a thing."

"No," Doc said.

"Did you, by chance, use this creature's blood to cast?"

"Absolutely," Doc said. "Better his than mine."

"And did you, by chance, steal part of his life essence?"

"I wouldn't even know how to start doing that," Doc said.

Charlie raised a smug eyebrow at Doc.

"You were casting blood magic based on some theoretical bits and bobs I gave you over a few drinks, baby," Charlie said. "I reckon you went and stole a bit of this creature's very life for yourself all on instinct. I think my favorite thing about you is that you are so dangerous and have absolutely no clue what you're doing sometimes. It's like hanging out with an alligator."

"That's the best analogy you can come up with?"

"I'll think of something better later," Charlie said. "I'm too busy assessing how you went and changed your whole physiology."

"Any idea how to figure out if it's fixable?"

"I'd have to know what you are now if you want me to help you figure out a proper diagnosis."

"And how would we do that?" Doc asked.

"Well," Charlie said, and smiled widely, showing off his fangs.

"Oh, come on," Doc said.

"Wouldn't be the first time you've been bit by a vampire and I know it," Charlie said. "Hell, wouldn't be the first time you got bit by me."

"We were literally fighting to the death when you bit me last time," Doc said.

"And look how that turned out! Now we're truest friends," Charlie said.

Doc sighed and threw his arms up.

"Why do you have to bite me?"

"Because I taste things in the blood, Doc," Charlie said. "And, on account of our previous violent encounter, I actually have a baseline for what you are made up of. I'll be able to tell the difference."

Doc stared at the Baron blankly. The vampire stared back, then smiled sheepishly.

"Can I just say, a staring contest with you is not nearly as much fun now that you have a pair of magenta candles where your eyeballs used to be."

"I can't believe I'm going to go through with this," Doc said.

"So is that a yes?"

"Try not to enjoy it too much, huh?" Doc said.

"I'll say the same to you," the Baron said.

Doc held up a finger and pointed it at Charlie.

"A taste."

"Of course."

"No more than you need."

"I'll try my best."

"I don't want to need orange juice and a cookie to get back on my feet after this."

"How about barbecue and a beer?"

"This is getting awkward," Doc said.

"Let's fix that," the Baron said, and, with a movement so quick Doc only observed it because of his enchanted vision, the vampire was upon him, piercing his neck with stiletto-like fangs.

Doc had faced more than his fair share of vampires in his adventures, some friendly, some not, and he had a few scars to prove it. The Baron himself had gotten behind him in the fight and managed a bite before Doc used a spell to summon sunlight indoors and scare him off. Somehow, being attacked and volunteering for a bite were alarmingly different experiences, and without the adrenaline of combat, Doc's legs almost went out from under him. He realized quickly he had no idea how long the bite went on, but he felt the Baron steady him, and then help him down onto a nearby stool. Doc slapped hand over the bite, but there was no blood there – he'd forgotten that some enchantment in the vampire bite seals the wound immediately, almost like a mosquito.

He shook off the haze of the bite – an enchantment, like a point in the teeth, and set his eyes upon the Baron. He expected to see the vampire looking smug and delighted, but instead he saw him drinking bourbon directly from a bottle and wiping his mouth aggressively.

"You okay?" Doc asked, his voice sounding distant and slurred.

"Oh, Doctor, you should've warned me you're packing the strong stuff now," Charlie said. For the first time, Doc saw the vampire flop down in a chair – or rather a beer keg in this case – to keep from teetering off his feet.

"The what now?" Doc said.

"You would think after enough centuries I'd learn some gods-damned caution, but no, never had any self-control, just jump right in," Charlie said. "I recognized it in time, though. The taste in your blood. Congratulations. You're demon-blooded now, Doctor

Silence. You upgraded to the top shelf. Or the bottom shelf, depending on your thoughts on the matter."

"Wait, demon-blooded?" Doc said. "That's a real thing? The creature called me that, but I just thought it was an insult for magicians."

The vampire stood up and wobbled around the room, picked a bottle of warm beer at random, popped the cap off with his thumb, and drank half of it in one pull. He opened a second for Doc and handed it over.

"It's a real thing," the Baron said. "You've taken some of his power, this Mage Slayer. Stolen his essence. It's in you now."

"What does that even mean?" Doc asked.

"Well for one, congratulations, you're going to live a hell of a lot longer than the average human, so you and I should be having grand adventures far longer than we anticipated," he said. "And your eyes, I don't know what to tell you about those, must be a side effect."

"Are you okay?" Doc asked.

"Oh, I'll be fine, I figured it out soon enough," Charlie said. "Which is good because if I'd gotten carried away, too much demon blood will kill me and mine. In moderation though, it's a heck of a rush."

"You're... welcome?"

"Appropriate response," the Baron said, wiping his forehead. He seemed to regain his composure a bit between sitting and drinking. "I wish I had more to tell you, darlin', but there are fewer demon-blooded out there than vampires or wizards. You're in some uncharted territory."

"Slightly more charted than before," Doc said. He clinked his bottle against the Baron's and lifted it up in a salute. "I owe you one."

"Tell you what, my young wizardly friend," the Baron said, the façade of his public persona returning now that business was done. "Come tear up the town with me tonight and we'll call it even."

"This is going to end up being a week of my life I'll barely remember, isn't it," Doc said.

"Probably," Charlie said. "But what's the point of having vampire friends if they don't help you live a little?"

Chapter 23: The Lady Grey

Doc hated Christmas.

Well, he thought, hate is the wrong emotion. But Christmas made him feel terrible about everything. About the family he left behind, about the friends he no longer saw. The way the world found a brief moment of magic to celebrate together while he lurked in the shadows alone. What he felt, he knew, wasn't so much hate as resentment. Becoming a magician had given him so much, but it took away the little things. The reasons to celebrate. The people to celebrate with.

He tended to seek out places of celebration on Christmas Eve. Concerts, or ice rinks, or tree lightings. Anything to make him feel more a part of the world than apart from it. On this Christmas, his loneliest yet as he continued to avoid those he did not want to explain his transformation to, he found himself on the streets of Boston, alone, his dark coat wrapped tight against the evening chill. He pulled his collar up and listened to carolers, and watched families meet and embrace, saw cars with silly reindeer horns stuck to the sides drive by through a newly fallen snow he knew would be gray and grimy by morning. It was snowing, too, but just ever so slightly, the kind of faint, delicate dusting that would stick to your clothes and hair but leave no trace of itself on the sidewalks.

He wanted to hate Christmas, but even here, in his loneliness, he felt a kind of love for it, like an outsider looking in, like staring into a beautiful snow globe. The shaman on the hill, he thought, that's what Erasmus always taught me we were. On the outskirts, keeping the monsters at bay so others could live in safety and love.

It was somewhere near Boston Common he knew he was being watched. At first he was unbothered by it; old cities are full of ghosts, and ghosts can't help but follow magicians when they see them, like moths to flame. But after a few blocks, the sensation grew more intense. He headed toward the theater district and stepped into the first alley he found, walking swiftly into the shadows, trying to keep his clunky boots from making too much noise.

When he turned back, he saw a woman standing at the mouth of the alley. She wore a dark short coat over a skirt, thick, ornate tights disappearing into ridiculously high heeled boots. Her hair was nearly white, and cut into a sharp, angular bob. She wore the sort of sunglasses old movie stars would wear, despite the evening's darkness. The snow did not melt when it touched her coat, but clung there like stars.

Doc felt his heart pounding in his chest, and he did not know why, and for that reason, he readied himself for a fight.

"Doctor Silence?" she said. Her voice was hypnotic, practiced. Others might find it alluring. Doc knew a dangerous voice when he heart one, and this woman radiated danger.

"If you're asking, you know the answer," Doc said.

"It's impolite to assume," the woman said. "May I call you Doc?"

"Everyone else does," he said. "What do I call you?"

"I'm Lady Natasha Grey," she said, her lips quirking into a smile. Doc couldn't help smiling back.

"Is that a real honorific?" he asked.

"Are you a real doctor?"

He shrugged, admitting defeat.

"You've got me there," Doc said.

"I was hoping we might talk," the Lady said.

"About what?"

Lady Grey stepped further into the alley, never making a noise.

"You're going about this all wrong," she said. "A man of your talents doesn't have to do what you do."

"And what is that, exactly?"

"You don't have to fight them, darling," she said.

She removed her glasses, then, slowly, setting the scene. She showed him her eyes, and they blazed with flames just like his, only rather than a pale purple, they were the color of true flames, gold and red flickering and dancing.

"Most everything that goes bump in the night can be reasoned with," she said. "Can be bought. You just need to know how to make the right deal."

"The right deal."

"You've been learning the hard way to do magic," she said. "Don't get me wrong. I get the appeal. To be a hero. To be a warrior. And there's beauty in the magic of words. But sometimes it's just better to get them to give you what you need."

"Are you offering to teach me how to bargain with demons?"

"Have dinner with me. You can always change your mind."

She held out a hand. Doc accepted it.

***

They had dinner together in a restaurant too nice for Doc to feel comfortable in. The staff took no notice of their burning eyes; they spoke to Natasha as if she were a client of the highest caliber. She drank expensive wine, which she shared with Doc, but the food and drink tasted like ashes to him. He was too worried to take pleasure in the taste.

"I used to be like you," Natasha said between bites of a

shockingly expensive steak. "Well, not like you, I never really had that kind of ethical line, but I learned magic the hard way, same as you."

"All magic is the hard way," Doc said.

"True," Natasha said, pointing a knife tip at him. "But after a while, I started seeing patterns. Value in information, in secrets. I started bartering for power. A secret for a spell. A spell for a fortune. A fortune for an artifact. An artifact for power."

"All magic is balance, though. You just had a different way of setting the scales," Doc said.

"It's a bit of a balancing act, yes. But it's a skill, just like any other spellcraft. And it just has this wonderful way of getting easier the longer you do it."

Doc leaned in, trying to take a bite of the expensive fillet in front of him and failing.

"I have to ask. About your eyes."

"Well, I heard about yours," Natasha said.

"You heard what," Doc said.

"Thole magician community is talking about it, how you ripped part of a demon's life force out of him to drive him off," she said. "Wild stuff. You have fans. Frankly, though, that's what I'm talking about. That's the hard way to get demon-blooded."

"So you didn't kill a Mage Slayer."

"First, you didn't kill him, you sent him home, but that's neither here nor there," she said. "Demon-blooding yourself to win the fight scared the living hell – pardon the horrible joke – out of him. They won't send another after you."

"He's not dead?"

"No, and the fact that you permanently took a slice of his living power from him is a good way to make sure the Mage Slayers leave you alone," she said. "Bravo, darling."

"How did you even hear about this?"

"My lawyer is a devil. He told me about it over drinks in Los Angeles a while back."

"You've got to be kidding," Doc said.

"I love, I adore, how innocent you are," she said. "This is the thing about the hard way. All your little magician friends, out there fighting monsters, saving the world – have they ever told you how many monsters there are with healthy business endeavors on the prime material plane? They're everywhere. And they need people like me. People, potentially, like you as well."

Doc leaned back and rubbed his eyes, feeling naked without his glasses.

"So I take it you didn't become demon-blooded in combat," he said tiredly.

"No, I bought mine. Or traded for it, really. There's a lot of benefits to being demon-blooded. Well worth the bargain," she said, moving on to a sliver of asparagus.

"And no Mage Slayer was ever sent after you," he said.

"I paid mine off," she said. "By the time I'd gained enough attention to scare anyone, I already had demi-gods in my day planner. The benefit of not being a hero, Doc, is that you are, instead, an asset."

"Are you a villain?"

"That's a silly question. There are no villains, Doc. Or rather, there are, but they're boring. If you want to insult me, call me an opportunist. At least that's a nasty name I think I deserve."

Doc rested his elbows on the table, remembered something about how that was rude, removed them, then leaned forward and spoke softly.

"What do you want from me?" he asked.

"I see a highly trained magician in word magic and blood magic," she said.

"I am not highly trained in blood magic, that was completely an accident," Doc said.

"Fine, a highly trained word magician and an idiot savant blood magician," she said. "I'm curious what you'd do if you knew bargaining magic. I want to teach you what I know."

"I don't know that I really want to work in sales," Doc said.

"Fine," Lady Grey said, taking a deep sip of her wine. "Then just hang out with me for a while. See how the other half lives. Get out of dusty libraries and dark sewers and see if this life suits you."

And Doc made a decision that would change his life. He said yes.

***

Doc Silence traveled with Natasha Grey off and on for almost two years. It was, strangely, the least violent period of his entire life as a magician, not a sewer or cave in sight, not a swordfight or even a bar fight, for that matter. Conflict was resolved through words, and sometimes through money, and Doc learned how to deescalate a situation through confidence and charm where once he used spellcraft or combat.

He learned very little true magic in those years, at least not the kind he was used to. Natasha did not gain her magic through old books or ancient runes, but she knew the value of magic, the worth of it, and how to exchange one thing for another and always come out on top. It felt slimy to Doc at first, but he saw a sort of mathematical neutrality to it, as well – everyone entered an agreement with something they wanted and something they were willing to give up, and though the bargains were rarely, if ever, fair and balanced, the writing was there in ink, or in blood. Doc had assumed that bargaining magic involved a great deal of lying, but the fact was most people, most creatures, really, could be swayed far more easily by the truth.

And everyone was willing to give up something to get what they wanted. It was Lady Grey's specialty to see when those deals were in her favor, and to walk away when they were not.

Instead of demons and cultists, Doc met movie stars and warlocks – often the same person, he found – all of whom owed Lady Grey some favor, or had done business with her in the past, or better yet, were looking to do business in the future. He met presidents and dictators and generals. Some he hated instantly, but Natasha taught him to hold his tongue and hide his disdain. A good poker face, she said, is worth more than any illusion or charm spell.

Some of these people, though, Doc found he genuinely liked. He wanted to warn them when a deal wasn't in their favor, but in the end, they got what they wanted, be it money or fame or love or something else. Natasha left every deal so that everyone was happy, even if her cut was always the choicer one. When he voiced discomfort, she let him sit in on a few bad deals, ones she knew about but would not take part in, and Doc saw first-hand how truly vicious bargain magic could get.

He watched a man sell his soul for money, and he wanted to warn him, to say it wasn't worth it, but Natasha put a hand gently on his shoulder, and whispered: "We do not determine the value anyone puts on their soul. That is a price only the seller can determine."

Doc knew, knew without being told, that Natasha Grey traded in souls, but she never did so around him. He wasn't sure how, but he would have felt compelled to stop her, and that was a line she didn't want either of them to cross.

Doc thought he had traveled the world before meeting Natasha, but there are different layers to the world, different ecosystems, and his explorations had been limited by scope and by experience. He saw cities he thought he knew like the back of his hand with fresh eyes. He often did not like what he saw there, and soon came to realize he preferred the gutters to the high rises.

There were parties and galas, awash in wealth and privilege. He played his part, sometimes as the Lady Grey's bodyguard, sometimes as her partner, sometimes as her second, occasionally as her date. He saw gods trade favors with devils; billionaires offer up ancient artifacts for longer lives; once, at a party, a blood sacrifice so violent it startled even Natasha herself, who apologized and said she was unaware that was part of the evening's entertainment.

Doc learned that you can always trust a bargain with a hellspawn but you'll never win a deal with a fae creature, because the latter think linear thoughts and the others are avatars of chaos.

But he also found that the fae made more sense to him, in the long run. He'd been buried in myth long before he was exposed to the order of deal making, and myth need not make sense.

He'd been warned to stay away from the fae at parties, but this was one piece of advice he ignored. It was at an event in Venice when a fae noble put a hand on his shoulder when she caught him alone, separated from Natasha as she would wheel and deal with the rich and powerful there. The touch startled Doc, who found himself near-enchanted by the impossible green eyes of the faerie noble standing beside him at the bar.

"You're at the wrong party, you know," she said. Doc knew she spoke in her native language, but the words translated through magic; the sound of her voice made his heart race.

"I think maybe you are as well," Doc said.

The faerie shrugged.

"We do what we must to survive," she said. "The world has forgotten us and made us small, and we sell little pieces of ourselves in the hopes we may one day rise again."

"I'm sorry," Doc said.

"It's not your fault. You believe in us," she said. "I see what you're doing, you know. And I think you're a bright little star. But don't stay forever in this world, wizard. Learn from it, and go back where you belong. The chaos misses you."

Doc saw Natasha eyeing their conversation from across the room, gaze darting to the fae noble beside him. Doc nodded to her and raised a glass, which seemed to assuage the Lady slightly as she turned back to her business.

"This world makes me so tired," he said out loud.

"I'd fear for you if it didn't," the faerie said. "Be safe, Doctor Silence."

"You know my name?" Doc said.

"I should. You carry a sword my people made."

He opened his mouth to apologize, but the faerie waved him off.

"It's in better hands with you," she said.

"The Forgotten Way needed a new Flame," she said, in such a way Doc could hear the proper names in her inflection. "The Summer Court does not have enough knights in this world anymore."

She touched his arm once more and stepped away, blending into the crowd and disappearing. He wondered briefly if he'd imagined the entire exchange, but then an aging British movie star came over and slapped a hand on his arm and teased him about the elf hitting on him.

Natasha found him not long after, looped her arm through his, and walked him from the party, their business concluded.

"Poor you," she said. "The weird ones always find you. What is it about you and the fae creatures?"

"Must be my nature," Doc said.

"We'll knock that out of you eventually," she said. "Dancing under the moonlight with pixies sounds fun, until you have to deal with the mosquito bites."

***

Things were different after that night, though. He continued to travel with Natasha, to learn her art, and even find ways to apply it to his own magic. He made a few bargains, but not the lasting kind, mostly wheeling and dealing a collection of magical trinkets and talismans that would be useful down the road. It was beneficial, but he didn't enjoy it, and the longer it all went on, the emptier it felt. Or perhaps, more accurately, the emptier it made him feel.

Natasha sensed it in him, of course. He could hide very little from her. That was what made her so good at what she did.

"You miss being a hero, don't you," she said one night as they lounged in her luxury apartment overlooking Paris. The Eiffel Tower was lit up in the distance.

"I suppose I do," Doc said.

"You really want to go back to a life in the shadows after all I've shown you?"

"There are shadows in this life, too, Natasha," he said. "We pretend they are velvet curtains, but the bargains I've seen made…"

"You can't have light without darkness, Doc," she said. "There can't be people like you without people like me."

"I suppose not," he said.

"It's funny," she said. "I suppose I envisioned myself as a bit of a devil, trying to tempt you into this life. I was curious if you'd fall. I'm surprised you stayed as long as you did."

"I stayed because I came to love you, Natasha," he said. The words surprised him as much as they did her, and Natasha Grey was nearly impossible to surprise. "It wasn't this life that kept me here for all this time. It wasn't even the magic I learned, though I've learned more than I thought I would. You are singularly remarkable in your darkness."

She stared at him blankly for an uncomfortable amount of time, expressionless, unblinking.

"People flatter me all the time, Doc Silence. They think it will get them a better deal, or put them in my good graces, but mostly it makes me feel contempt for them. It makes them sound weak and stupid."

"Do I sound weak and stupid?"

She put a hand on his cheek. He wondered what it might be like to observe them here, eyes uncovered, four tiny infernos locked in an eternal cycle of eldritch flames. It felt simultaneously distant and intimate, unable to truly look within each other's eyes, but seeing something they both hid from the real world.

"No, no you don't," she said. "It's just so rare when someone means what they say."

She dropped her hand from his face and picked up his hands.

"There will be times, you know, when we are on opposite sides of things. Our world is a cycle of conflict, even more than the mundane world," she said.

"I know."

"I wish you hadn't been… I wish you hadn't been you," she

said. "You're a terrible enemy. Because you are difficult to hate."

"You're good at what you do because you are impossible to hate," Doc said.

"Tell that to my enemies," she said. "I'll miss you on my arm, you sad, strange boy. Will you miss me?"

"More than I thought I would," Doc said.

"Well you know how to find me," she said. "Don't get yourself killed saving babies from bogeymen."

"Don't make any deals you will regret," Doc said

"I haven't lived this long by making that kind of mistake," she said. She leaned in, kissed him on the lips, and took his glasses from the pocket of his coat and placed them on his face for him. "Goodbye, Doctor Silence."

"I'll see you soon, Lady Gray," Doc said. He started the spell to open a portal, but instead began walking toward the door, feeling as though he might want to walk the streets of Paris a few moments longer.

As he reached the door, she called out to him one last time.

"Doc," she said. "I do love you, you know."

Doc looked back, hand on the antique doorknob of her apartment, half-turned.

"I didn't," Doc said. "But now I do."

It was raining in Paris as Doc Silence left the hidden home of the Lady Natasha Grey. He knew he left a piece of himself behind there, a bargaining chip she would someday use in her games. But she taught him well, and just this once, he knew, the deal made would fall in his favor.

Chapter 24: The weight of things

Doc Silence and Erasmus Hawksmith sat together in Central Park, sipping coffee from paper cups. Erasmus looked better than when Doc pulled him from the Dreamless Lands; but the fact remained that the old wizard had not aged a day in the first ten years or more Doc knew him, and his time in that other plane seemed to have caused all those years to catch up to him, as if a punishment. He was visibly aged, slower, though his eyes were as clear now as the day Doc first met him. He kept his beard longer these days, his hair less tidy, but Doc suspected it was more an affectation than a sign of growing decrepitude.

They didn't talk as much as they used to. This was Doc's fault, he knew; he didn't want to hold a grudge, but he resented Erasmus for those years when he was gone, without a word. They talked about it only once, and it became a fight, as Erasmus pointed out how much Doc learned on his own, and Doc raged at how many times he risked his life trying to bring Hawksmith home.

But Erasmus was the only person Doc knew with any memory of his life before magic, and he couldn't stay mad, not forever.

There was a distance between them, now, and Doc realized this must be what it's like when a child outgrows their parent.

"How's the school," Doc asked casually, shaking his coffee to stir up the detritus at the bottom of the cup.

"It's interesting," Erasmus said. "I don't interfere anymore, and it's growing, like a farmland allowed to return to nature. And it's spreading – there are Hawksmith Academies in different worlds, now."

"You must be proud," Doc said.

"I suppose I am," Erasmus said. "It's a strange feeling, to make something from nothing."

"As opposed to nurturing something you found," Doc said.

"Oh, don't be passive aggressive," Erasmus said. "I'm proud of you, more than the school."

"I wouldn't blame you if you were prouder of the school," Doc said. "I'm just one wizard."

"A wizard who has done more before his thirtieth birthday than most do in a lifetime."

"Feels like I've mostly made mistakes," Doc said. "And made enemies."

"If a magician has no enemies, he's not doing it right," Erasmus said.

"You do know normal people don't have enemies," Doc said.

Erasmus let out a soft, coughing laugh.

"Normal people don't teleport themselves across the world or summon objects out of thin air," he said. "We're not normal people."

"I know that for sure," Doc said. "I can't even walk around without lenses to disguise my eyes anymore."

"You never did explain how you cast blood magic in that duel," Erasmus said. "I might have failed you on any number of counts, but I didn't teach you that."

Doc shrugged.

"While you were gone, I decided I wanted to learn more about the other kinds of magic," Doc said. "For theorycraft purposes. I spent some time with a bunch of vampire spellcasters."

Erasmus made a dramatic gurgling sound, halfway between amused and disgusted.

"Well, if you want to learn about blood magic, go to the people who can't get enough of it," he said.

"I never tried to cast anything, but I guess I just internalized some of the tricks I saw them use, and when I was losing the fight with the Mage Slayer, I got desperate," Doc said.

"Which is how blood magic gets you, when you're willing to do anything," Erasmus said. "I'm sorry I wasn't there to help with that fight."

"Did they ever come for you?" Doc said. "A Mage Slayer?"

"I was a late bloomer," Erasmus said. "By the time I was strong enough to get their attention, I wasn't someone they were worried about anymore. Someone like you though, you have so much time to get better at your craft, and you're so openly idealist..."

"People hate an idealist, don't they."

"In magic, and in reality," Erasmus said.

"Anyway. If I'd known it would do this," Doc said, gesturing to his eyes, "I wouldn't have cast the spell. I just didn't know what else to do. I was dying. And no need to apologize for not being there. You were here on the prime material plane, but Culler caught me alone on purpose. He never would have come after me if I had help, I think."

"You're probably right," Erasmus said. "His kind prefer an ambush to a fair fight, even as tough as they are."

"Speaking of theorycraft, though, are you still spending time with the princess of bad decisions?"

"Natasha?" Doc asked. "No. I think I learned all I could from her."

"Really," Erasmus said.

"No, not really," Doc said. "But if I stayed, I'd start to be more like her, and I don't want to be that kind of magician. I want to be better than that."

"That's my boy," Erasmus said. "I suppose you're going to

apprentice yourself to a necromancer next."

"Absolutely not," Doc said, laughing earnestly. "That's one place I don't need to go. I was thinking of asking Bláithín to teach me to do arcane tattoos, though."

"Word magic by a different name," Erasmus said, sounding mildly impressed. "She likely won't, but don't be offended."

"Why not, do you think?"

"Because it's a rare art, and that makes her valuable. Being a rare thing in this world keeps you safe and keeps you strong. But it's worth asking. I've never known her to take an apprentice, and the man who taught her retired long ago."

"We're all rare things, aren't we."

"Yes," Erasmus said. "We are."

Doc watched joggers and dog walkers make their way past, sipping his coffee, sitting in comfortable silence with his mentor.

"Erasmus," Doc said. "When I saved my brother, the woman in the Fens said she cursed me. That a dark cloud would follow me all my days, and that I'd never be happy."

"Sounds like something one like her would say," Erasmus said.

"At the time I thought she was just spitting out nonsense."

"She may very well have been."

"I think about that moment, sometimes," Doc said. "And if she really did curse me."

Erasmus leaned back and looked at the sky.

"Have you ever been happy, Doc?"

Doc knew he had. For a moment he thought about lying, but he could tell Erasmus would see through it.

"Of course I have," Doc said.

"And have those happy times made your life better?"

"Yes."

"So you have not, in fact, known nothing but sorrow. You've had more than your fair share of sorrow, for sure, but you're a magician, and that's the risk when you play with magic. But in between that darkness there have been points of light."

"Yes, there have."

"You have loved, and been loved. You have seen wonders. You have done things both good and great, and left the world better than you found it," Erasmus said.

"I think so," Doc said. "I hope so."

"Then she was wrong," Erasmus said. "She cursed you, that's true. She cursed you with the sort of doubt that would follow you forever and make you look past the joy in your life, waiting for sorrow to return. She played a great and vicious trick on you, my boy."

Doc nodded and cast the smallest of spells to heat up his coffee. Erasmus held his cup toward Doc for him to do the same.

"This is a heavy life, Erasmus," Doc said. "The weight of things feels unbearable sometimes."

"Does it though?" Erasmus said. "I know what you've seen and done. I know who you are. Has the weight ever felt too much to carry?"

Doc thought about it a moment. He thought about the scars on his body, about the faces he no longer saw, about the darkness he'd faced and come out the other side. And he was here, drinking coffee in a park with his oldest friend under a bright sun, and the world was at peace, at least for this moment.

"No," Doc said. "No, it's never more than I can carry."

"And that's why I chose you," Erasmus said. "Or why the world brought us together. It's a lie to say that life will not give you more than you can handle. Life will absolutely give you more than you can carry. But you, Doc Silence, are singularly capable of shouldering the weight of the things to come. I'm very proud of you."

"Why you *chose* me?" Doc said. "You knew my brother would get into trouble with that creature in the Fens, didn't you."

"She'd been devouring children for centuries," Erasmus said. "I wasn't hanging out in a magic shop lurking, waiting for the moment for you to be desperate and afraid. But I saw something in you in that moment and chose to intervene. A singular convergence of luck. That's magic in its purest form, Doc, when it

213

opens a window. You can choose to climb through it or stay behind. We both chose the window that day."

"You really don't think she cursed me that day?"

"Oh, I'm sure she tried," Erasmus said. "But I wouldn't worry about it. In our line of work people curse us every day. All the time. A litany of curses. Who can keep track?"

"So I should just keep looking for the light," Doc said.

"Best advice I can give you, my boy," Erasmus said. "The light is right there in front of you. It's up to you whether you embrace it or let it pass you by."

Chapter 25: The wedding

Doc Silence kept his promises, and he had promised to attend a wedding.

He wasn't particularly looking forward to it. The Dreamless Lands were unsettling at best in his previous visit, and he didn't like the way reality seemed to decide on a whim what the rules were there. But he made a promise, and so at the appointed time, he put on his best clothes (which were not, to be fair, very nice), cast a glamour spell on them to make them look presentable, and buckled the planar knife onto this belt. He drew the blade, preparing to cut into the veil between realities, when the light from a teleportation spell sparked across the room. Erasmus Hawksmith walked through, wearing a three-piece suit and looking jauntier than he had in recent months.

"What are you doing here?" Doc asked.

"Great way to greet your old teacher," Erasmus said, checking his watch. "Are we going or not?"

"We?"

"What, did you think you're the only one invited to this fiasco of a wedding?" Erasmus said. "I've known Lady Dreamless longer than you have, you know. You really are starting to develop that over-inflated sense of self-importance all proper wizards have."

"You really want to go back there?" Doc asked.

"It's just a wedding," Erasmus said. "Not like I'm going to conduct epic arcane experiments to build interdimensional wizarding schools. Now are you going to use that knife or not? I didn't get dressed up for nothing. Also, they are going to see right through your illusions on that outfit."

"It's the best I have," Doc said.

"I'm mostly kidding," Erasmus said. "This is a wedding between the Dreamless Lands and the Nightmare Kingdoms. Half the guests will be naked."

"You're really selling me on this," Doc said, and then, with a flick of his wrist, slit a hole in reality, which he and Erasmus walked through.

***

I got the calculations right, Doc thought, as he stepped through the portal onto a patch of silver grass beneath a lavender sky. A castle that appeared to be made of quartz rose before them, a nonsensical structure that felt more at home in an M.C. Escher drawing or a *Gormenghast* novel than in any reality. A road of sapphire stones led up to the castle, and wedding guests made their way toward the open portcullis.

"So remember, tread cautiously here," Erasmus said as he eyed a pair of creatures, which appeared to be bipedal giraffes with leathery bat wings, stroll by carrying a candy-colored gift box.

"This from you," Doc said. "I don't usually like to bring it up, but I'll remind you that I spent years of my life trying to rescue you from this place, not the other way around."

"Well, learn from my mistakes, kid," Erasmus said. "The Dreamless Lands aren't fae, but they're fae-adjacent. They have rules, but the rules only make sense to the people who make them up, so you've got to recalibrate your expectations with every conversation."

"Sounds like how I live every minute of my life with magic," Doc said.

"True, but you and I both know magic will conform to the rules *you* set for it, not the other way around," Erasmus said. "This place is made of dreams. It's as stable as a marshmallow in a microwave."

Doc felt a tug at his pant leg, and looked down to see a black and white cat, with a half-mask of black over the right side of her face, looking up at him expectantly with bright green eyes. The cat was comically stumpy, just compact in every way, short legs, short tail, tiny torso. She held a letter in her paw, between two toe beans.

"Can I help you," Doc asked.

"You Doc Silence?" the cat asked in a close approximation to a Boston accent.

"I am," Doc said. "And you are?"

"Halfmask Troublemaker," the cat said. "The Lady told me I should give this to you."

She aggressively held out the letter to him again. Doc hesitated, and the cat whacked his shin with her other paw. Finally, Doc took the envelope from her.

"No need to get aggressive about it," he said.

"No need to be such a wimp about it,' she said.

"Are you going to the wedding?" Doc asked.

"Do I look like I'm going to a wedding?"

"I don't know how cats dress when attending weddings," Doc said.

Erasmus laughed. The cat hissed.

"I'll have you know I was invited, but I'm going to watch from the rafters," Halfmask said. "I sense there will be trouble, and it will be trouble I did not cause, that that is the worst kind of trouble. So I will watch from afar. And I will laugh, and then run."

"That sounds like the most sensible advice I've heard in years," Erasmus said.

"When you need advice on how to survive trouble, ask a cat,"

Halfmask said. "We always know the best time to leave a party."

The cat held out her other paw expectantly.

"What," Doc said.

"Tip," the cat said.

"You have no pockets," Doc said.

"Do I look like I care?" Halfmask said. "Tip."

Doc looked at Erasmus, who was still laughing. The older wizard just shrugged.

Doc held out his hand, made a few small arcane gestures, and suddenly a small, clear pearl appeared in his palm. He held it out to Halfmask, who eyed it greedily.

"What is this," she asked.

"It's a spell," Doc said. "If you crush it in your paw, you will become invisible for one hour. It will only work once, but if there is to be trouble…"

"Cats do not need magic to be invisible," Halfmask said, though she still eyed the pearl with curiosity. "We are invisible when we want to be."

"Then I'll keep the spell," Doc said.

"No, no," Halfmask said, snatching the pearl from his offering hand. "Perhaps this will be fun. I accept your tip, magician."

"Thank you," Doc said.

"Good day to you," Halfmask said, before she bounded off into the tall grass. And then, from a hidden vantage point: "Don't die."

"Fae adjacent," Doc said.

"All cats are fae adjacent," Erasmus said. "It's why we love them."

The older magician pointed at the envelope in Doc's hand. It was an elegant, cream-colored parchment, sealed with a lump of wax the color and texture of a glitter bomb.

"Well, are you going to open it?" he asked.

Doc sighed and broke the seal, half-expecting the wax to explode. Instead, he found a hand-written note inside. The letters were jumbled at first, but as he tried to read them, they reformed into a coherent message, dancing across the page.

My Dearest Doctor of Silence,

It is on this day I ask a great favor of you. This is a wedding made out of promise and obligation, not of love or honor. It was made not on my behalf but on my station's, and I do not will it. A merging of the Dreamless Lands and the Nightmare Kingdom will have long-reaching effects across the planes I am not willing to make; and to be truly honest, I do not wish to merge my life forever with this Prince of Nightmares.

Save me from this fate, and save the Dreamless Lands from encroaching darkness.

Sincerely,

Lady Dreamless

Doc showed Erasmus the letter, who couldn't help but burst out laughing.

"Oh, this is funny?" Doc said.

"Better you than me, that's all," Erasmus said. "This is what you get for letting people know you've got a heroic streak, Doc. They expect you to save them."

"I have to do this, right? Long-reaching effects—will it destroy dreams everywhere? Will everyone have nothing but nightmares?"

"I have no idea," Erasmus said. "But then again I've always thought more about the smaller impacts. If you redirect the butterfly, you might sway the hurricane."

Doc lifted his glasses, which he realized he didn't need here in this place where flaming eyes would go all but unnoticed, and rubbed the bridge of his nose.

"How do I do this?" Doc asked.

"Well," Erasmus said. "I suppose when they ask if there are any objections, you object."

Doc looked away and back over the gleaming treetops of a nearby dream forest. In the distance, the sky turned from lavender to a grim, bruised purple, and beyond that, the dark black-gray of a storm.

"What's that," Doc asked.

"The Nightmare Kingdom is particularly close today," Erasmus said. "You can't always see the border."

"Well, that's wonderful," Doc said.

"How's that objection feeling now?"

"Like maybe I should start working on what I'm going to say," Doc said, and then started hoofing it toward the castle.

***

Doc and Erasmus were greeted as any other guests, their names checked off a list—which wasn't really a list, but some kind of performative verification process made by a four-foot-tall rabbit in a tuxedo—and escorted inside.

"Bride or groom?" the rabbit asked.

"Bride," Doc and Erasmus said in unison. They looked at each other, then back to the rabbit, then at each other again.

"Right this way," the rabbit said, and led them to a massive chamber lined with pews, like a church. A grand dais stood at the end with two thrones, one silver and one onyx. The ceiling was filled with stars, and Doc could not tell if it was magic, or art, or both that made them glow. The gathered guests were a cacophony of whimsy and terror, and it was easy to see which side belonged with which. On the left side, a hodge-podge of beings, ranging from identifiable mythical creatures to cartoonish animals to creatures like abstract paintings come to life, milled around looking excited and worried. On the right side, the picture was far more grim. Some looked quite clearly like demons; others like eldritch horrors with too many eyes, or tentacles where their mouths should be. But the ones who were most unsettling were those who were, on the surface, the least strange—ordinary, even conventionally attractive human faces, but the faces showed no sign of emotion, of joy or fear or remorse. The faces of killers, Doc thought. The faces of nightmares.

They were shown to their seats, midway down on the left side, aligning with the silver throne. Doc found himself sitting next to a hunched old woman, her face like a carved and dried apple, eyes dark pits with no irises. A pair of ram horns curled from her forehead, framing her face.

"Aren't you a strange one," she said, looking up at him.

"Nice to meet you as well," Doc said.

"Nice is an odd choice of words on this day," she said. Her voice was squeaky and cracked.

Doc turned his attention to the other side of the aisle. The nightmares were strangely beautiful, in a way, spiky and dark, threatening but enthralling. The distinct division between the two sides was palpable out here in the pews. It was not fear and joy, or but rather regret and indifference. No one seemed particularly happy to be here.

Doc noticed Erasmus rubber-necking the crowd as well.

"What are you looking for?" Doc asked.

"Wondering if anyone we know is here," he said. "I've seen a few entities from the higher planes but no humans. Figured I'd at least see some of the Council Prime here, or the Forgotten Way, but…"

"This is how we'll be remembered. 'They went to a wedding and were never seen again,'" Doc said.

"Don't worry. If the nightmares tear you apart I'll make sure to survive and tell your story," Erasmus said.

"Story?" the old woman with the ram horns said. "Have you ever heard the story of Lady Dreamless?"

"I—I mean, we've met, yes," Doc said.

"No, the story. The faerie tale. About how this all came to be," the old woman said.

"I don't think I have," Doc said.

The old woman inhaled sharply and closed her strange, deep-set eyes. And then she began to recite:

Have you heard of the Lady Dreamless?
Promised to a nightmare Prince,
Raised to the sounds of the songs of the Damned,
Queen of the Citrine Tower,

Heir to an empty throne?

Have you heard her story?
Trapped for a millennium in a black gem,
With only the whispers of passing nightmares
To keep her company?

Have you heard of her escape?
How she crossed the black and starless paths
Of faded lands, armed with only her wits
And a wisp of fire to guide her?

"So she was a captive of the Nightmare Prince?" Doc asked quietly.

The old woman leaned in conspiratorially.

"No, the Nightmare King," she said. "She escaped, but the two kingdoms thought the best way to make peace was to keep this promised union. To make dream and nightmare whole once more."

"How long has the engagement been?" Doc asked. He heard Erasmus chuckle softly behind him.

"Oh, a few centuries, by your standards. Time is meaningless here, you know."

"I assumed," Doc said.

Their conversation was interrupted as music, which swung wildly from delicate to discordant, began to play. From the left side of the dais, Lady Dreamless emerged, wearing a shimmering, translucent gown the same color as her pearlescent skin, her tail emerging from a slit in the back. Her fluorescent red hair had grown out a little since he'd last seen her, and it was styled into a cascading wave down one side of her face. Her shoulders were bare, her back straight, and she looked much more the queen than when last they met. He caught her scanning the crowd, and somehow, amidst all the chaos and madness, they locked eyes. She offered him the tiniest of worried smiles, and the expression in her eyes took his breath away.

"Oh no," Doc said. "How'd she spot me?"

"Probably looked for the guy with the glowing fireball eyes," Erasmus said.

"I didn't have these when I met her," Doc said.

"You think she doesn't keep tabs on the waking world?" Erasmus said.

And then, the Nightmare Prince entered the room.

Impossibly tall, he had strange, long limbs that seemed to both dance and articulate in inhuman ways. It was hard to tell where the living creature began and his clothing began, as his visible skin had a nearly identical texture to the sleek, gleaming black of his armor. A great head rested atop a muscular neck, eyes glowing with an internal fire, like a furnace. His mouth, when he opened it to speak, emitted that same light. Doc couldn't tell if he wore a crown, a helmet, or neither, as two immense, jet-black horns swept back from his forehead, a magnificent adornment impossible to distinguish from the Prince's own body.

The Nightmare Prince, dwarfing the Lady Dreamless, offered his hand to her, and she took it. Doc could sense the reluctance even from here, and wondered if the Nightmare Prince detected it as well.

A third creature appeared just then, flying along the aisle from the back of the chamber. He was man-shaped, but had the head of a raven, and wings like moth, each wing marked with an eye-like image. He fluttered between aisles and arrived at the dais, where a podium waited for him.

As the bride and groom settled into their respective positions, the moth-winged priest began to recite the words of ceremony.

"Gathered dreams and nightmares," he said. "We are here today to celebrate the union of these two sovereigns, and the union of our two lands."

His words were very formal in tone, but much like gibberish in other ways; he said names of places and things, referenced historical events, of legends and historical figures, and none of it made any sense to Doc—it was as if listening to a child make up a story on the fly. But the audience was rapt, either out of fear or true interest, and the room was alarmingly, dangerously quiet. Doc's stomach rumbled with worry and acid.

"Maybe they won't ask for any objections," he whispered softly. Erasmus raised an eyebrow at him and shrugged.

"If there be any objections to this most magnificent and glorious of unions," the priest said, holding two clawed hands in the air before him. "Speak now, dreams, speak now, nightmares, or forever hold your peace."

"Dammit," Doc said, and pushed past Erasmus into the center aisle.

The crowd gasped in such a dramatic and over the top fashion it almost sounded like a comedy. Doc himself might have laughed if he were an onlooker and not the one causing the disruption. His heart pounded so hard he could feel it in his throat, and his stomach was a pit of fire.

"Who... dares," the Nightmare Prince growled.

"This is the Doctor of Silence," Lady Dreamless said. "He is an ally, and welcome in this land."

"He is not welcome in mine," the Nightmare Prince said.

"Please, my lord, my lady, tradition dictates we must hear him out," the priest said, though he did not sound particularly convincing, Doc noticed. He might be the only one in the room Doc felt almost as much fear for as he did himself in that one moment.

The Nightmare Prince turned a withering gaze on the priest, and then onto Doc. He could feel Erasmus's eyes on him, but the old man didn't step in to help. Probably for the best, Doc thought. *One of us should make it home to tell the story of how I got myself killed interfering in an interplanar wedding.*

"On what grounds do you object," the priest said.

"I know the Lady Dreamless, and I know her hopes," Doc said. He could sense a growing rage in the Nightmare Prince at that, and immediately regretted his phrasing. "What I mean to say is, I know she wishes… I… this is a wedding out of duty, am I right?"

"All things are out of duty," the priest said.

"Even here, in a land where the rules bend to your will, and not the other way around?" Doc asked.

"Get on with it, magician," the Nightmare Prince said.

Doc stole the fastest of glimpses at Lady Dreamless, who stood stock still on the dais, frozen like prey, watching without blinking.

"I… Might I tell you a story, my Prince?" Doc said.

"This is not a time for stories," the Nightmare Prince said.

"These are the Dreamless Lands," the Lady said. "There is nothing but time for stories here."

Doc approached the dais and took a knee a few respectful rows back. He cast a tiny spell on himself to help his voice project more clearly, and then looked up at both sovereigns, and the priest between them.

I can't challenge him to a duel, Doc thought. I can't win a war in a room built with magic. I don't have the strength, but this is not a place for strength. He'd spent his whole life making magic with words, Doc thought. Let the words do the job, just this once, you stupid magician. Just tell them the truth.

And so, he began. He kept his pace even, his cadence soothing; he used phrases he knew had meaning in myth and folklore. He told a faerie tale, but there were no faeries in it. Only a life, but now seemed as good a time as any to tell it.

"Once, there was a boy who loved his brother very much," Doc said. "And one day a great and terrible magic came for them both. The boy escaped, and thought he would never see his brother again, but he met a magician, who told him he could save this brother, whom he loved so much, in exchange for his name. By becoming a magician himself. But this choice was a terrible one, because once he gave his name away, the boy's brother would forget him. They would never see each other again. He would have to give up that which he loved, in order to save it."

He swallowed hard and steadied himself before continuing.

"The boy," Doc said, "Chose to save his brother, of course.

Because that is what you do for love. That is what you do for the people you love. You give up everything. You make the sacrifice. You do that which you know is right, and you take on the burden of pain and loss so that they might be free. You have no choice, not if you love them. You give what is asked, all of it, without hesitation."

"The boy made the right decision," the Nightmare Prince said. "To do otherwise is selfish. Self-defeating. To sacrifice others for yourself is the height of villainy."

The room murmured in agreement, on both sides of the aisle, both bride and groom.

"When the boy was grown, he loved again," Doc said. "He found someone, who knew nothing of magic, who cared nothing for magic. By then, of course, the boy had grown to need magic. It was who he was, it was what he was, it was all of him, as everyone in this room has, I'm sure, felt as well."

"Of course," the Nightmare Prince said, leaning in.

"But the boy, now a man, tried to live in both worlds," Doc said. "He tried to be a magician, and he tried to be a good man, someone this woman could love back. He wanted to be a part of her world, but needed to remain apart from it, because this was what duty demanded, this was what magic demanded, this was, of course, the right thing to do."

"One cannot live in both worlds," the Nightmare Prince said.

In her place beside him, the Lady Dreamless watched silently, eyes filling with tears like mercury.

"No, one cannot," Doc said. "Truly, one cannot live in both worlds. It will tear you apart at the seams. But the boy tried, he tried with every fiber of his being, every cell in his body, to love and be loved, but to do the things his work demanded, to fight the creatures who rose up from the shadows or fell from the stars, to be the shaman, the sentinel, the guardian."

Doc inhaled sharply. He felt much older than his years in that moment, and very alone in this room full of people and monsters. He sensed the weight of his entire life, from the moment he walked into the Fens with his brother to this very second, like a burden dragging down upon his spine, upon his skull, upon his heart.

"The boy chose duty over love," Doc said. "But that's not true, is it? He chose duty because of love. Because doing what he had to do would keep this woman he loved safe. By staying away from her, he would keep the demons and monsters from ever finding her. By saving the world a little bit each day, he would make that world safe for her, and for all the people he loved. For the brother and parents he never saw again. For the next little boy who walked into a swamp and found a wicked thing there waiting. For every mortal pairing, ordinary people whose only true magic is, in act, love itself. He gave up every ounce of happiness because he knew what was behind the curtain, what lurked in the shadows or under basement stairs, and someone had to shoulder that burden. He did it so no one else had to. He chose loneliness over love, so that love might prevail. For everyone else."

"Your story doesn't make sense," the Nightmare Prince said. "Not for what you are trying to do here. Do you not argue, with every word, that what we do here tonight is the right thing? To follow our duty, to listen to fate, to forego true love because duty demands it? Are you not saying with perfect clarity that denying this marriage is wrong, and that love is less important that duty?"

Doc's lungs felt thick and slow. He took a deep breath, swallowed hard, and looked up to stare the Nightmare Prince directly in his glowing red eyes, matching him flame for flame.

"No, my prince," Doc said. "The boy chose duty over love first because he had no choice, and you have a choice here today. You are not bound by fate. You are the Nightmare Prince and the Lady Dreamless. You rule over the sleeping minds of mortals, in a realm where rules have no power other than that which you give them."

"But the boy chose duty twice," the Nightmare Prince rumbled.

"Yes," Doc said. "And when he had a choice, he made a decision he will regret until his dying day. And you know magicians live a very long time. Love and duty are not binary things, Lord of Night Terrors. They can coexist. And he did not choose duty that second time. He chose the greater aspect of love. He did not make a sacrifice for honor. He did so because he loved too much to stay."

The Nightmare Prince stared down at Doc without a word, waiting. Waiting, Doc knew, for closure.

"If this wedding occurs, my Lord, my Lady, will love prevail? Or will you look back with longing for a better time? Because magicians live long lives, but we are not immortal. And this, I know, you both are."

The Nightmare Prince rose from his throne. He could have been ten feet tall, or twenty, or more. The illusory nature of this place made it seem as if he were all things at once. When he spoke, not a sound was made in the chamber.

"You have proven your name to be a lie, Doctor of Silence," he said. "Silence is not your purview."

A soft laugh chittered across the room, then fell away. Doc wondered if this was how he would die. Finally die, Doc thought, despite his young age; there were days he felt his twenty-some-odd years were instead centuries, that this was the culmination of many lifetimes, none of them pleasant. He'd walked toward death every day since he was twelve years old. This seemed as good as any a place to finally meet his end.

"When I first looked upon you here in this place, I saw a man upon whom true nightmares hold no sway," the prince said. "You are not a man without fear, but your fears were not simple, and nightmares like a simple theme. We shouldn't have to work that hard to scare you. But here you are. And now I know what scares you. And know this, Doctor of Silence, regret is not the darkness my kind weaves. Dreams of regret belong to my betrothed. She knows melancholy the way I know fear."

Doc nodded, and looked to the Lady Dreamless, whose calm had faded, who now fidgeted and looked back and forth between the wizard and the prince.

"Truth has a magic to it, doesn't it," the Nightmare Prince said. "Magic is so often lies, but perhaps that is why the truth is so powerful – lies are petty magic, and honesty is so much more. Today you presented the latter, and though I am loathe to admit it, I find myself swayed. I do not wish to look over my shoulder for eternity, filled with regret."

"I've only felt this way a short time, my Prince, and it is a heavy thing," Doc said.

The Nightmare Prince nodded almost imperceptibly to Doc, then reached a hand out to Lady Dreamless. She took it, and drew closer to him, voluntarily for the first time. Physically, the prince dwarfed her, but somehow in that moment their stature, in all other ways balanced equally.

"I release you from your promise," the Nightmare Prince said. "I will return to my realm and leave you to yours. This mortal has given us that rarest of gifts tonight. A chance to not make an eternal mistake."

"I then release you from your promises as well," Lady Dreamless said. "I would part as allies, and share the sleeping realms as equals, if you would."

"I would," the Nightmare Prince said. He glanced back at Doc, who still knelt before the dais. "What would we do with this one, who showed such terrible impudence to both our kingdoms?"

Lady Dreamless also looked down at him, and Doc thought, for the briefest of moments, now that she had what she wanted, she would obliterate him from all of existence. Instead, she smiled.

"I would reward him," she said. "And name him a High General in the Army of the Dreamless. For he has shown the courage of a warrior, but the wisdom of a good man."

The Nightmare Prince gave the Lady Dreamless a sidelong assessment, then smiled, his mouth glowing red with flame.

"It would not do for your forces to gain such an ally on this day while mine does not," he said. "So I name him a First Mage of the Nightmare Kingdom, with all this title requires and offers. A place on both our councils. To balance the scales between dream and nightmare."

"I agree to this," Lady Dreamless said. She held out a hand to

Doc for him to rise. "Do you accept these titles, wizard? Will you make them a part of you?"

Internally, Doc swore relentlessly and with every curse word he'd ever heard, while fighting off the urge to vomit and pass out. Externally, he rose calmly to his feet and bowed.

"It would be my greatest honor, my Lady, my Prince," Doc said.

"Then welcome, First Wizard," the Nightmare Prince said.

'Welcome, High General," Lady Dreamless said. "And thank you."

"Oh dreams and figments, terrors and delights," the Nightmare Prince said. "A wedding will not occur this day, but a feast will. Make merry, cause joy, for today our kingdoms have made peace without sacrificing love."

The room erupted into absolute chaos, music from too many sources discordantly playing over each other, wild dancing, food flying, drinks being poured fit to drown the imbibers. The Lady Dreamless and the Nightmare Prince had a quiet, intimate conversation on the dais, perhaps working out details, or perhaps simply making small talk. There seemed to be a relief between both of them, as though a catastrophe truly had been averted.

A hand clamped down on Doc's shoulder. He almost jumped out of his skin.

"My boy," Erasmus said, his eyes red-rimmed. "I am so very sorry I did not warn you of the darkness of this life."

"You did, in your way," Doc said. "And what you didn't teach me, I learned along the way. It's okay. You've done nothing wrong."

"I've done something right, by setting you on this path," Erasmus said. "Not for you. You deserved a better life than this. But for everyone else. You... I am so proud of you, you know."

Doc put a hand over Erasmus' on his shoulder.

"I know," he said.

"Someday, I hope some of the good you put into the world comes back to you," Erasmus said. "It would be a right and just thing if it did."

"But it won't," Doc said.

"Most likely not," Erasmus said. "Magic isn't fair."

"And that's fine," Doc said. "That's the life we chose."

Chapter 26: Not alone in this world

Doc had come to realize that, for better or for worse, he'd become a vigilante.

It wasn't an intentional choice, he supposed. There were simply things in this world the proper authorities weren't able to handle, and only so many magicians willing to put themselves at risk to deal with, and fewer still who did so for the right reasons. And so he spent his early twenties delving in caves, and talking to ghosts; getting into brawls with demons and corralling vampires into plying their trade more ethically.

It was exhausting work, and unappreciated, though he'd never say that out loud. Yes, the occasional person would thank him for driving off a huddle of Puk-Wudjies kidnapping hikers on a popular trail, or discouraging a pack of cultists from summoning an elder god in a mall, but for the most part, it was quiet, unseen work.

It was better that way, Doc knew. The less the world at large was aware of the monsters under the bed, the better they'd sleep. But still, he wished he had more people to talk to about it. More allies, too, as his friends were mostly aging wizards growing weary of the life, or jaded sorcerers who no longer cared to do any good in this world.

Nobody wanted to be a hero. And, as Doc hung his coat up in the closet of the apartment he kept hidden by mystic wards in the City, he couldn't blame them. Who wanted to do this sort of thing for their entire lives? He opened his refrigerator and took out the last remaining slices of yesterday's pizza and ate them cold without sitting down. With a flick of his wrist he turned on the television, wishing he could settle his mind enough to watch something fun, but instead, the channel was eternally tuned to the news.

War and tragedy, humanity being cruel to each other. Mundane evils. I could try to do something about that, Doc thought, if I didn't have to stop the monsters that go bump in the night. Monsters just take up too much time.

The newscasters shifted their attention to something unusual this night, though: footage of a man in a blue and silver suit of armor, stopping a horrific shooting with blasts of instantly freezing ice. The man approached reporters in a news conference and removed his helmet. A young face, too handsome by far, hair slick with sweat from the helmet, emerged. He talked about turning his family's fortune into something better. About how the things they built always ended up in the wrong hands. And that maybe it was time they ended up in the right hands.

"Are you saying the right hands are yours, Mr. Winter?" a reporter asked.

The man in the suit smirked and shrugged, a comical image in the burly metal armor.

"Until someone better comes along, sure," he said. "Show me someone I can trust more than myself and I'll step aside."

"What is this technology called?" another reporter yelled.

"I don't know yet," the man called Winter said.

"Come on, you never miss a chance for branding, Henry!" someone yelled from the back of the press conference. Again, Winter laughed.

"I call it the Coldwall armor," he said. "Impenetrable to protect the user, non-lethal to protect everyone else. We don't need more guns. We need more shields."

Doc found himself staring at the television as the man spoke, the cold pizza warming unpleasantly to room temperature.

"Henry Winter," Doc said, making a mental note. Someone doing good with the means he had. Doc had no idea what to do with this information, of course. He knew nothing of technology, and had a hard time imagining even the best man-made armor would stand up to a walking nightmare or an angry spirit.

But still. Someone else out there, doing good in the world.

***

The aliens began making headlines a few months later.

No one actually knew for sure they were aliens, of course. Doc didn't believe in alien life, but at the same time he didn't disbelieve in it either; it was simply that he hadn't encountered it first-hand and would reassess when that time came. He'd been to other planes of existence and seen all manner of impossible things, so aliens were not a big ask for him to stretch his belief. But calling glowing men who flew through the air "aliens" seemed a bit of a reach to Doc. He knew plenty of glowing creatures who flew through the air. He could fly himself, if he wanted to, and he glowed more than he preferred.

There wasn't much footage of them, of course. They darted around like illusions, and would have been terrifying if they weren't so actively kind. There were reports of them freeing hostages in one situation; saving the passengers of a plane crash in another; evacuating flood victims during a monsoon in Southeast Asia in another. It took months before anyone got a clear photo of them, and then the rumors swapped from aliens to angels. Two dashing young men, faces half-hidden behind their masks, who were surrounded by a halo of blue-white light as they danced around the sky.

Doc knew with absolute certainty they were not angels. He'd met angels, and the ones he'd met were not inclined to interfere with mortal affairs. Drowning victims were far below the purview of celestials. This line of thinking made Doc wonder, briefly, why he preferred the company of werewolves and vampires to angels, and what that said about his character, but in the end what he knew was he just didn't like snobs.

The aliens-turned-angels were finally named when an international space station sent out a distress signal. There was no way to help the men and women drifting through space. All, it was assumed, would be lost. But then two blue-white lights darted into the atmosphere and beyond, stabilizing the space station, and later delivering the tools and equipment needed to finalize the repairs. Afterward, no one from the government would talk about what they saw, but one astronaut, furious at the gag order, spoke out.

"They told us their names are Straylight and Horizon," she said. "I don't know what they are or how they get their powers. But they both had lovely accents and were very sweet, and we'd have burned up on reentry without them. They're heroes. Not monsters from another planet."

Straylight and Horizon, Doc thought, watching the astronaut speak on a television set in Times Square. He was there to deal with an immortal serial killer who jumped from body to body after each kill, and he did not have the time to deal with aliens or angels. Maybe later, Doc thought, sensing his quarry on the move in the subway. Right after I deal with this monster.

***

A god fell from the sky one fine November morning, and both Doc Silence and Erasmus Hawksmith were there to see it.

There had been signs and portents, of course, because there are always signs and portents, and while some in the wizarding community thought this was a terrifying prospect—the first true god to make his appearance on Earth in decades, maybe longer,

Doc and Erasmus both found the idea, simply put, tiring. They'd just worked together to stave off an incursion from a particularly dreary corner of the plane of Shadows, and the idea of dealing with a god was just more than they wanted to add to their schedule. But still, it was beneficial to at least see which god fell. A somewhat unreliable witch in France told Doc it would be one of the Greek pantheon, which, Doc was ashamed to admit, he found somewhat tedious, the idea of trying to teach an immortal that Olympus was long gone.

Instead, a burly, blue-haired man plummeted from the clouds and landed with a violent thud in a crater in the Balkans.

Doc and Erasmus watched from a safe distance as the thick-bodied, bearded man dragged himself from the hole in the earth his own body had caused, shook his head like a dog, and then jumped, as if attempting to fly.

He did not fly. So he jumped again, with equal lack of success.

The god hopped back down into the crater and emerged once more, this time carrying a long-handled battle axe. He puffed out his cheeks, exhaled, stretched his back with an awkward crack, and started walking away.

"Should we help him?" Doc asked.

"I mean, he seems harmless," Erasmus said.

"He's got a giant axe and is walking around like he didn't just fall from space and belly flop on the side of a mountain," Doc said.

"He'll be fine, then," Erasmus said. "I'm all for helping the helpless, but I've dealt with gods before and they are not worth the trouble, kid."

The blue-haired man stopped, walked backward, looked up at the sky, and sat down on a rock, looking despondent.

"I'm going to go talk to him," Doc said.

"I'm not going to stop you," Erasmus said. "I'm just not god-sitting."

Doc threw up his hands irritably and strolled up to the god, who was scratching at his beard like a dog.

"Hey," Doc said. "You lost?"

"Mortal!" the blue-haired man said. "I am Korthos of Aramaias, the Truthbringer, the Dragon's Son. I am… I think I'm lost."

Doc wracked his brain for any reference to a Korthos or Aramaias in all the old tomes he'd read in his studies. This was, potentially, a man from a pantheon modern writings had completely forgotten about. Part of him was intrigued; the other part regretted instantly letting himself be known to this being.

"Okay, Korthos of Aramaias. How'd you end up falling out of the sky?"

"I don't know, mortal." Doc didn't even need to work hard to hear the lie.

"Really."

"I don't explain myself to mortals, mortal!"

"You speak to a High General in the Army of the Dreamless, and a First Mage of the Nightmare Kingdom. Is that pedigree enough for you to explain yourself to me? I am a guardian of this world, and your reason for being here is my business." Doc tried to sound official throwing around the ridiculous titles, as true as they were, but his tone felt more like scolding a misbehaving dog.

"I choose not to tell you."

"Then go home," Doc said. "You are not welcome here."

Korthos looked at his shoes like a chastised child, and muttered, "My mother threw me out. She said I needed to go learn how to be a hero again, or something."

Doc looked at Korthos, then looked at the crater, then looked back at Erasmus, who was nowhere to be found, and back again to this blue, miserable god.

"I can't believe I'm saying this," Doc said. "But Korthos, are you hungry?"

"I would break bread with you, First Mage! I am famished, as though I have been thrown across the cosmos without a snack."

Doc shook his head, a wave of irritable exhaustion seeping into his very bones.

"Call me Doc, Korthos," he said. "Come on. Let's get you a cheeseburger."

"This word 'cheese' I know," Korthos said. "But 'burger,' that is a foreign thing. What is it?"

"It's easier to show than explain," Doc said. "But you strike me as the cheeseburger type."

***

Doc stood in line at an Ishmael's Coffee and wondered if anyone in line could see the blood on his coat.

It wasn't human blood, and it was more blue than red, but still, it looked blood-ish, Doc thought. Blood-like. He hoped nobody noticed.

Certainly the barista either didn't see it or didn't care as she took his order for the largest coffee they could legally sell him. He phrased it exactly like that, and she laughed, though Doc assumed she was just humoring him. He was a mess and he knew it, and anyone laughing at his jokes would have to overlook that.

"Hey, Doc," a strangely familiar voice said in line behind him. He couldn't quite place it right away, and, because most people who knew him also wanted to kill him, he prepared for a fight and hoped they wouldn't destroy the Ishmael's. He liked this one. It was close to his loft.

Before he could turn, the voice spoke again.

"Buy a girl a coffee, huh? I don't have any money from this timeline."

And then Doc knew who he'd see when he turned around.

Anarchy Annie had her tattooed arms folded across her chest, wearing the same olive green tee shirt as the last time he met her. Her pink hair was sloppily brushed back from her face and held in place by her sunglasses, which she had perched on her head. Annie smirked at him with a crooked smile.

"Sure," Doc said. "We'll make that two."

Coffees in hand, Doc and Annie found a seat at a black iron table outside. The chairs were uncomfortable, but the air was not, the first hint of autumn fighting off the heat of summer. Doc didn't have a favorite season, exactly, but he always welcomed autumn. It was when things ended, so change could come.

"Did you miss me?" Annie asked, adding an absolutely nauseating amount of sugar to her coffee. Doc drank his black.

"I barely know you," Doc said.

"I keep forgetting that part. Time's a funny thing. I've known you forever."

"Starting now," Doc said.

"Sure, something like that," Annie said. She looked around, taking in the sight of the City as dusk drew itself around them like a blanket. She smiled.

"I've seen what happens when you don't step up, you know," she said.

"What do you mean, step up?"

"I mean some timelines you're not here. Maybe you never become a wizard. Maybe some manticore eats you as a teenager. Maybe you're the Mirrorverse version of yourself and evil. But I've seen a lot of futures, and this places isn't always here."

"I'm not that important," Doc said.

"Nobody's that important," Annie said. "Or really everyone is."

She moved her hand through the air in front of her like a bird on the wind.

"Time is bendy and break-y. Change one thing, a whole new world is born. But some events are more pivotal than others. Y'know? It's not that some things matter more; it's that some things just alter the stream instead of letting the waters of time wash over it."

"And I'm, what, a rock in the stream?"

"You're a fisherman," Annie said, wrinkling her nose at him. "So am I. Maybe not fishermen, exactly. But sailors. And if we're lucky, we're sailors on the same boat."

"So we're crew now," Doc said.

"It's an imperfect metaphor, baby, but you get my meaning."

"I can't say that I know with absolute certainty that I do."

"That's fine. I'll stop being cute about it," Annie said. "I know you've been paying attention. You're not alone in this world. There are people out there doing good things. Ever consider doing good things with those other folks?"

"I met a blue god in a crater," Doc said. "And the last thing I wanted to do was invite him on an adventure."

"But he's useful, right? He can do things you can't. I can do things you can't. You definitely can do things the rest of us can't. There's what, a hundred people in the entire world who know how to use magic? And how many of them do anything to leave the world better than they found it?"

"There's a few of us," Doc said.

"Not as many as there should be," Annie said, taking an uncouth gulp of her still steaming coffee.

"No," Doc said.

"So why not lead by example?" Annie asked.

Doc shook his head.

"The others won't change. It's not in the nature of magicians to change," he said.

"But the idea is appealing anyway," Annie said.

"I didn't say it wasn't," Doc said. "But I work by myself. It's better that way."

"Because nobody gets hurt."

"One reason, yeah," Doc said.

"But what if your allies were forgotten gods, and alien warriors, and guys in military-grade armored suits? What then?"

Doc stared into his coffee and shrugged. He heard something rattling across the table and looked up to see a ring of metal rolling toward him. He caught it.

"Look, I know you'll come around, because you're my future best friend and I know you can't help it. But I get it. You need time to process giving up your lone wizard against the world schtick. That's cool. But when you're ready, you use that and I'll be here, okay?"

"I'm a magician. I can just send you a message with a spell."

"Can your magic... travel through time?" Annie said, waggling her eyebrows.

"I have absolutely no idea," Doc said.

"Use the thing. It's a communicator. It'll ping me. It's like a text message, but across time."

"So your technology is more powerful than my magic," Doc said.

"All technology is magic if you don't know how to use it," Annie said, polishing off her coffee and tossing it into a nearby barrel. She missed, sending the paper cup careening in the air, but Doc reached out with a simple telekinetic spell and caught it, placing it gently in the trash.

"See, we're a team already," she said.

"I didn't say that."

"But you felt it," Annie said. "I'll see you soon, Doc. And by the way, when the doorbell rings later, answer it."

"When what?"

Annie didn't answer. Instead, she winked, tapped the device on her wrist, and disappeared in a sliver of light.

He picked up the metal band on the table and saw it was basically a bracelet. He hesitated for a few seconds, almost put it in his pocket, but instead, he snapped it on his wrist.

***

Doc stood in the darkness of his loft in the City, watching the lights wink on like stars as evening set. He absently traced one of the tattoos on his right arm with his left thumb, the raised scar tissue of the ink strangely comforting in its familiarity. Annie's words bothered him. He didn't want to be a part of something bigger than himself; containing the knowledge and terror of magic pushed his willpower to the limits. The idea of taking on more simultaneously terrified and exhausted him.

He didn't need anyone else. Any time he tried to need anyone else, he failed them, or they failed him. It was better this way, alone. Wasn't that how all wizards were in the old stories, grim loners or crazed hermits, madmen on the outside looking in? Maybe the stories were unfair to those wizards. Maybe they stayed outside the lines of society to protect themselves from caring too much.

He knew what Erasmus would say. They had enough work to do on their own. They were already doing everything they could to leave this disaster of a world better than they found it. Don't lift more than you can carry. Magicians who tried to take on too much, those were the ones that magic consumed and destroyed.

Yes, Doc thought. This is for the best. The pink-haired woman meant well, but Doc did his best work alone. He'd been on his own since Erasmus first disappeared all those years ago. He grew up alone.

And then he heard a knock on his door.

No one ever knocked. No one even knew someone lived here. Doc had made sure to cast illusions to make the space appear vacant, but not derelict, and used spells to hide his presence when he was here at all. He waited, assuming the knock was a mistake, perhaps a neighbor who wandered onto the wrong floor.

Another knock. Still polite, but more forceful this time. The sort of knock one does when you're not sure you were loud enough the first time.

And then the doorbell rang. Doc hadn't even been aware there was doorbell installed. It must've been there all along. How was he to know? No one visited him.

"When the doorbell rings, answer it," Annie had told him. He wasn't entirely sure he believed that she was a time traveler, but Doc had seen more things in this reality than should exist, and he was willing to give time travel the benefit of the doubt. Maybe she did know what happens next.

He crossed the room and opened the door.

A man stood in the hallway, and nothing about him was ordinary. He tried to appear casual in jeans and a light jacket, but the clothes fit wrong, as though he didn't know how to properly size clothing to over his massive shoulders and broad chest.

Piercing eyes regarded Doc with an unexpected nervousness, and Doc realized that for the first time in as long has he could remember, he'd forgotten to put his glasses back on before interacting with a stranger. He could see the pale lavender light flickering across the man's face, deepening the striking lines and crags of his cheeks and eyes.

His hair was a little long, and messy, iron gray fading to stark white, and from that hair, tiny flames danced and drifted like a halo.

"Hi there. You must be Doc Silence," the stranger said. His voice was grainy but almost soft, gentle, with a distinct New Zealand accent layered in.

"I am," he said. "How did you find me?"

"Mind if I come in?" the man said.

Doc frowned, then relented, and stepped aside to let the stranger inside.

The man looked around at the barren loft, the only light within from the ambient streetlight outside the windows, and from the fire in his hair and Doc's eyes.

"We treat ourselves well enough," he said, turning back to smile kindly at Doc. "I have a house back home. My uncle left it to me. I have no idea what's in it."

"Who are you," Doc said, though the flames in the man's hair gave him a clue.

"Name's Te Parata," he said, offering a huge hand, which Doc begrudgingly shook. The hand was shockingly warm, almost hot to the touch. "But I guess the news outlets are calling me Sunstar."

"The Solar-Powered Man," Doc said. Long before reports of aliens and men in armor, there had been story after story of this man, faster than a camera could capture, bright as daylight, with hair of flame, appearing across the globe. He never spoke to the press. Never spoke to anyone, really. Just showed up, saved the day, and flew away. Doc could understand that. Sometimes you just wanted to do the job and be gone before anyone asked you why.

"That's me," he said. "I've been at this longer than you'd think.

But the world is changing, and I guess people know I'm real now. Probably not too long before they know you're real, too."

"I doubt that," Doc said.

Te shrugged and pursed his lips.

"I don't know much about magic," he said. "I've seen strange and amazing and horrifying things, but magic, that's my blind spot. If I can't hit it or burn it I don't really know how to fight it. I'm... I have this theory, that folks like us, we're the immune system of the world. I figure I'm a white blood cell. You're an antibiotic. We both stop the darkness from spreading. Keep the world healthy, despite its best efforts to sicken itself."

Doc said nothing, though he had to admit he didn't hate the analogy.

"Why are you here Sunstar?"

"Please call me Te," Parata said. "They give us names. Straylight and Horizon. Coldwall. Like cartoons. Is your name really Doc Silence? Don't tell me your real name if you don't want to, no pressure. I'm just curious."

"I..." Doc was surprised to feel his voice catch in his throat unexpectedly. He had told the story of giving his name away to people over the years, but somehow, standing in the presence of someone else whose identity was altered without his permission, he felt a shockingly acute kinship to him. "Magic cost me my name. Doc Silence is the only one I've ever known. The only one I can remember."

Te Parata smiled warmly at him.

"It's not a bad name, as names go," he said.

"I could have done worse," Doc said. "I picked it myself."

Te laughed. It was infectious.

"If we could all be so lucky," he said.

Doc leaned back against the doorframe and folded his arms across his chest.

"Why are you here, Te?" Doc asked.

The big man sighed and threw his hands out to his sides.

"There's always been one of me," he said. "I guess there always will be one, even after I'm gone. But I didn't have anyone to learn from. I didn't have a teacher. I thought I was alone in the world. And I saw those alien boys. I met this woman who says she travels through time. And I heard about you—quietly, don't worry, you're still a mystery to most. And I thought: we don't have to be alone in this world. We could work together. We could be something. And maybe…"

"Share some of the burden," Doc said.

"Yeah," Te said. "Or at least share what we know. I don't want the next kid born like me to start from scratch. I don't know if you had a teacher or not—"

"I did," Doc said.

"That's good," Te said.

"Arguable, but at least I had someone to give me a place to start," Doc said.

"That's all we need, sometimes," Te said.

Doc relaxed his hands, paced a bit, stuck his hands in his pockets.

"Say we do this," Doc said. "Say, hypothetically, we bring a group of impossible people together. What do we do?"

"We save the world, Doc," Te said. "One day at a time. Like we're doing now. But together."

Doc rubbed the bridge of his nose and tried to ignore the squirming anxiety in his guts. He took a deep breath and looked Te Parata, the Sunstar, in his eyes. Doc had looked a lot of creatures, human and otherwise, directly in the eyes, and he thought he was a good judge of intent.

The sincerity he saw there broke his heart. I've been in the shadows for so long, Doc thought. Even at my best, I'm still a creature of darkness. And I am so tired of being alone.

"Where do we go?" Doc said. "My loft? Your uncle's house?"

Te gestured out the window, toward the cityscape outside. He pointed directly a tall tower overlooking the downtown with an odd, angular shape at the top.

"Did you know there was a spaceship hidden in the City?" Te

246

said.

"A spaceship," Doc said.

"Yeah," Te said. "And I have the keys."

Chapter 27: A continual farewell

Once upon a time, Doc Silence left the City because he could not avoid running into his father.

Unlike most people who move to get away from their father, it wasn't because he did not love him, or because his father was cruel, or demanding, or unkind. It was because his father looked at him as a stranger.

This was the cost of magic. This was the toll paid to save his brother's life. This was how Doc Silence became a magician.

And it broke his heart.

He came back to the City eventually, because this place was in his soul. It was a part of him. And the City grew in his absence; it became easier to avoid people, almost effortless to go months or years without ever seeing someone you knew. You had to seek out the people you wanted to find here, and that growing anonymity, that ability to fade into shadows, made it possible for Doc to call this place home once more.

Well, one of his homes. Magic allowed him to dart across the world with a single step, and he rarely stayed in once place long.

But he learned that all wizards get a little predictable after a while, because, in a life weaved of chaos and change, you couldn't help but want some sliver of reality to call your own. Your wizard's tower, your barrow, your laboratory, your hole in the ground no one could take from you.

And so, for a while, Doc felt safe there.

Until the day he saw a ghost he never expected to see.

Doc was downtown, clearing his head by disappearing into the crowds. Somehow the distraction of people going about their ordinary lives all around him let him forget about the worries of his own, to stop obsessing about spells and shadows for a while. He was beginning to warm to the idea of working with others, but it still made him anxious and uncomfortable, and often spent more time apart from Te Parata and Henry Winter and the others for days at a time.

It was on one of these solitary excursions he saw his brother crossing a busy intersection.

Doc was surprised at how alike they looked. His brother, of course, still had ordinary hair, and eyes that did not appear as small bonfires; but the bone structure, the shape of his mouth, Doc recognized him instantly.

Self-consciously, feeling like a creep, he followed him.

He won't recognize me, Doc knew. The same magic that stole Doc's face from his father's memory effected his brother, too. In fact, after following him for a few blocks, his brother looked over his shoulder as if looking for someone, and for just a second they made eye contact; but he regarded him like a stranger. Just another passerby on the street.

Still, Doc wove a spell of invisibility upon himself, and another to mask his footsteps, more to lesson his anxiety than to hide.

His brother got on the subway, so Doc did as well; and then into a car in a parking lot at a station on the edge of town, heading out into the suburbs. Am I really doing this? Doc thought, but before he could even talk himself out of it he transformed himself into a raven and flew above the car, following his brother home, to a lovely, two-story house perhaps ten miles outside the City. Another car was in the driveway, and Doc noticed immediately that it was laden with suitcases, a bike rack on the back already loaded up. His brother went inside, and Doc sat on a wire, still looking like a raven, and watched through the windows. A grumpy grackle squawked at him, and Doc told him in the language of beasts to get lost.

Through the window, he saw his brother give a quick kiss to a woman, also dressed for work, as she closed a laptop and slid it into a carrying case. Two children ran into the room soon after, a boy and a girl, very close in age. His brother picked up the little girl and pointed at a small, turquoise backpack with a unicorn on it, then set he back on her feet.

There was some packing; both his brother and his wife disappeared and returned dressed more casually, and all four headed back out to the car, both children swinging little colorful backpacks (the boy's was dinosaur themed).

The family climbed into the car, and Doc exhaled sharply. You're being a fool, he thought. Go home. This is disgusting. Leave these people in peace.

But his curiosity got the better of him, and so when the car pulled out of the driveway, he followed once again.

The family traveled for over an hour, all the way to a seaside suburb, one where Doc and his family would go during the summer when he was small. It was a bit ragged back then, and had gentrified some, though the houses here still had the low-slung feel of summer homes. The lawns were nicer now. Doc could smell the beach. It made him nostalgic in ways he didn't think he was capable of anymore.

Eventually, his brother's car pulled into a driveway of a small yellow house with a single SUV in the driveway. The kids flew from the backseat nearly before the vehicle had come to a complete stop. Doc dropped to the ground and re-cast his invisibility spell, finding an out of the way spot near an utility pole, watching his brother and his wife start to struggle with the bags in the hatchback.

That was when Doc saw his parents emerge from the little yellow house. They looked so well, Doc thought. Older of course, but happy, and healthy; his mother held her granddaughter on her hip, the girl looking maybe just one year away from outgrowing this sort of thing. The boy had launched himself onto his grandfather's back, who carried him like a parcel as he helped Doc's brother unload bags from the car. They talked, though Doc, self-consciously, made a deliberate effort to hang back far enough to not hear their words. Maybe he was afraid to know what they'd talk about. Maybe he was afraid he'd want to join in.

They soon went into the house, and Doc stayed long enough to watch the windows grow bright against the encroaching darkness. A car pulled up to deliver pizza. He heard the sounds of a baseball game on the television.

It was an ordinary life, and it was beautiful, and it was safe.

Doc liked to believe he never regretted his decision to give away his name. Given the choice, he would have traded his name for his brother's safety a million times over. He would have given his entire life for him, handed himself over to the creature in the Fens so his brother could go home.

But there were days, dark and long when he wondered about the life he'd lost. All magic has a cost, Erasmus Hawksmith taught him in that very first moment, and Doc Silence knew that magic took its cut from his life every moment of every day of every year. What it gave back, the things he'd seen and done, were nothing short of miraculous.

But his life also felt like a continual farewell.

After a while, Doc felt silly standing there, a ghost in the gathering night, a specter of someone these wonderful people once knew and now never would.

But here there was joy, and here there was love.

And the cost of magic was not too great to bear, Doc thought. Not for this. Not for them.

Epilogue: The plane crash

Doc looked out over the wreckage of the plane and felt tired to his very bones.

He was first on scene, and still too late. Maybe when they were younger they might have gotten here faster, though he knew that was delusional. The team Sunstar and Doc Silence built were fast, but they weren't prescient. They couldn't stop every terrible thing that happened in the world. They couldn't be everywhere at once.

And they were not at full strength, Doc knew. They were getting a little older now, slowing down. Well, everyone but Anarchy Annie, but she'd always moved to the speed of her own clock. Sometimes a plane falls out of the sky and we can't be there to catch it, Doc thought.

Te would have caught it. But Te was gone, dead these past six months, and Doc could barely feel the sun pass over his skin without wondering why someone would snuff out a light so bright. But that was what they'd found, this band of heroes: that the harder you tried to make the world a better place, the more some people would resent you for it. They had nemeses now, all of them.

Doc had always had enemies, he had enemies before he cast his first spell, but the others had found antitheses to their natures, true archenemies, horrible inversions of themselves.

Te Parata always knew it would end. There's always been someone like me, he'd say, and the implication of course was that whoever that someone was, they were gone before he arrived. They'd come to call Te's powers the Gawain Gene, or sometimes the Gawain Mutation, drawing power from the sun. He had always seemed unstoppable and impervious, but over the years they'd all lost friends fighting threats that grew more and more dangerous, more and more excessive, as if the world were upping the stakes to keep pace with their powers.

Sometimes Doc wondered if they'd made a mistake, combining forces. As if they'd dared the universe to take them on. And they hadn't all survived. They buried friends before Te, and they'd bury friends after. Magicians live a long time, Doc knew, but he was beginning to worry he'd outlive them all. His allies were warriors and heroes, but they didn't grow up the way he had. Doc always knew the escape route, like a pest.

He heard the distinct zipper-like sound of Annie's gear activating behind him, and heard her boots crunch on the broken earth as she joined him overlooking the crash site. Parts of the plane were still on fire, but Doc knew there were no survivors. He'd cast a spell on his eyes to find signs of life and saw none.

"This is awful," Annie said, the sun blaring down on them like a furnace. At least the plane crashed in the desert, Doc thought. Better here than a busy city.

"What are we doing here, Annie," Doc said. "We're not medics. I can't bring someone back from the dead."

"We go where we think we might be needed," Annie said.

Doc took off his glasses and rubbed the heels of both hands against his eyes. He blinked away the blind spots, and when he opened his eyes fully again, he caught a glimmer of light on the far side of the crash.

"You see that?" Doc asked.

"See what," Annie said.

Doc didn't wait for her response, but rather took off running across the carnage. He was sure this was some sort of violation of federal or international law, disrupting a crime scene or disaster, but he didn't care. The light he saw wasn't literal—it was a glimmer of life, a tiny spark his spell had picked up on.

He waved his hand and sent a slab of shrapnel flying, only afterward realizing in his haste and sloppiness he might have killed whomever lay hidden underneath. But those fears were assuaged when he saw the mystic light remain in the same spot as before, a small shape on the ground, the earth blackened by flames all around.

A baby carrier, torn and scorched, rested there, still buckled into the seat it crashed in. The blankets were shredded and blackened, the plastic melted and warped. But buckled into the carrier was a tiny infant, little hands raised up as if trying to touch the sun.

Doc stopped a few feet away, his breath caught in his throat, as he saw the impossible: her hair, it seemed, was on fire.

But no, not on fire, Doc knew instantly—this infant possessed the same corona of fire Te Parata had, dancing wicks of fire playing through her reddish locks.

Doc knelt down beside the baby, who looked up at him with calm curiosity, as if nothing had happened, as if she had not just fallen from the sky. She smiled toothlessly at him, and Doc couldn't help but smile back. There wasn't a scratch on her.

"Hello, little one," Doc said. He held out a hand and the baby gripped one finger in her chubby fist. Her skin was hot to the touch. Not feverish, not sick, but radiating the warm of the sun. Doc knew someone with hands like that once.

Annie sidled up beside them and put her hands on her hips.

"Well look at that," she said. "I think she likes you."

"Annie, I think she's…"

"No kidding," Annie said. "You think it's the literal fire in her hair that gives it away?"

Doc could hear sirens in the distance, helicopters approaching quickly. He gingerly removed the baby from her carrier and cradled her in his arm.

"Doc, she's got powers," Annie said.

"Yeah," he said.

"Do we… I can't believe I'm saying this, but do we want, like, the government to get their hands on a baby with Sunstar's abilities?"

Doc thought back to what Te had said when they first met, about wishing he could have learned from someone when his powers manifested. About feeling alone in the world.

"She might have family," Doc said.

"Or her family was on this plane," Annie said. "Doc—I've seen futures where the Gawain Gene is weaponized. We can't just leave her here."

"Then we take her," Doc said, and all hesitation was gone. He glanced down at the infant once more, and saw her reflexively squeezing the lapel of his jacket. The next Gawain mutation. The successor to his friend. A hero or monster, depending on what happened next.

Doc reached out with a weave of complex mystical energy, erasing their footsteps, removing the presence of Annie and Doc from the memory of the land and the living. He opened up a portal back to the Tower and bit his lip.

"Are we doing the right thing?" Doc asked.

"Doc, I never know the right thing. That's why I always ask you," Annie said.

"I… we'll find out where she belongs, then," Doc said. "You and I. We'll do this right."

"We always do," Annie said.

"We always try," Doc corrected her. "I hope this is the right thing to do."

Together, Annie and Doc stepped through the portal and away from the wreckage, unaware that Doc carried the future in in his arms.

ABOUT THE AUTHOR

Matthew Phillion is a writer, actor, and film director based in Salem, Massachusetts. He is the author of the Indestructibles Young Adult superhero adventure series, its spinoff series, Echo and the Sea, and the RPG-meets-high-fantasy Dungeon Crawlers series. A "recovering journalist," he has written on everything from hospital safety to cybersecurity to the opioid crisis.

Also by Matthew Phillion

Novels in the Indestructibles Series – in print and e-book formats

The Indestructibles (Book 1)
The Indestructibles: Breakout (Book 2)
The Entropy of Everything (the Indestructibles Book 3)
Like a Comet (the Indestructibles Book 4)
The Crimson Child (the Indestructibles Book 5)

Tales from the Indestructiverse

Echo and the Sea
Poseidon's Scar

The Indestructibles One-Shots (digital shorts)

The Soloist
Gifted
Blood & Bone
The Monsters We Make
Krampus in the City
Roll for Initiative (an Indestructibles Story) – also available in print

The Dungeon Crawlers Novella Series

The Player's Guide to Dungeon Crawling (The Dungeon Crawlers Book 1)
The Dungeoneer's Bestiary (The Dungeon Crawlers Book 2)
The Ghoul Slayer's Guidebook (The Dungeon Crawlers Book 3)
The Tomb of the Maker (The Dungeon Crawlers Book 4)
Splitting the Party (The Dungeon Crawlers Book 5)
Lost in Revery: Tales of the Dungeon Crawlers Vol. 1 (Collecting Books - 3 in print)